Braley's Road

Copyright © 2025 by Lesley M. Avery
Contact: lesleymavery.author@gmail.com

All scripture quotations taken from the King James Version of the Bible
King James Version KJV (public domain)

"How do I love thee?" From Sonnet 43 by Elizabeth Barrett Browning

Sonnets from the Portugese (public domain)

Cover, interior design, and formatting by Aubrey Labitigan
Jai Design
Contact: facebook.com/designjai
Published by Autumn Hearth Publishing
ISBN: 978-1-965906-10-1 E-book
ISBN: 978-1-965906-07-1 Paperback
ISBN: 978-1-965906-08-8 Hardcover
ISBN: 978-1-965906-09-5 Dustjacket

AUTUMN HEARTH
PUBLISHING

This book is lovingly dedicated to my sister.

She who read my half-finished stories and waited nearly forty years
for the endings.
She who has helped me stand up when necessary
and stood by me always.
She who so valiantly tried to convince us both, all those years ago,
with the brave words—*It will be all right*—when we both knew
it never would, and for far too many other reasons to list here or
anywhere else.

BRALEY'S ROAD

LESLEY M. AVERY

Prologue

January 1865
New Bedford, Massachusetts

Two months, the doctor had said.

"Just pick one, how hard can it be?" Papa Joe pushed the morning paper toward her from where he lay in his bed, and Braley looked at him with horror in her dark brown eyes. "I thought you were teasing."

She studied the man who had married her mother when she was seven, hoping to see a familiar twinkle in his eye, or his ready grin. She had adored Joe for these past fourteen years. He had two sons from a previous marriage, but it was her image that sat framed on his desk at the sawmill, and even after her mother had died, he had never faltered in his love for his *brown-eyed girl.* But *two months,* the doctor had said, and it would all be over. He was not teasing, and she stared, trying to come to grips with the truth. Her world would change.

"The boys will inherit the farm, Braley. It belonged to their mother's family. Do not stay here." He looked into her eyes, hoping he could convey the things he could not speak of. "I know you worked hard to keep it a home, and you did a fine job. I thought I would be here to see to you having a place of your own. I'm sorry."

"Shh. It'll be all right." She *had* worked hard, taking over the household chores and helping run the small farm while he worked at the mill. For the most part, it had been her and her Pappy. Her Papa Joe. The boys had come and gone as they pleased as they got older. "I understand, Pap." With fear gripping her heart, she took his work-worn hand in hers and kissed his weathered cheek. She had grown up with her step-brothers and learned to wrestle and fight well enough to hold her own, but now she did not like the way they looked at her when Joe was not around. She had no other family. Her only hope was Brian Grant, the boy who had said he loved her, promised her the world, and sailed off to make his fortune. But that was three years ago. She hooked a length of straight brown hair behind her ear and sat on the edge of the bed to present her case. "But Brian said…"

Joe studied her with pleading dark eyes much like her own, "Face it, Bray, Brian is not coming back. Men like him are a dime a dozen, full of promises and full of…"

Papa Joe mumbled something under his breath that she did not hear. She was no longer listening. Her heart beat faster as the constrictions of the harsh reality closed in around her, crushing her hopes and swallowing her dreams.

"There's some money I saved up for ya. It's out in the old kiln in the shed. You take that. Don't let the boys know. And you be brave, my brown-eyed girl… *be strong*."

She studied the pleading look in his eyes with tears rolling silently down her cheeks, her throat tight, and could only nod. *This was goodbye.*

Papa Joe nodded too and took a deep breath, "This one looks good." He plopped a stout finger down on an ad under the heading, *'Object Matrimony.'* "We're running out of time, Bray."

He was right. Like a kitten lost in the rain, she had no place to go. Ignoring the lump in her throat, she began to search the personal advertisements for the man she would marry.

Part 1

Chapter 1

March 1865
Ohio

She knew it was wrong to wish him dead, but she did.

Jacob Turner had advertised himself as a man of God. That was why she had chosen him. Papa Joe had not made the eight weeks the doctor had predicted. It was scarcely a month before his sons had moved into the house, and Braley was on a train to Ohio. If you had to marry someone you had never met, *a man of God* would seem a good choice, or so she had thought.

She arrived with the clothes on her back, a small valise with a few extra items, and a volume of sonnets that once belonged to her mother. The town was smaller than she had imagined, dusty and disappointing, but she'd had more than enough of coaches and trains, and he was there to meet her.

"Braley Stuart?" He asked.

"Jacob?" With shining dark eyes and hair darker than hers, he was a good-looking man. *Better than his description*, she thought, which was a good beginning, and she was impressed with his black suit with its long frock coat. *Was this it? Was this how one met a husband?* He had helped her down from the coach and taken her to lunch.

"Was that your church I passed on the way in?" She asked for the sake of something to say.

"No," he said.

"Oh. Is there another church in town?"

"No."

She sipped her coffee until the silence grew uncomfortable. "How long have you been a minister?" She tried.

His dark eyes studied her. "I will be."

Was he angry? He looked angry, but she couldn't be sure. "Oh. I see." She did not see, because he wore a white collar of some sort.

Much like joining the scraps of a patchwork quilt, and with nearly as much effort, she was able to piece together that he *considered himself* a man of God. He was building his own church. He wanted a son to inherit the grand parish he would create; therefore, he needed a wife. He had a large farm. He grew corn. And oats. And wheat. He was thirty-two years old.

"It's time," he said, placing payment on the table and coming to assist with her chair.

Braley took a breath. *He seemed clean and well-mannered… and she had no place else to go.*

The red-headed Sheriff Murphy and his wife, Constance, who cuddled and cooed and made marriage look inviting, offered to serve as witnesses, and the woman who ran the boarding house would play the church organ.

Constance, a pretty, buxom, dark-haired woman who was a bit older than Braley, pulled her aside on the pretense of readying the bride. She handed her a bouquet of wildflowers. "Are you sure this is what you want, honey? Are you sure you don't want to take some time to get to know him? Jacob is… Well, he doesn't mix much, and he's kind of quiet… sullen sometimes, I know it's none of my business, but you seem pretty young."

But she had no place else to go.

They had been married within the hour by the friendly, blond, blue-eyed, and newly appointed Reverend Keats. Braley liked the reverend, but in spite of his ready smile, a suffocating tension pervaded the room. She put it down to nerves. Her groom placed a plain gold band on her finger. The tension reached its pinnacle when Reverend Keats, seeming to speak for Jacob's benefit alone, informed him, "*By the power vested in me,* I now pronounce you man and wife."

They had left soon afterward, with Braley full of hopes and dreams for the future, traveling to Jacob's home miles from town, far from anyone, except, as she understood it, for one distant neighbor and the men who worked on the farm and the church.

Jacob was quiet on the ride, and Braley could not seem to calm her racing pulse. "Have you lived here long?" She asked to break the silence.

He nodded yes.

"Have you family in the area?"

He shook his head no, not turning to look at her.

Braley bit back her disappointment. *She would have liked a sister-in-law and some nieces and nephews.* After several more attempts that brought no better response, she decided he must be as apprehensive as she was. She studied his profile and watched his long fingers manage the reins. *How strange that this man she did not know was now her husband.* She swallowed hard. *It will be fine,* she told herself, turning her attention to the surrounding countryside. *They would build a life together, and perhaps the love that she longed for would follow.*

Her hopes lifted with the first view of her new home. Rolling hills and green pastures stretched as far as she could see. The farm included a large barn and several smaller buildings, all encouragingly well kept, and a two-story clapboard house with a welcoming front porch. Her first thought was *flower boxes. Window boxes spilling over with wild flowers would be perfect.* She was busy dreaming of color combinations when they rounded the corner.

It sat in the far pasture, a mass of bare wooden bones, putting her in mind of a mastodon graveyard, until she registered the men working. It was not the remains of something, but the beginning. Its sheer size was overwhelming, and she looked to Jacob for explanation.

"*Is that your church?*" She whispered, feeling the stupidity of the words even as they left her lips.

For the first time, he smiled. "More than just a church," he replied, his eyes caressing the lumbered framework, "A monument to the glory of God!"

She looked from the building site to her new husband, and back again, feeling the blood slow in her veins. "*But isn't it too large?*"

That was the last comment she ever made about the church.

It was not a happy home. It was dark and cold without the ring of laughter or the excitement of visitors, and it was not long before Braley discovered Jacob Turner was not a man of God. Not a man with a kind and loving heart. Perhaps her first clue, had she not been so naïve, would have been that he brought the buggy whip into the house and stored it in the corner. His obvious resentment of Reverend Keats had put him in a foul temper from the first day, and each day after that, there seemed to be a reason she was in the wrong and was made to pay for it. *She had to learn*, he had said, and it had become clear to her she was to be the perfect wife of the perfect preacher in the grandest church for miles around. She *learned* a lot in the first week, and more in the ones that followed, all against the background of constant hammering, the heartbeat of the church, as it rose to life. Whether she had burned the bread that the Lord had provided, not cleaned the house as close to godliness as expected, or not kept his two identical suits immaculate, and his three white collars starched and ready, she couldn't seem to do anything right. There was her comment about the church, and the time at supper when she asked him why he was not a real minister. That was the first time he had struck her. He hadn't spoken to her for three days after that, and not a day had gone by since, that she hadn't found herself confined to her room at some point, expected to repent for her sins and her wrongdoings. What she had learned best was that trying to please him was like swimming against the tide. She doubted it could be done. *Was this married life?* She wasn't sure, but she felt more like a prisoner than a wife, and she had never been so lonely. Papa Joe had once said, *"Some people are only happy when they are unhappy."* She had never truly grasped his meaning until now. Jacob Turner had no visitors because he had no friends. She had come to understand he preferred it that way. What she would never understand was why.

At one time, she consoled herself with the friendship of a kitten she discovered in the garden. A little gray tabby with one white foot. She called her Pansy. The stray followed her everywhere and became the one bright spot in her world.

"We don't need a cat." Jacob had said. "I hate cats."

"But you have cats." She had pointed out.

"Mousers, in the barn where they belong. Everything here serves a purpose. You would do well to remember that."

The risk for defiance was great, but she was beyond caring. She fed the kitten when he wasn't around and sheltered it, giving it all the love she had nowhere to share, and receiving the love she needed in return. She had smuggled it into her room to keep her company at night; the little warm body curled on her chest. A vision of the contentment she longed for... until it disappeared.

"Did you take her!?" She had dared demand of Jacob when she could not find her anywhere, her thoughts racing to conclusions, none of them acceptable.

"You must have left the door open," he said, but he did not meet her eyes.

"She is always free to go out, but she always comes back."

He shrugged in dismissal. She had searched for days and cried for weeks.

Her only solace became the occasional trips to town, and of course, church on Sundays. But that brought her little relief, as the ride home was always about what was wrong with Reverend Keats and his sermons, and how Jacob would do so much better when his church was completed. The congregation, too, made her uncomfortable. Some looked at her with awe, and some with pity, and she wondered what they knew.

And she had another concern. In the nearly two months since they had been married, she had slept alone. Jacob had not consummated their marriage and seemed to have no interest in doing so.

She was not completely sure how it was supposed to work. Her mother had died when she was ten. Papa Joe had done his best to explain how the cat at the sawmill had kittens, and he had gotten a neighbor lady to talk to her when she had started to bleed. But other than being relieved that she was not about to die, and a few hints about what it meant, that was about it. She did remember catching a glimpse of Mama and Papa Joe kissing on occasion, and it was nothing like the impersonal brush she had received on her wedding day. Even Brian Grant, an awkward seventeen-year-old, had done a more respectable job, but that was as far as it went. She was painfully short on the details.

The first night she had washed and changed and waited in her room, her heart thudding in her ears until it was the only thing she could hear in the silent house. She had awoken sometime in the early dawn, dismayed that the night had passed no differently than any other, and she had waited each night with the same result. Now, though, her anticipation had turned to dread. *What had she done wrong? Was she so terrible? Was she too tall? Too short? Too clumsy? Was it because she had burned the bread?* She knew she was not the prettiest girl in the world, but she had never been made to feel ugly, as she did now. *After all, men always wanted women, didn't they? That was why one had to be so careful.* Papa Joe had warned her about it when she was seeing Brian. *Why then would a man not want a woman that was his to take, unless she was completely unattractive?* She sat on her bed and drew an already damp sleeve across her face to banish unwelcome tears. She was hungry and thirsty. Gathering her anger and resentment around her like a shield, she took a deep breath and concentrated on her plan.

She no longer wanted him to come to her. She knew as long as he did not, they were not truly married, and that was for the best. She no longer wanted to be his wife. There would never be anything here for her if their only interaction was when he struck her. Then there were the days he pretended she did not exist...

She wasn't sure when it became a plan, but she did know when she got the chance, she was going to leave. She had come with such high hopes that things would work out, but anything would be better than this. She wasn't even allowed to go into town by herself. She could not imagine spending the rest of her days sitting across from an angry, unhappy man who wouldn't speak to her. One who spent his time waiting for her to do something wrong so he could punish her. Somewhere, somehow, she would find a way to support herself. She had some money Papa Joe had given her, and before she'd had a chance to tell Jacob about it in their first days, he had yelled at her for something, and in her shock, the thought had left her. Now she was glad. She would use the money to get away. She had seen Constance several times on their trips into town, and they were becoming fast friends. *Perhaps she would help...* Braley paused. The constant hammering had stopped, and there was a different kind of commotion outside. She rose from the corner to peer out the curtained window. The men were by the barn struggling with a huge stallion, before letting him loose where a mare waited within the confines of the corral. *Poor girl,* she whispered, *There's no escape for you.*

The horses were out of her line of sight now, but she watched for a moment until the rough shouts of the men made her sick to her stomach. And then her gaze fell on Jacob. He stood apart from the others, taking in the scene, and then did something that sent a chill up her spine. He turned and looked up at her window.

No! Not now. It's too late now. I don't want you now. She turned and looked around the room for escape, but she knew it was useless. She was locked in.

She was relieved when he did not come to her room in the middle of the day with the men outside. She spent the days that followed even more on the edge of her nerves whenever he was near, until one night when he began to talk to her at supper.

He talked about the weather, the crops, and how he didn't mean the things he said. He didn't mean to yell. He wouldn't, if she didn't make him. He wanted what was best for her. She had misunderstood. People had always misunderstood him. He smiled and touched her hand.

She felt sad for him. *Could she have misunderstood? Everything? Could they make a new beginning? Maybe it wasn't his fault.* He pulled her chair out for her when they were done, and waited while she did the dishes. One night, when it was time for bed, he took her hand and led her up the stairs to her room.

Braley was undecided. *Should she let this happen? Was there hope for this to be a real marriage? Could she be wrong about his treatment of her? Did she misinterpret his actions and the things he said? Maybe it was her fault. Maybe he really did have her best interests at heart… And he was her husband.*

It was over before it had begun, and it was more horrid than she had ever imagined. He left her without a word. He hadn't even taken off his boots, and it was done. *Except for the hurt. The pinching and prodding. And the pain. The neighbor lady hadn't told her how much it would hurt.* He had kissed her once at the beginning, his lips cold and hard against her mouth. Even that had hurt, crushing her lips against her teeth. He hadn't held her. There had been no soft words, no caring caresses, as she had imagined there might be… *Because there was no love. And now she was truly his wife.*

Chapter 2

She had stayed for the sake of the child. A child needed a proper home, or at least, a roof over their head. And too, because Jacob's behavior had changed somewhat when he learned she was expecting. It was part of his dream, and she thought she could see a difference in him. He no longer hit her, and she made the most of the fragile peace. She was cautious in her words and her actions, kept the house clean, did her chores, and made sure supper was on time. It was exhausting, and she was not at all sure how long she could keep it up. Especially now, with her time getting closer, when she found she was so often in need of a nap.

She was still not allowed to go into town unless she went with Jacob, and those visits were few and far between. She looked forward to even a short visit with the sheriff's wife and what little she saw of the pastor, who was always pleasant and cheerful. It was one of these visits that now caused the promising lift in her spirits.

"What a beautiful day!" She tried, as they rode along in the buckboard, forgetting he was once again not speaking to her. Her latest offense was falling asleep. She had sat for a moment after sweeping and doing the breakfast dishes, and almost instantly dozed off. It was only for a few minutes, but, of course, he had chosen that time to return to the house, and he had caught her. Now she was being punished. He had thrown out passages from Proverbs—something about *sloth* and being *slack in her work*—she should know them by now. He read the bible to her for hours every evening, but she could never remember well enough to quote chapter and verse like he could, except for a few of her favorites that she had already known. She didn't care. And she didn't care anymore if he chose not to speak to her. She had gotten quite used to these treatments and caught on to the fact that most of them lasted three days, although she had no idea why. Occasionally, when the offense was bad enough, the silence would extend to five days. *That was fine too.* There was nothing she could do about it.

In the beginning, she had kept trying. She made pleasant comments and took the time to carefully word her questions so that they would require more than a nod or a shake of the head. She had tried getting him to tell her what was amiss. She had even begged him to talk to her once, because she truly had no idea what was wrong. It hadn't worked, but it *had* left her with a burning shame, and she had resolved never to beg again.

As a result, in addition to no affection, there was less and less communication. Surely, they were the only couple in the area who had not turned out to celebrate the ending of the war or to mourn President Lincoln. She hadn't learned the war was ending until Constance had told her. *Jacob had to have known. There were parties and celebrations…* Invitations to weddings were turned down as a matter of course. There were fundraisers and church socials they did not attend, and barn raisings with food and dancing that were to be avoided. '*People should learn to take care of their own.' 'Neither a borrower nor a lender be,'* and *the Lord helps those who help themselves.'* Those sentiments did not come from the bible. Neither did they follow its teachings.

Over time, she had given up. There was nothing she could ever do or say to bring him out of his angry moods. She had learned to wait them out and had eventually begun to think of these periods as a reprieve from the daily toll on her nerves. *Three days off. Three days of peace.* It gave her time to think. She didn't have to worry about what to say or how to say it. When he was not speaking to her, he acted as though she were not there, as he did now. It was as if he did not see her when they passed in the hallway or sat at supper together. At some point, she began to prefer the blank stare in his eyes. If she didn't exist, at least she couldn't be wrong, and of course, if she were not there, he could not possibly love her as a husband loves a wife, and she had no need to feel the shame of rejection or indifference. She only wished she could really disappear.

The baby sat heavily on her bladder in the hard riding wooden seat, and she had to relieve herself, but she didn't dare say so. *He wouldn't stop anyway; it would put them off schedule.* As they neared the town, Braley sat forward in excitement, but then forced herself to relax for the last few miles. It wouldn't do to let him know how much she enjoyed these visits, lest they be taken away. *Like the window boxes...*

With so many men gone in the war, help had been difficult to come by. The workers on the farm were a ragtag collection of those who had avoided the war altogether, deserters, and those who had returned from the fighting wounded and angry. She didn't blame them, but she had feared them, until early one morning when Jacob had ridden out to supervise the fields for the day, and she ventured out to face them.

She had dreamed of having window boxes since the day she arrived and mentioned it numerous times to Jacob, who had scoffed and put her off by naming all the reasons they were unnecessary.

Well, it may not be necessary, but it *was* time. She couldn't see the harm, as it would cost nothing but a little effort. Gathering her nerve, she had left the house and crossed the considerable distance to the pile of scrap lumber that sat off to one side of the church. The hammering came to a stop, and the men stared, but she felt nothing but respect, and possibly a little sadness in their regard for her. Some in the back wandered away, and there was an awkward silence before the hammering started again, and one of them, doffing his hat, stepped forward.

"May I help you, missus?" His glance surveyed the yard and looked toward the house.

Braley held to her resolve. He was a rough-looking man, thin and not too tall, with a jagged scar on his cheek. She tried not to stare. *How awful it must be to always have everyone stare.* "Yes, please, I wanted to gather some scrap boards to make some flower boxes. Is all of this being discarded?"

A few of the other men who stood watching had doffed their hats following the first one's example, but soon, they too, drifted back to work. "Yes, ma'am, most of this here is too short to be put to good use. "Here, let me help you," he said, as he stooped to sort through the pile. "How many boxes would you need?"

"Four would be perfect, they're for the windows on the porch," she replied, as she too began to dig through the pile, careful not to catch her skirts.

"Here now, ma'am, you'll get splinters. I'll find you some good-sized pieces." He peered up at her. "Did you say you're going to make them yourself?"

Braley straightened. "Yes, I've built them before, back home; they're fairly easy except for the cutting. Maybe I could use those pieces over there." She pointed to some boards that seemed to be all the same length and about the size she had in mind.

The man rose and went to where she pointed. "Why don't you leave it to me? I'd be happy to make them up for you on my lunch hour and bring 'em up to the house. Won't take any time at all."

"Thank you so much, if you're sure it won't be too much trouble…"

"Rusty, my name's Rusty, ma'am. No trouble at all."

"That would give me time to gather the flowers, Rusty. Thank you again."

And she did. She took the garden cart and set off with a mixture of excitement and determination. She walked for miles, digging and gathering the best blooms in the summer heat… Purple Cone Flower, Black-Eyed Susan, Blazing Star, Wild Bergamot, and Sweet Everlasting.

The grass is always greener... And so too, the flowers further away, beckoning her with more colors and larger blooms. She had wandered further than she should, and that was how she met Lucy… *But that was another story.*

The wagon bumped over a particularly unkind rut, jolting her out of her thoughts. A glance at Jacob told her he still stared straight ahead, not concerned with her welfare in the least, and she drifted back to her memories… Rusty was true to his word, and she couldn't have been happier when she returned to find the four stout boxes waiting for her at the porch windows. He had even filled them partway with good garden soil. She had thought to make it a point to thank him again and perhaps pay him something from her own money.

She had mixed some sand in with the soil, carrying it a little at a time, and spent all afternoon getting the boxes planted just so, before lugging the water to water them in. This was when *she* felt closest to God, she thought. When she spent time appreciating nature and working to create something beautiful with the strength and ability he had given her. There was nothing wrong with reading the bible. She was raised on it and often enjoyed the scriptures when she was alone and quiet, and could give thought and contemplation to the beautiful words, but a forced four or five hours a night on a regimented schedule was not enjoyable to her. She worried so much about not being able to answer the questions Jacob asked afterward that she retained very few of the verses, and of course, there were consequences. She was *learning* them the hard way. No, there was nothing wrong with reading the bible, the fault lay in twisting the words and fitting them to suit a different purpose. Besides, she would dearly love to read other books too, the way she used to...

There had been her mother's book… The last thing she had that those loving hands had touched. Her prized possession. He had caught her reading one night when he had burst into her room to berate her for some other discretion, and snatched the volume from her hands.

"What is this?" He questioned, before he began to read. "How do I love thee?" *The beautiful words of a love she could only dream about.* His scowl said everything. "You don't need this… this… Desire and lust are tools of the devil! What else have you been hiding? How else have you desecrated my house?"

"Give it to me!" She had scrambled from the bed, grabbing his arm, but he had held the book out of her reach and tossed it into the fire, blocking its demise from her view.

"All you need to read is in the Good Book." He had stormed out of the room, and she had sat on the floor watching the flames destroy what was left of her past.

That was yet another story. One she seldom allowed herself to think about. She closed her eyes against the memory that threatened to overwhelm her and drew her thoughts back to the planters… How the blooms had bobbed in the breeze, a riot of color, exactly as she had pictured them. Despite the ache in her back, her heart had swelled with happiness. She had been pleased and proud of her hard work.

Too pleased. And too proud. They were gone the next day. Something about vanity and pride—*Proverbs again.* The budding friendship had also ended, as she was forbidden further contact with any of the helpers. Rusty was gone. She had never seen him again.

Braley shifted on the hard seat, growing exceedingly uncomfortable. They were getting closer to town. She only hoped she would make it in time. *She would have to make a run for the privy.* The memory of the window boxes always made her think of the day she met Lucy, as the two went hand in hand.

She had wandered so far gathering the flowers that she was nearly at the boundary with their one and only neighbor. Lucy, too, had been out gathering, although she, in a more practical purpose, sought wild onion and garlic to store for the winter. Her husband had been injured, and they were behind in getting everything planted.

Braley had, of course, offered to help so the work could get done. Jacob had lectured her time and again, in his superior-than-thou tone, that crops could mean the difference between life and death, but Papa Joe had taught her that. *Everyone knew that.* She had thought at the time to get Rusty and a few of the men to help out, but of course, that was not to be. She had been excited to learn that Lucy and her husband had three children and another on the way. With so much in common, they had become almost instant friends and Braley had visions of their children growing up much the same. She didn't mention this to Jacob, of course. She had learned to keep things to herself. She had gone to help the very next day, after he had left, taking a straighter path than the day she had wandered in the fields.

"Oh, do come in!" Lucy invited, "I do appreciate this so much. This is Annabelle," she indicated a little girl playing by the hearth.

Braley stared, the chill that ran up her arms turning to heat in her face.

"Is something wrong? Do you need to sit down?" Lucy took her arm in concern.

There was no mistaking the markings and the little white foot on the kitten playing with the little girl. *How could he have possibly wandered this far?* "That kitten..."

"Oh yes! Your husband stopped by on his way to town one day and offered it to the children. He had never stopped before. I thought him stand-offish, to be honest. I guess I was mistaken. Such a kind man, the reverend. You're very lucky."

Braley heard without listening and stared without seeing. She managed to hold back tears as she kissed the tiny head, contenting herself with the knowledge that the kitten was still alive and loved by this little girl. She could visit. It was for the best. *It was.* And much better than the thoughts that haunted her at night. Her relief was bittersweet, but still, she had been excited at the prospect of having friends.

Jacob had not, and once he found she had been visiting, he let it be known with a multitude of questions and snide comments about what she was doing over there so often. In fact, she was quite surprised he had not resorted to locking her in her room, but she was beyond caring. She had explained multiple times what she was doing, and considering she came home muddied and tired, she would have thought it was obvious she was telling the truth. She was quite sure he believed it was the truth; it was just his way of wearing her down until she gave up. But she had refused... Until the day she had been late coming home, and he had returned early from his ride.

"What are you smiling about?" He demanded.

"Sorry," she answered out of habit.

He sat at the table in the shadows while she washed her hands and hastily prepared to make supper, bracing herself for the remarks that were sure to come.

"If it weren't for you, the world would come to a standstill."

Braley froze, not sure how to answer. "What does that mean?"

"Well, you're always doing other people's work, aren't you?"

"Oh, I thought for a moment you were giving me a compliment." It was a half-hearted attempt to make a point. To make him see the harshness of his words. "I guess I should know better."

"Well, when you're doing everybody else's work, yours doesn't get done, does it? Who's going to help you with your work? Who does anything for you? Nobody but me. You belong here."

Braley stopped what she was doing. "Maybe I went to visit my kitten!"

The look on his face was both priceless and frightening. "That was none of your concern. It was mine to do with as I saw fit. You had no business over there! You shouldn't have gone."

She knew to have caught him out was unforgivable. "But she's my friend, and she needs my help. Our own garden is all planted and doing fine. There is no reason I can't help her."

"*Your friend?* Someone you just met? There are no friends, only people who want something from you. If you're too nice, people will take advantage of your good nature. You are too naïve, too stupid to know when people are using you. It's my job to protect you."

She stared, speechless for the moment. *"My God. What kind of people raised you? What about loving thy neighbor?* And you call yourself a man of God? *You have no idea what that even means!"* She knew she had gone too far. She hadn't seen the riding crop until it was too late. She had run, but not fast enough.

It was not as bad as the whip, which curled around her sides and sliced her flesh, but it did its own damage, heavy and blunt. It was the words, though, that hurt the most. They wounded in a different way. The pain and humiliation, the punishment for kindness that tore her on the inside.

She had never gone to the neighbors again. By the time she had healed enough to leave the house, it was long past time to plant. There were a few awkward times she came face to face with them at church, and being too embarrassed to explain, she had mumbled some excuse.

At last, they pulled onto the main street of the town. Jacob dropped her off at the sheriff's house, helping her down for appearance's sake, and even giving her an odd one-armed hug in front of Constance, careful, of course, not to make any bodily contact. He always left her there while he went down the street to get the supplies. She was not allowed to shop. Her visits with Constance were the only time he let her out of his sight, and Braley wasn't sure why, but she was grateful. She suspected that it was also for appearance's sake, and he wouldn't leave her at home with the men. And, too, because she was only visiting the sheriff's wife. After all, they were only two women. What could they possibly do?

"Goodness, you're as big as a house! How are you feeling?" Constance asked, her wise blue eyes taking in everything, as soon as Braley had come in from the privy. "It won't be long now," she said, giving her friend a warm hug in greeting.

"Yes," said Braley, her eyes widening. "I'm so tired, and I'm getting nervous."

"And how are things?" The older woman went to peer out the curtained window to make sure Jacob had gone about his business before she sat to pour the tea.

"About the same. I cannot say they are good, but they are not as bad."

"Has he struck you?"

"Not since that last."

"That is not good enough, you know."

Braley braced for a lecture. It was both comforting and uncomfortable to have a friend who knew her secrets. The choice had been taken from her when she had shown up on the doorstep on one of her earlier visits, barely able to move from the slashes on her back and a bruise around her eye. Jacob wanted to leave her home, she knew, but he didn't trust her, and he didn't trust his workers to take care of his business dealings. *Make an excuse,* he had instructed, but Constance had known instantly and been horrified, and Braley didn't even try to explain it away. Both women simply pretended that she had.

"I know," she answered. "I think he may change when the baby comes. Maybe he will be happier then."

"And if he is not?"

Braley had no answer. She hadn't thought that far ahead. She hadn't wanted to.

"We should have a plan. In case it gets worse. There is the baby to think of. You're going to have to be strong. Do you know how to ride?"

"Yes, but I don't think…"

"People don't change, Braley. I had no idea he was that bad. I never would have let you marry him. He won't change."

"But he wants the baby."

"He wants his dream. It's not about the baby."

"He is looking forward to it. Someone to follow him in his ministry, and carry on with the church."

"And if it's a girl?"

Braley hung her head, "I don't know. He never mentions a daughter. It's as though it's not even a consideration. I'm hoping for a boy."

"And what if it is? What if he doesn't measure up? You know yourself how hard it is to not cross Jacob. Most of the wrongs are perceived in his own mind. You said there are times when you don't even know what you did to set him off. How is a child supposed to know?" Her voice rose. "And you will be caught in the middle, always defending, always on edge. Always wrong, no matter what you do. What kind of life will that be for either of you? It's hell to watch your children suffer."

Braley stared at her friend, tendrils of sympathy entwining her heart as understanding grew.

"Oh yes. I was married before. My boys are from my first marriage. The Sheriff is my third husband. I left the first one, and the second one was worse from the start, kinda like yours… The difference being, *I* didn't put up with it. He's dead."

Braley nearly spit out her tea and her eyes widened.

Constance burst out laughing. "Oh no, honey, I didn't kill him. Not that I hadn't thought about it."

"Don't mind me, ladies." The sheriff entered, letting the screen door slam, "I'm just passing through. Wouldn't dream of interrupting the witching hour." He winked at Braley. "Forgot my notes," he said to his wife, stopping to give her a hug and a kiss, and a squeeze where Braley pretended not to notice, before making his way out.

"There are good men out there," Constance continued without so much as a blush when he had left. "I wouldn't trade my Warren for anything in the world. Of course, I had to throw a few back before I got a keeper," she said, looking after him. "I met him during the war. I was a nurse, and he came in with the wounded. To think I could have lost him the same day I found him, and I would never have known." She shook her head. "Trust me when I tell you, people don't change. No matter how many times they say they will."

"You love him," Braley said, not sure why, except that it was so evident in the woman's face.

"Yes, I do."

"And he's… *Is he always like that?*"

"Like what?"

Braley blushed, regretting venturing into such embarrassing territory.

"Don't be shy, you can ask me anything."

"I was wondering…" She studied her hands in her lap. "Does he always kiss you and hug you? For no reason? He seems very… *affectionate.*"

Constance laughed, "It's not for *no reason*. The reason is love. And he is," she lowered her voice to a whisper, *"most every night."*

Braley's eyes widened. "You mean…"

Constance nodded.

Braley studied her, "Oh, I'm so sorry," she whispered. "But you already have children… surely you don't need to…"

"Oh, honey. You need a plan. Listen…"

Braley sat in confusion, not believing half of what Constance told her, and doubting the rest. "I had thought to leave before the baby, and then I had decided to stay, but now, I don't know…"

Chapter 3

Jacob had slammed out of the house, but Constance was there and placed her beautiful baby girl in her arms. "Be strong. Never mind him, Braley, he hasn't the sense God gave a goat." She gazed at the child with a mixture of awe and longing. "I always wanted a little girl. She's beautiful."

And she was. Braley looked at her daughter, small and pink and helpless, with a head full of dark hair, and her heart melted. She looked to her friend, "I need a plan."

"Soon as you're up and around, we'll work something out. Meanwhile, I'll be here as much as I can. My Warren will help."

Jacob came back after a week, as brooding as ever. He rarely spoke and never looked at her or the baby.

"Don't you want to see Eliza?" Braley dared ask.

"Eliza?" He scoffed, making a face of distaste.

"Yes, after Elizabeth, *righteous before God, walking blamelessly—It's from Luke 1:6,*" she threw at him. She had worked at remembering the verse.

Constance, washing the dishes, smiled to herself and kept her head down.

"You had her. You can take care of her. She is of no use to me. Now we'll have to try again," he said before quitting the room.

Constance looked up to catch Braley's look of alarm.

The hammering continued, and the church rose majestically on the hill. The steeple, now higher than the barn, could be seen for miles around, and the money and the work now began to be concentrated on the inside.

It was no longer an empty shell, but Braley was. She stood gazing out the window at the mammoth structure. She saw the rolling hills, the pastures, and the white picket fence. *What a shame.* Here was everything most people could want. A man and woman, land to sustain them, and room to grow. A beautiful child, and a sturdy house with more rooms to fill. But that was it. It was a house and not a home. They were a man and a woman, not a husband and wife working together. There was nothing to temper the harshness of life, to warm the coldhearted winters ahead. Nothing to stand between them and the world. No sharing of joys or dividing of sorrows. Not without love. Her dreams of growing together had long ago been cast aside. She existed to care for her baby, trying to stay healthy, walking in the sunshine, and getting her strength back, feeling all the while like a non-person. She lived for her child and the visits from her one friend. Human contact. A hug and a voice. A voice that answered and acknowledged her existence. She knew now she could not stay here, could not expose her child to the same harsh treatment. It mattered little where she went; she already lived alone.

All of Jacob's time was now spent working on the church. The crops were poor and withering in the summer heat. Without the crops, there would be no food for next year, and no money to pay the men or finish the church. Eliza was nearing three months old, and Braley did not know how long she could use healing from her birth as an excuse between children. He had believed her so far. She loved her daughter, but she did not want another child belonging to Jacob. Aside from an occasional pinching or prodding meant to humiliate her, he had never touched her or tried to be with her since that one night, and she hoped to keep it that way. If ever a prayer were answered, she hoped with all her heart it would be this one.

They had finished another silent supper when Braley, hearing a buggy, looked out to see Constance. It was long past her usual visiting time, and surprisingly, the sheriff had joined her. "Come in…" She stopped, reading her friend's face. "What's wrong?"

Jacob did not get up, nor acknowledge them, and she felt the room flood with tension.

"We have news." Constance put down her basket and hung her coat by the door before hurrying to the nervous woman.

Braley hugged her and handed her the baby as usual.

"The Lord works in mysterious ways," she whispered in Braley's ear, as she settled Eliza on her shoulder and began a rapid patting of her back through the blanket.

Braley saw a warning in her eyes, but a smile that threatened, and she did not know what to expect.

"The strangest thing." Constance turned to her husband, giving him the floor.

"Now don't be alarmed." Sheriff Murphy removed his hat and addressed them both, "It's not your fault, and it is easily remedied. There's a preacher on the way."

Braley questioned Constance with a frown.

"Now ya see, I've arrested Reverend Keats."

"Oh, why?" Braley whispered. She liked the cheerful clergyman who was always so pleasant.

"Turns out, Reverend Keats weren't no reverend after all. He was wanted for bank robbery and was hiding out in plain sight. Can you believe it? No wonder he was always smilin', he was playin' a big joke on all of us. I turned him over to the county this morning."

Braley was feeling sad for the reverend before conflicting waves of joy and fear washed over her, stealing her breath. She stared at Constance, who nodded, looking much too pleased, and then she whirled to face Jacob, who sat with a look of horror on his face.

"Sinners. We are sinners! Fornicators! God forgive me!"

"Now, don't take it too hard. You're not the only ones. There're three other couples got hitched since the reverend came to town. I've sent for another minister, and he'll be here next month to fix everybody up right. You can get remarried and ain't nobody gonna think nothin' of it, but there's no papers, nothing was ever filed, so you'd have to take care of that." He stopped to rub his whiskered cheek, "Or, I think, under common law, you can claim yourselves married in good faith, that could work. All you have to do is swear to mutual consent. We thought we should let you know as soon as possible so you could decide."

Consent? She had a choice? Ha! Braley could hardly take it in. *Were they truly not married?* She glanced at Constance for confirmation, reading encouragement and triumph in her eyes, and at Eliza, and made the choice for both of them. "No! Not now. Not ever."

Jacob leapt to his feet. *"But you have to! It's your fault!"* He yelled. *"Jezebel! Temptress! You and that devil Keats! Always laughing together. You have damned me to hell!"* Before anyone could move, he upended the table, sending the kerosene lamp to shatter against the wall, showering the women with fuel and flame and broken glass. Ignoring the cries of panic and pain, he pointed to Eliza, *"And she's a… a misbegotten curse!"* He stormed out, running to his church.

The sheriff used his bare hands to put out the flames in his wife's hair and on the back of her arm, and Braley's shoulder, where she had shielded Eliza. They stomped on the scattered patches burning across the floor, and Braley snatched up the tablecloth to beat at the flames on the wall where the kerosene had splattered, unaware that her skirts had caught.

The sheriff went to his knees and smothered the fire with his hat, all accompanied by the endless screams of the baby. *"Are you all right?! Are you all right?!"* He yelled, still brushing at the shards of glass and the smoldering ruins of their clothing.

"Yes," Braley said, taking Eliza to comfort her, while Constance nodded, brushing at her hair.

Eliza would not be quieted. "Here," the sheriff righted the table, and Braley placed the baby down to unwrap her and examine her with shaking hands.

Constance stepped in to help. They removed her clothing, their hands nicked and cut from the broken shards, but found nothing. "Here, turn her over," she said, and there, caught in the folds of the blanket, was a piece of hot glass that had burned the child's neck.

"Oh, it's burned her and she's bleeding!" Braley cried, tossing the piece of glass to the floor, tears blurring her vision.

"So are you," her friend pointed out, pressing the edge of the blanket to Eliza's neck. "You've a cut on your cheek."

Braley put a hand to her face, swiping at the blood and tears.

"Come on," Warren said, "grab your things before he comes back. You're not staying here. You'll come with us and we'll see the doctor."

Battered and burned, blistered and bandaged, the small brigade slowly recovered. Constance had cut her hair back where it had been singed; she had a burn on her upper arm and various cuts and nicks. The sheriff's hands were the worst, and he had badly burned his knees while helping Braley with her skirts. Braley would be left with deep scarring on the back of her left shoulder and a mark on her left cheek to remember that night. She would count it a small price to pay for her freedom if it weren't for the pain Eliza had been through. The young mother would never forget the sound of her child's screams and never forgive the brand on the back of the tiny neck from the combined cut and burn from the bit of curved glass. She would never forgive Jacob Turner. Never.

It had been over a month, and there had been no sign of him, which she considered a blessing. "You know," she said to Constance, as they sat over coffee one morning, "when the doctor is done treating my shoulder and the annulment is filed, I'll have to think about leaving. I'll stay and help with Warren if you need me, but I can't be running into Jacob for the rest of my life."

"I understand," Constance said, "but I hate to see you go. You'll have to write and…" She rose at a knock on the door. "Well, speak of the devil, and he appears," she muttered, peeking through the curtains. "Should I let him in?"

"Braley stood and took a step backward, her inclination to flee, before she caught herself. She was free. She did not have to go with him, or do as he said ever again. She glanced at Eliza, sleeping in a makeshift crib in the corner. The sheriff was confined to a bed in the back storage room while he recuperated, but he was home. She nodded.

"Jacob." Constance gave the only greeting she could muster.

"I've come to speak to my wife."

"What do you want?" Braley asked.

"Will you come outside so we can talk?" He stared at her face, but said nothing.

"Here will do, although I can't think what you could possibly have to say after what you did."

"I'd like to speak in private."

"I'll go in the other room," Constance volunteered, letting Braley know with a look, she would not be far away.

"What do you want?" Braley asked again.

"It's almost time for the new preacher to arrive. I thought we should make plans."

"Plans?"

"To get married. To be saved from our sin. It is the only way. We shall have to repent and pray for forgiveness, of course."

"Do you think I would marry you now? You could have killed us. As it is, you've scarred us all."

"But it's the only way, don't you see? It is our best chance to correct this wrong that we have done. To save ourselves. *To save our souls.* I have given it a lot of thought. There is no way to correct the… *her* being born out of wedlock, but you and I can start over."

Braley knew what wrong she had done, but it was long before a month ago. "You and I?" She looked at him warily. "What about Eliza?"

"I have an idea."

Braley backed away, the fine hairs on the back of her neck rising in alarm.

"We can put her on the orphan train."

"Are you insane?" She whispered, barely able to breathe. "She is not an orphan! She is our child!"

"Now, listen to reason… She'll find a new family. It's a good organization, started by a minister. She's too young to be of any use to anyone right now. Families mostly want workers, but some couple that can't have children may want her. She'll have a family, they won't know what she is, and we won't be saddled with the error of our ways, even though it wasn't our fault," he added. "We can have more children. Legitimate children, worthy of the glory of the church."

They won't know what she is? "Is that what she is to you… *An error? An error to be cast aside?"* God loves all children. She sank into the nearest chair. "You need to go."

"You can't do this to me! It's unfair!"

"Unfair to you? You would throw away your own child?" Her voice rose, "It wasn't her fault either! She is innocent! *And you would condemn her to who knows what kind of life to save yourself?"*

His voice rose as well, "It's the only way, don't you see? You have to marry me!"

At the sound, Eliza began to cry. Braley went to her and lifted her to her shoulder, patting her back and rocking back and forth.

"What is that?" Jacob stepped closer, staring at the small curved scar ending in an angry red splotch of tortured skin.

"That is what you did. You and your temper."

His eyes widened, and he stepped away. *"It's a six."*

"What?"

"It is a number six!"

"What are you saying? It is not."

"She is marked with the number of sin. The day of man, the sinner, one short of seven. Short of perfection. *He knows!* Satan knows her. She must be dealt with."

Braley stared at this man she had once thought she could build a life with. *"You've lost your mind,"* she whispered. "You did that! Not God, not Satan, you! You are the evil here! Get out. Get out and stay away from us. Stay away from my daughter!"

Chapter 4

"Where will you go?" Constance asked.

Braley paused in packing the few items she had. "Back East, I guess. I miss New Bedford. I think I'd be more comfortable there. I do know I can't stay anywhere near him. I still have the money I came with. It will be enough to get me there and for a place to stay for a while, and I can find work."

"I agree you shouldn't stay here, but are you sure you'll be all right, traveling alone with the baby?"

"Yes, unless… *Do you think he would come after me?*"

Her friend took a deep breath, considering, "I don't think he'd leave his church."

Braley nodded, not wholly convinced.

"I'm going to miss you," the older woman said into the quiet.

Braley embraced her, unable to stay the tears that started. "And I, you. I'll never forget how much you helped me. If it wasn't for you, I might not be here now."

The morning would bring both routine and revelations. Constance stirred first as usual, started the fire, put the coffee on, and got her sons fed and off to school. She brought the sheriff a tray, poured herself a cup of coffee, and went to join him, sitting on the edge of the bed. "Braley's usually up by now. She must have been tired out from dealing with Jacob yesterday..."

Warren watched as her face drained of color and her smile faded.

"I haven't heard the baby cry either." Blindly, she placed her cup on the dresser and fled the room.

"She's gone," she reported moments later. "She's gone and she's in trouble. He's taken her."

"Now, we don't know that, darlin', hold your horses." Her husband tried to calm her. "Maybe she decided to get an early start."

"She wouldn't have left without saying goodbye."

"But we can't know that," he said, sounding less sure of himself.

"I know it," she said, every nerve on edge. "She wouldn't. And she wouldn't have left her belongings."

Braley paced in her old room like a wild animal trapped in a cage, her nails bloodied and torn from trying to claw her way out. She found herself once again locked in, and this time the windows were boarded from the outside. The once incessant hammering was no more. From what little she could see through the space between the planks, no one stirred out by the holy aberration. She could only assume the men had left because they were no longer being paid.

It was dark when she had woken in the buckboard. Her hands were tied, and she was nauseous, but Eliza was there beside her. The next thing she knew, she was in her room listening to the buckboard drive off. She jumped up, fighting the nausea, hoping against hope, but she was alone. Eliza was gone.

Dawn crept in through the barricaded window as she put up the sash. She grabbed a small table, hammering it against the boards until it splintered in her hands. A straight chair met the same fate. Neither rendered any progress. The fire poker and tools had been removed long ago, but the iron grate made of metal bars was still in the fireplace. Swinging it proved too difficult, but holding it with two hands, she rammed it again and again against her wooden prison. The boards didn't budge. She attacked the door with the same result and returned to batter the blockaded window, resting only when she could no longer lift her arms, and beginning again, blinded by sweat and tears, her injured shoulder a searing agony.

She opened her eyes but saw nothing, thoughts forming through a fog. *It was almost dark. Her head ached. She must have passed out. No, no, no! She had wasted precious time. He would be further away with Eliza.* She stood waiting for her eyes to adjust to the dark and heard someone on the stairs. Her heart began to pound, and she picked up the grate.

There was a soft knock. "Braley?"

"Constance! Can you get me out?"

The key was in the lock, and Constance opened the door to find her friend covered in soot, the pale trails of tears streaking her face, her hands bloodied from the rough iron bars. She opened her arms.

Braley dropped the grate and collapsed against her in heartbreaking tears of relief and terror. *"She's gone. He took her!"* She choked out. *"He's put her on the train, I know it! I don't know what happened. I don't remember."*

"I know. I know. We'll find her. But we've got to get out of here before he comes back."

In the kitchen, Braley guzzled water and washed her hands and face.

"Put these on," Constance instructed, handing her some clothes from a bundle she had brought, and eyeing several bottles of ether on the sideboard.

Braley put on the tan duck trousers, long-sleeve work shirt, and oversized canvas jacket. She finished pulling on the stockings and boots and looked to the older woman. Constance was dressed much the same.

"Those were my son's. You need a disguise, and it will be easier to travel," she said, adding a wide-brimmed hat. "He'll likely be watching the trains and the coaches. I've got a mount and a pack mule with food and supplies for you outside, that's what took me so long. I packed your things and some extras, and your money is in the saddlebag. You'll have to go back toward town and then head west, but take the back roads. When you get far enough away, you can catch a train. Ask around and follow the trains transporting the orphans. They have stops where they show the available children, and there will be advertisements—pamphlets and newspapers. The train that came through today is headed for Iowa. They make a lot of stops, but you don't have to. You may get ahead of them. We'll do everything we can from this end to see if we can find where she was sent. Warren will get the other lawmen to help, so check in at the sheriff's offices whenever you can. Write me with any news and let me know where to reach you and…" She froze at the look of horror on Braley's face.

"It's the buckboard. He's coming!"

"This way!" Constance glanced around the kitchen and bundled up the dirty clothes before ushering Braley out the side door, leading her into the bushes where she had hidden the horses. She gave her a hug. "You go," she whispered, "I'll create a diversion. He'll be furious when he sees you're gone."

"But I want you to come," Braley pleaded, even as she mounted the horse. She grabbed her friend's hand. "At least as far as town, so I know you're safe."

"Don't worry about me. I'll be fine. Be strong."

"How many times?" Braley's voice cracked.

"What?"

"How many times do I have to be strong?"

"One more. Always one more." Constance squeezed her hand and handed her up the lead to the mule. "Now go before you get us both caught!"

Choosing the lesser of two evils, Braley put heels to the horse, "I'll be back." She set off at a slow pace at first to not make too much noise and picked up speed as she got further away. She gave one last look over her shoulder, but it was pitch black now, and she focused her attention on the road ahead.

Jacob entered the house, fumbling to light a lamp from the hall table. It had been a long day, but the preacher would come tomorrow and all would be put right. A little more ether would take care of that, and it would help him get his son as well. He glanced at the sideboard. The ether was not there. He frowned, holding the lamp higher, and had to look closer to make out the mess of damp sooty towels that littered the kitchen. He bolted up the stairs.

The door to her room was open and he slammed it back against the wall. A strange glow outside caught his attention, and he moved toward the windows, forgetting they were boarded up. Turning, he tripped over the grate in the middle of the room, striking his shin and sprawling headfirst onto the floor, dropping the lamp. A line of flame shot across the rug. He stomped on the flames and rushed to the next room to look out the window.

Constance took the long way home. The situation was a weight on her heart, but it was a pleasant night, with a soft wind and the scent of rain in the air. The kind of night that made you feel closer to God. It had been a long while since she'd had a little time to herself to reflect. She needed it now. Her heart broke for her friend. She hoped Braley would be all right on her own and prayed she would be able to track down Eliza. Now and then, she looked over her shoulder at the orange glow on the horizon. It was growing brighter, but it was not the sun.

How dare he? How dare he use ether to kidnap a woman and child from her home and separate them? Rip them apart. *And who knows what he had planned for Braley?* It was fitting that Jacob had come home. Fitting that he had been there to see it. And fitting that ether was flammable.

Jacob ran to the church, a strangled cry tearing from his throat, but it was too late. All he could do was drop to his knees and watch it burn. *"Burn in hell!"* He screamed aloud. *"Why God? Why? What did I do to you? Have I not suffered enough?"*

The flames reached the roof and climbed the stairway to the steeple—*much like he had dreamed of doing for the grand opening*—they peeled back the shingles and the layers beneath, revealing the massive skeleton to the night sky. It was too hot. He had to move away. It was then that he saw the flames in the house. In her room. In his haste to get to the church, he had failed to put out the fire upstairs.

Part 2
Chapter 5

Braley had ridden for miles. She was not hungry and stopped only for water and to rest the animals. Her back hurt from hours in the saddle, and the pain of her full breasts brought tears to her eyes. She had no idea where she was going, except west. *West toward Eliza.* It had rained during the first night, hopefully covering her tracks, and she now followed the setting sun, staying out of sight of the main roads. Constance, bless her, had packed everything she could possibly need, including a rifle. She knew how to use it and take care of it, but she wasn't a very good shot. Papa Joe had taken her hunting many times, and they had camped, but she had mostly gone along to keep him company and to enjoy the time spent together. Now she found herself trying to remember all the things he had shown her.

She thought she had cried herself out over her baby, so much a part of her that she could still feel her in her arms, but tears started again at the thought of Papa Joe. *What would he think about the mess she had gotten herself into? What would he have done? He would have helped her, as always, that's what.* She kept the rifle beside her as she bedded down for the night alone in the woods, and cried herself to sleep.

She wanted to cry again the next morning, when she opened her eyes and found herself trapped in a body of stone. She couldn't move. Every muscle and bone screamed in protest and refused to do her bidding. Her breasts ached, and her shirt was soaked through. But she had to get up, saddle the horse, and pack up the mule.

She could barely lift the saddle, and the horse shied from her failed attempts. "*It's okay, Pap. Whoa, Pappy,*" she quieted the chestnut gelding. She didn't know why she started out talking to Papa Joe and ended up talking to the horse, but it had worked, and calmed both of them. Maybe she was losing her mind, but the horse was saddled. It had taken much too long, and she still hurt all over, but she didn't cry.

Day after day, she traveled much the same, but forced herself to eat, knowing she had to keep up her strength. She had hard tack and jerky, and she cooked rice and beans. She hated the extra time it took to prepare the food, and the chance she was taking by making a campfire. She compromised, cooking every few days, making enough to last until the next time, and eating it cold. On the off days, she missed the coffee.

She no longer ached when she moved and had no trouble saddling the horse. The pain in her breasts diminished day by day, the heavy burden replaced by the guilt she carried instead. Her long hair was bothersome, snagging twigs and getting in her way. It wouldn't fit under her hat, so she tied it back, and when that wasn't enough, she grabbed the ends in frustration and cut it just below her shoulders. When she began to lose count of the days she had traveled, she found a stick and carved notches to keep track, tying it to hang from her saddle. In the evenings, to pass the time, she carved Eliza's name and the date of her birth and added small blossoms to the design. It was better than concentrating on the questionable sounds in the woods.

After a few weeks, she headed northwest following the railroad tracks, hoping to find a town. It took longer than she thought, and the first small town she came to did not seem very promising. She went straight to the railway office, afraid they wouldn't take her seriously because of the way she was dressed, but there was nothing she could do about it.

"Can I help you, young fella?" The pleasant man behind the counter looked in her direction.

Braley turned around, but there was no one behind her.

"Can I help you, son?"

He thought she was a boy! She saw no reason to correct him. "Please. I'm looking for the orphans. The ones on the train from Ohio." Her knees were shaking as if her whole life depended on his answer, because it did.

"Train came through yesterday, but I only saw two kids get off. They were older and got picked up right away. Sometimes they're headed for specific destinations further up the line. Sometimes there's a whole bunch standing right out there on the platform for a look-see. Ain't you kind of young to be looking to adopt?"

"I'm not. I'm looking for one child. A baby. Have you seen a baby? A girl with dark hair?"

"I didn't, but they don't all get off the train. Sometimes, the little ones go straight to a home if nobody wants them. Let's face it, until they're of working age, they're nothing but another mouth to feed. We don't actually have one. A home, I mean. If they were on that train, my guess is they kept going." He stopped to peer at her over his spectacles. "You know, there are hundreds of miles of track out here. And that's just in Iowa."

Braley left sick to her stomach; the odds of finding Eliza seemed insurmountable. Her hand trembled as she finished a letter to Constance to let her know where she was and where she was going.

The man in the post office also thought she was a boy. Braley didn't mind. It felt safer being disguised as a *young man,* and emboldened by her new identity, she went to the hotel for a room, a decent meal, and a bath, before continuing on her way.

In the care of one sheriff's office, there was a letter from Constance. *Keep going,* was what it said. Sheriff Murphy had contacted other lawmen down the line and was still trying to get information from the Children's Aid Society. Eliza had not been located, but there was no indication she had been dropped off anywhere. '*Keep going,*' the letter said. *And she would.*

There were no outbound trains leaving soon enough to satisfy her, so she rode off again to search the next town, and the next, with much the same result. *Keep going.* She checked the newspapers and read the heartbreaking flyers until she saw them in her sleep. *Wanted: Homes for Children. A company of homeless children from the East will arrive at…* This was followed by a date, time, and location. *It was not unlike an auction for livestock*, she thought.

When she no longer feared Jacob would travel this far in search of her, she switched to riding the train to cross the Mississippi, loading the horse and mule in the stock cars. Some of the trains were transporting children, and it sickened her to see them displayed on platforms, being inspected like animals, the biggest and strongest often fought over. *They would be the best workers.* The lucky ones had been *ordered,* and she found it difficult to hold her temper or her disgust when she learned such a thing existed. *Want a ten-year-old boy with brown hair and blue eyes?* All you had to do was ask, and he would be delivered, much like a load of lumber or a bolt of cloth. Some, of course, were grateful to find a home, and she supposed it could be a good arrangement in some cases, if love were involved, but she wondered about the *ordered* ones. *Were they actually in need of a home?* Or were they someone's beloved child, mistaken for an orphan, snatched off the streets by accident or because they fit the bill? *Had anyone ordered a beautiful dark-haired baby girl?*

The next train she boarded had only six children as riders, four older boys who sat squabbling amongst themselves, and a younger boy and girl with sandy-brown hair who sat huddled together. The little girl was crying.

"Hello." Braley sat across from them, her attention drawn to the little girl with her hair in braids. "Are you all right? Do you need help?" She looked around for an attendant and got the attention of a woman sitting near the older boys. It was apparent she had her hands full keeping them in line, and gave an encouraging nod in Braley's direction. "Do you want to tell me what's wrong?"

Both heads turned in her direction, and two sets of identical blue eyes looked her over. "My sister can't stop cryin'," the boy said. "Our ma and pa died, and we're gonna' get somebody to take care of us."

"I'm very sorry." Braley tried to keep her voice steady, feeling the threat of tears she thought long gone. "What's your name?" She asked the little girl.

The child hid her face and whispered to her brother.

"I'm Curtis Kittle, and this is Olivia. She's six," he explained. "I'm ten. She wants to know if you're a girl or a boy."

Braley smiled. "I'm a girl, Olivia. My name is Braley, and I have a little girl of my own." *Somewhere.* "Would you like to come and see me?"

The little girl reached out her arms, and Braley lifted her and sat in her place, holding her on her lap. She tried her best to calm them, talking about how nice it would be to have a family and someone to take care of them. Before long, the little girl stopped crying and snuggled into her neck to sleep. Braley sat with an arm around Curtis, asking him preposterous questions to make him laugh. "You're a good brother to take care of your sister," she complimented, and watched his eyes light with pride.

"I promised my mom, and she's only little. I will always take care of her," he said, dozing against her shoulder.

Braley cherished the moments until the stop where the children got off. It was hardly big enough to qualify as a town, with no main street to speak of, so she waited on the train. She wished them well with an aching heart and watched them out the window. She hadn't asked if they had been *ordered* or if they were being picked up. Her stomach churned as one by one the older boys were examined, poked and prodded, and went their separate ways, claimed by different families, until only the brother and sister were left.

Braley decided they had not been ordered, as no one had been waiting for them. They looked so small and alone standing out in the open, hope their only possession. Hope and their love for each other. It broke her heart, and she was afraid the train would leave before she found out what would become of them.

The whistle sounded, the bell rang, and the engine started to chuff when a wagon pulled up. A man climbed down while the woman waited. The train began to move. Braley had to walk down the length of the cars to keep them in sight, and then her blood ran cold and she began to run. *No! No! Dear God, no!*

The man picked up Curtis and put him in the wagon, kicking and screaming, and drove away, leaving Olivia with the attendant holding her back when she tried to run after her brother.

Braley could not get off the train. She had no way to stop it. She ran back through the cars screaming for help, tears streaming down her face, trying to find someone, anyone, and when she did, it was too late. She would have to wait for the next stop, miles away. *The wait wouldn't be very long*, she was told. But they were wrong. It would be a lifetime.

It was not to be the last time she would witness the separation of siblings, and it was a sight she knew would haunt her for the rest of her days. Brothers and sisters crying and reaching for each other as they were claimed by different parties. It was one of the saddest things to her. That, and the ones not chosen at all. The ones left standing on the platform when the crowds drifted away. The look on their faces when they realized they had not measured up. That they were somehow lacking, not good enough to be claimed. *Not wanted.* They would get back on the trains, of course, to try again at the next stop, but not before watching the others drive off with new families. The nights she could not sleep, she poured her heart out in tear-stained letters to Constance.

The rocking and rolling of the train came to a gradual stop, and Braley woke, grateful to have escaped, for a time, the mixture of anticipation and dread that were her constant companions. She roused herself and went to collect her animals before wandering into yet another town. Each had been louder and rougher than the last, but none like this, with shooting and shouting in the streets and piano music coming from the saloon. *This town was trouble; she could feel it.* As she walked past, two men tumbled through the swinging doors and began fighting in the street, a crowd gathering to watch and cheer.

She posted another letter before making her way to the general store to replenish some of her supplies, her foreboding not yet diminished. Inside, it was dark and cool, and empty of other customers. She let out a sigh of relief, inhaling the wonderful scents of spices and leather, and herbal soaps. A giant of a man greeted her, and she was taking her time gathering a few things in the relaxing environment when a man burst in.

"I told you I'd be back, you damn cheat. Now give me my money back." His hand hovered above his holstered gun in an obvious threat.

The proprietor stepped out from behind the counter, already

reaching for his gun. Braley had ducked for cover instinctively, doing her best to become part of the woodwork, when a small towheaded boy appeared from the back room, running straight into the line of fire.

She was never to remember how she had leapt, tackled, and rolled with the youngster, as three shots rang over their heads; she only knew she came to a stop holding the boy, and the proprietor was kneeling beside them, crying. The other man lay still.

"My God, my God, Klaus, Klaus," the boy almost disappeared in his father's embrace. It was a few minutes before the man seemed to remember Braley was there. Tears unashamedly falling, he took her hand, dwarfed in his, shaking it nonstop. "Thank you, thank you. You have saved his life. You have saved us both, because I would die." He placed a hand over his heart. "And my wife…" He rolled his eyes. "You have what you want." He spread his arms encompassing the store. "All you want. Anything."

Braley, shaken by everything that had happened in the space of a few moments, opened her mouth to say the polite words that would decline his offer, and changed her mind. She knew what she wanted. *"Anything?"*

He nodded.

"I want that," she said, pointing to his waist where he wore a cross-draw holster.

"You want my gun?" He asked, reaching to unbuckle the belt.

"No," she said, "Teach me. Will you teach me how to shoot like that? I'll pay you."

"You will not, there is no need. I will show you, and find you the right gun… to fit," he said, looking her up and down.

"But it's too much, I want to pay."

"It is not the cost of my son. Let me do this for you." They shook hands again to seal the bargain, and he turned his hand over to study hers before he released it. "You are a girl?"

"Yes. But I'd rather you didn't tell anyone."

"I understand. It is safer for you. But I will tell my wife, because that is safer for me." He laughed and helped her to her feet. "My name is Herkules."

The wife of Herkules was blonde and pretty and as petite as he was large. He had told her that Braley had saved the little boy from danger and of the bargain they had made, leaving out most of the pertinent details. That was all she needed to hear. Braley was her hero. "I am Astrid. Come, you will stay."

She stayed with the little family at the wife's insistence, checking in town each day for a message from Constance. True to his word, Herkules brought her an ivory-handled revolver more fitting to her size, with a holster like his that he had crafted himself, and practiced with her each evening.

"Learn to draw first, then we will worry about the aim," he instructed. "Wearing the holster across makes the draw faster. It is safer and will not fall out or catch the brush when you ride. More important is the care and the cleaning we will do next. Never draw your gun unless you mean to use it, and always shoot three times."

"Three times?"

"Yes, make sure it counts. Easy to remember, one for the Father, one for the Son, and one for the Holy Ghost. A prayer for them if you don't miss, and a prayer for yourself if you do, because then you are dead."

They practiced until she could not lift her arm. "Now again."

Afterward, while he finished his chores, the women would sit on the porch in worn rockers the couple had brought with them on their journey west from Pennsylvania.

"Your husband is a good teacher," Braley said, breaking the comfortable silence. "He has a lot of patience."

Astrid smiled. "He is a good man, and a good husband."

She knew it could be true; she had seen it more than once, but it still struck Braley as odd to hear those words together, and see the dreamy look in the eyes of a wife speaking of the man she had married.

"I will tell you a secret," Astrid decided. "*Herkules* is not his real name. His name is Heiko. It is like your *Henry*, but he was so big as a child, his father called him Herkules. He likes it better."

Braley smiled, just as Klaus did her the honor of climbing into her lap and laying his head on her chest. She didn't know why… the hypnotic rocking, a woman to talk to, the warmth of the child… But she told Astrid her story. She left out many of the unpleasant details, but her husband was not a good man, and she told her so, and how it came about that he was not even her husband. She told her about Eliza and how and why she was there. The awful story came pouring out, but she didn't cry.

Astrid did. "Oh, how awful for you," she said, putting a hand over her mouth. "And you are traveling alone?"

Braley nodded. "I'm going to keep looking. I can't give up. I will never give up."

Chapter 6

She left her new friends behind with a promise to write and to practice. She was loaded down with the best of wishes, new supplies, and plenty of ammunition. Constance had sent word that there was a record of a child fitting Eliza's description, who had been sent to an orphanage to the north near Fort Leavenworth.

It was not her. The child was almost two years old, and although the little girl broke her heart, she was clearly not Eliza. She wished she could take her. *She wished she could take them all.* Braley wrote to Constance and headed west again. It had cost her almost a week's time. She had no idea if Eliza's name was included on the endless lists or if she were merely lost in the system. After several stops in Kansas, she headed northwest toward Fort Kearny in Nebraska.

Braley had never seen so much of nothing. Open plains stretched to the horizon. A sea of grass. It was hot and dusty and disheartening, with no place to hide at night. No trees, no brush, no shelter. She bedded down but slept little and was afraid to make a fire. She had never felt so alone, but she *had* felt more vulnerable; her frequent nightmares were a reminder of that. In them, nothing so terrible happened. It was only that Jacob was coming, and that was frightening enough.

The route she followed was little more than a path through the grass, but it soon widened into a trail that was obviously well-traveled.

She followed the wagon tracks and made good time until it started to rain so hard she couldn't see ahead. The poor animals, frightened by the thunder and lightning, bucked and tossed their heads, their fear making them too hard to handle, so she stopped. She couldn't lose them. It could mean life or death. Holding their bridles, speaking softly in the drenching rain, she became their anchor. Her strength, the nearest thing to shelter, she prayed for deliverance. "Whoa, Pappy, whoa, Joe. Easy boy. It will be all right. It will pass." Not sure if she were trying to comfort them, or herself, Braley closed her eyes. *See that ye be not troubled: for all these things must come to pass, but the end is not yet—Matthew, 24:6? Where did that come from?* It was Matthew, yes, but she could never quote scriptures even when she wished to.

The storm did pass, and she spent some time drying out her things in the sun. Most everything carried on the mule had been well covered by the tarpaulin and was usable. Feeling braver in the sunlight, she made a fire solely to make coffee in celebration.

Back on the trail, Pappy shied again at something up ahead. Braley pulled up and reached for her colt. What now? *A chair? It looked like a chair.* Braley looked twice. It was still a chair. An old rocker, much like the ones on Astrid's porch. *But why here in the middle of nowhere?* She rode along thinking it over until she rounded a bend and saw another in the tall grass, along with a table and a barrel, and it began to make sense. The ground was sandy here, and the wagons were heavy. Travelers had had to lighten the loads. It was but the beginning. For miles across the hot and windy plains were household goods and castoffs. These items were loved too much to be left behind when the owners set out on their journeys. They had been part of the dream, only to be sacrificed to make it come true, a burden too heavy to bear. She stopped and reached into her pocket. When she rode on, somewhere behind in the dust, lay a plain band of gold.

She had hoped to work her way further north, but being unsure which of the lesser paths would be best, she had stuck with the main route. *A passage so well-traveled had to lead to something.* At the last watering hole, she had come upon a group of travelers settling down for the night. The women, cooking and preparing to do laundry, while the men looked after the stock and made repairs to the wagons. They were on their way to Oregon and invited her to join them for the night. It was nice to see some signs of life, but she was leery. Papa Joe had warned her about cholera, dysentery, and the smallpox. *The more people, the greater chance of trouble,* he had said. She could not afford to get sick, so though she longed for company, with a few hours of daylight left, she decided to keep going. It was a decision she would regret.

She had pushed too long, ending up having to make camp in the dark, and so, had gone right to sleep, too tired to bother with a fire. She had no idea how long she had slept when she first heard the noise, her heart thudding even as she opened her eyes. There was the nervous nickering of the horses... *She wasn't dreaming.* It was close, whatever it was. She cocked her head to listen, reaching for the rifle, sitting up and staring into the pitch blackness as it moved closer. It wasn't footsteps, but something moved through the brush. Sweat dampened her shirt despite the cool breeze, and she forgot to breathe as she raised the gun, but she couldn't aim at what she couldn't see. The horses grew more restless, stomping and moving about. She reached for the lantern with one hand and fumbled for the matches, but it was too late. It burst into the clearing and was already at her feet. A cry escaped her throat as she fired into the night, but it didn't stop, tearing and scratching before she managed to push it off and send it on its way.

It had been a long time since she had risen to that level of fear and self-doubt. It would be impossible to sleep the rest of the night. She quieted the horses and sat for a long time calming herself—*Angry with herself. Cursing Jacob Turner, the God-forsaken prairie, and anything else she could think of*—not knowing whether to give rein to the hysterical laugh that rose in her throat or surrender to the tears that threatened, in her attempt to make peace with the fact she found difficult to accept. She had shot a tumbleweed.

It was becoming difficult to find room on her calendar stick to make another notch for each day that passed. She had caught up with several more wagon trains and met still more people. She was shocked to find they walked beside their wagons. The wagons were so full of provisions and belongings and perhaps, hopes and dreams, that there was no room to ride inside, and so they walked. They were walking to Oregon, clear across the country. That was too slow for her. She preferred to keep to herself, getting the most miles out of each day, and practicing her shooting as she had promised. She was getting better.

The ground became more barren and desert-like, and the heat was grueling. She rode with her shirt sleeves rolled up, but there was no relief. She spotted another wagon up ahead with a milk cow in tow, and thought she was gaining on it. She stopped to look again. *It wasn't moving.* It was too early to break for the night, and rather late for noon break. *Perhaps they were resting,* she thought, but as she approached, she didn't see anyone. She circled warily. "Hello?" She called out, not wanting to scare anyone.

There was no answer, and she drew closer, the cow lowing at her approach. "Hello?" She dismounted, tying her horse to a small bush. A sick feeling began to spread upward from her stomach, burning into her chest. "Hello?" She approached the team of blacks still hitched to the wagon, standing with their heads down. They did not look good, and she wondered how long they had been there, waiting in the heat without water. "Whoa boy," she lifted one large head, stroking the nose which felt rough, and then checked the other. The eyes were dull and the gums somewhat dry and tacky… *not good, but not too late.* Horses were not the best choice out here, as she understood it. Even those as large and strong as these drafts. All the wagons she had seen had used four or six oxen to pull the heavy loads. This wagon was smaller, but still… She had stalled long enough. She rested her forehead against the powerful neck and closed her eyes before walking to the back of the wagon. There was a buzzing sound, and she braced herself to look inside.

After she vomited into the brush, she paced, trying to decide what to do. *She couldn't leave them there.* She didn't want to leave them. She hadn't gone too close, but they didn't seem to have any wounds. The way the bodies were lying in the wagon, they were most likely laid up and died of sickness. *But what?* She was afraid. Afraid to touch them. *Oh God, help…*

In the end, she buried them, but did her best not to touch them. She dug a shallow grave by the back of the wagon and pulled them out with Pappy's help, tying a rope to the blankets they were lying on, and burying her gloves along with them. Her sight blurred by tears, she prayed as she worked, covering them over and leaving them there on the side of the trail, like so many others. It only took a few extra minutes to mark the grave with the shovel, a cross carved into the handle, something she had seen in her travels. *At least they were together.* It was the best she could do. She vomited again and went to unhitch the horses. It was a shame, really; the water barrel was almost full, but she did not dare let them drink from it. She did use it to wash her hands with the bar of strong lye soap that hung there before she set off to lead them to what she hoped was safer water. As they left the clearing, a large dog ran out from the brush to join them.

She had turned the animals loose after spending too long at the watering hole, seeing to their care. They followed her anyway, the cow plodding along behind with the dog, who sometimes ran ahead, or left them all together. He always returned at night, though, and Braley grew more comfortable having a campfire, with the extra eyes and ears around. She slept better, too. He was some kind of cur-shepherd mix, she guessed, judging by his reddish-gold coat and black face. A good farm dog and a better companion. She talked to him constantly, and at times even asked his advice, but she didn't think of him as hers, and she couldn't bring herself to name him. It didn't seem right. "You have a name, don't you, boy?" She took to calling him *Dog* and sharing her meals with him. More than once, he had growled and chased off something unknown in the night, perhaps saving her life, and the nights she woke from her nightmares, it was reassuring to have him nearby.

The grass along the trail was decimated by years of oxen and horses, goats and sheep, feeding en route, so she let the animals wander to find what they could, and followed where they went. It was much the same for firewood. At one point, she thought about burning her travel stick so she could have a cup of coffee, but decided against it. It wasn't enough to make a big enough fire anyway. Years of campfires alongside the trail had caused the countryside to be picked clean. *What did the overlanders do? Surely, they did not carry their own firewood on top of everything else?* "Buffalo chips." She spoke aloud to Dog. *Those would burn.* "Don't bring me any!" She yelled after him as he ran off.

She herded her little party toward the north, where the land turned increasingly rocky, and she was always on alert for coyotes, wolves, and snakes. Then there was that damn prickly pear cactus, *the spawn of Satan himself.* It was everywhere, and if you were smart, you only touched it once. She had learned to hate it as well as avoid it. The spines weren't so bad; it was the little bristles that were difficult to see and impossible to get rid of. One touch and they had haunted her for weeks. *Another lesson learned the hard way.*

It had been too long since she had contact with Constance, and she had lost far too much search time. She had to find somewhere soon; her food was running out, and she had precious little water. Two more nights passed without a fire. They left the prairie behind as they reached higher ground, and a stony carpet spread out ahead, heralding the majestic mountains that sat on the horizon. There was a welcome change as the air turned cooler and clearer.

She still had no idea where she was, but she had stopped to admire the view when Dog ran ahead and then returned to bark at her, and run off again. He had never done that before. Again, he appeared, barked, and ran off. The back of her neck tingled. *What now, Lord? Please, nothing bad. Did that qualify as a prayer? Should she pray harder?*

She spotted a riderless mount standing further down the path, ready to bolt at the dog's slightest movement. *Not again, please God!* Her stomach hurt with the hollow pain she had felt before. She couldn't do it again. She dismounted and walked closer, comforting the beautiful golden horse and securing it.

Dog darted off the trail, crashing into the brush, and Braley warily followed.

It was a man. Young, from what she could tell. He was lean and broad-shouldered and very still, dressed in a dark shirt, his straight blonde hair glinting in the sun. He lay face down with his hands tied behind him, a wide-brimmed hat by his side.

"Hello?" She didn't want to get too close. *"Mister?"* She stared, her mind drifting to the time a goldfinch had flown into the glass of her window when she was a young girl. She had heard it hit and gone out to find it on the ground. The memory had stayed with her. The feeling of loss, to see something so perfect, lying so still without a mark on it, seemed such a waste of God's beauty. She was sure the poor thing had died of a broken neck, and she had found a box, thinking she would bury it, but it was only stunned. It had woken up, and in a short time, it had recovered and flown away.

Was there a chance he would recover? She placed an unsteady hand on his back and snatched it away. *He was still warm.* She steeled herself to touch his back again and felt the faintest movement when he took a breath. Braley sat back on her heels, wondering what to do. *Should she move him? Perhaps he could breathe better if she turned him over.* She did, and he moaned.

He had a mustache, darker than his hair, about a day's growth of beard, and some dried blood by his temple that she hadn't seen. Still trying to keep some distance she moved his hair aside to examine the wound. She got her canteen and a cloth from her saddlebag. The water was warm, almost hot, from her day in the sun, but she used it, wiping his face and the back of his neck.

His eyes opened, *"Ah,"* he winced, squeezing them shut for a moment. "Did you shoot me?"

"Of course not."

A woman alone? "What are you doing here then?"

"Passing through. Not that it's any of your business." She held the canteen so he could take a drink. "What happened to you?"

"I told you. I got shot."

She looked him over again. "You don't look shot."

"I guess I hit my head when I fell off my horse." He glanced around, relieved to see he still had a ride home. "Thank you. My name is Laith. Laithram Demoranville. Would you untie me, please?"

"I don't know," she said.

"What?"

"You must be tied up for some reason."

"Well, are you going to leave me here to die?"

She thought it over while he held his breath, his eyes wide. "It looks like somebody already did that. What I'm wondering is *why*? What did you do?"

"Nothing. I promise you. I was on my way to buy some cattle and…" He swore, causing Braley to raise her brows. "I've probably been robbed. Can you at least check my saddlebag? On the left, there's a leather pouch with my initials on it."

She did as he asked, keeping her eyes on him as she undid the straps and searched the saddlebag. "Sorry," she said when she came back.

"Look, if you untie me, I'll be on my way."

She couldn't leave him here to die and pulled her knife from her boot to cut him free.

He sat up quickly. *Too quickly*. He winced again, pressing an arm to his side and raising a hand to his forehead.

Braley dropped the knife and scrambled backward on the ground, reaching for her gun.

"Whoa, lady! Jeez, what's wrong with you?"

Her eyes never left his as she handed him the canteen again, her heart beating rapidly.

He hated to think of her out here by herself if she were that nervous. "You any good with that?" He nodded toward the gun she carried.

"I'm working on it."

She knew she had overreacted. *Old habits die hard.* Still, she kept her distance when he rose and made his way up the bank, holding one arm against his side. Dog greeted him and he squatted to make his acquaintance.

"He found you," she said.

"Well, I'm grateful, even if you're not." He eyed the rest of her menagerie.

Braley blushed, embarrassed that he had read her thoughts.

He grinned, squinting at her, his eyes a light golden brown in the lowering sun.

She supposed he was quite good-looking. She also knew it counted for nothing.

"What are you doing out here all alone anyway?" He asked. "You headin' west?"

"The truth is, I'm lost," she admitted. "I need to get to a town. Do you know where we are?"

He swore again as he rifled through his saddlebag to check his losses. "Yeah, I do. I'm not that far from home." He reached into his pocket, pulled out some bills, and stuffed them back in. *At least they didn't get it all.* He studied her. She was an attractive girl, not too tall, straight dark hair past her shoulders. Her eyes were the deepest brown, earthy and warm, but full of suspicion. The small mark on her cheek only added a bit of mystery, and she had a pretty mouth… *Too bad she didn't smile.*

Braley grew uncomfortable under his gaze. "I didn't take anything."

"Never crossed my mind."

She nodded. "How did you know I was a woman?" She didn't mean to blurt it out, but she wanted to know before he left.

He laughed, "I'm not sure I should even try to answer that."

"Some of the places I've been, they thought I was a boy. You called me *lady.*"

"They must'a been blind," he muttered.

"Oh." She didn't know what he meant, but she had felt better when she thought no one knew. "So, you don't think I can pass for a boy?"

"Ha, sorry, no. I've never seen a cowboy with hips like that. That coat doesn't hide… as much as you think. *And with that face?*" He laughed again.

She regretted the direction the conversation had taken, and she wasn't sure what he meant about her face. She put a hand to the scar on her cheek and changed the subject. "Where are you headed?"

He looked around, "It's kind of late. I guess we'd better make camp."

Her pulse quickened, and she stepped back. "You said you would leave."

"I guess I did." He eyed the horizon. "I thought I might help you get where you wanna get. You know, for helping me out. I could bring you to the closest town. I hate to leave you out here by yourself, but I'll go if you want."

"I got this far."

"You just said you were lost."

Was a stranger's company better than none? Could she trust him? She needed to find a town. Braley stood battling temptation until she lost the fight. All that mattered was her daughter. She nodded. *She didn't have to trust him.*

"All right then. You got a name?" He put out his hand.

She winced, turning her face away, but then accepted the handshake. "I'm Braley Stuart."

His grip was gentle, his eyes full of questions. "I won't hurt you, Braley Stuart." He turned to unsaddle his horse, wondering what on earth had happened to make the woman so skittish, and grabbed his side in pain.

Braley approached warily, "What is it?"

"I told you. I got shot."

"I still don't see it," she said, examining the back of his shirt without moving any closer.

"It's here on my side. It must have bled. I think my shirt is stuck. It pulls every time I move."

"Here," she lifted the saddle off and placed it on the ground, conscious of his nearness and that she had turned her back to him. *Was he really hurt, or was it a trick?* "We'd better take a look."

There was a small tear on his side. He unbuttoned his shirt, and together they peeled it back until it resisted, and he made a face. "Come sit down," she said, going to get the canteen and the supplies she would need.

Laith had watched her. She looked scared to death until she saw the blood on his side, and then she had relaxed. A little. *Was she relieved that it wasn't too bad or that he was actually hurt? What the hell?*

She never met his eyes, but washed the dried blood away, inching the shirt back until it revealed a long graze across his ribs. It had started to bleed again when she disturbed it, and she patted it dry before applying an ointment. She hesitated, the roll of gauze in her hand, when it came time for the bandage, but he lifted his arms, so she wound the bandage around his chest, reaching inside his shirt at each pass.

Laith felt bad for her every time she put her arms around him to pass the bandage from one hand to the other behind his back. Clearly, she was nervous. The look of determination on her face touched his heart. She didn't like this at all, but she was doing it to help him.

Three days in, they sat around the campfire in the evening. She, resting with her back against a tree trunk, and he, keeping his distance, leaning against his saddle on the ground. He had been nothing but kind and considerate, drawing her out with stories and observations.

She had been quiet for much of the time. Although she had told him how she had acquired Dog when he asked about his name, and about the young couple she had stopped to bury, and somehow felt better for the telling. She was still wary of his motives, but she had decided, *almost*, that she was a bit more comfortable.

"You ever think about getting married?" He asked.

Everything in her roiled with alarm. *Surely, he couldn't mean that the way it sounded. She was overreacting again. Jumping to conclusions.* "You should be more careful. That almost sounded like a proposal."

He shrugged and glanced at her sideways.

He didn't jump up in denial and she'd rather he had. "I already dodged that bullet," she said.

"Just wondered." He was quiet for a time before he spoke again. "People marry out here pretty quickly. Mostly out of necessity, I guess."

"What makes you think it's a good idea to marry a stranger?" She asked, sipping her coffee and stroking Dog, who had settled beside her.

"I don't know. What makes you think it's not?"

"Because I did."

"Oh. So, you're married?"

"Not anymore." The surrounding darkness and the mesmerizing flames of the campfire made it easier to find the words. She told him about Reverend Keats and as much of her story as she thought he needed to know, which was very little. "It did not go well. I'm looking for my daughter. She came out here on the orphan train. I've been searching for months."

"How did she get on the orphan train if she wasn't an orphan?"

She was quiet for so long, he thought she wasn't going to answer. "Her father didn't want her."

Laith knew it wasn't the whole story, but it seemed as much as she wanted to tell at the moment. He had already guessed some of it, the way she seemed always on edge and ducked whenever he moved too fast. Her voice in the dark sounded tired and defeated. "I want to help you," he said. "There's no reason for me to go after the cattle without all the money. I'd only be going back home anyway, and they're not expecting me for a while."

He glanced in her direction, "My problems seem a lot less important compared to yours. I live with my father and my half-brother, Leland. It's a big spread with acres of timber and a saw mill my father built on the river. With the railroad coming, we added cattle. I want to grow corn, but they think I'm crazy. Anyway, my father hasn't been feeling well, and he wants to divide the property between my brother and me. He said first one of us to get a wife gets the main house and the lower acres, and the other gets the cabin and a bigger piece of the land."

"And you think that's a good reason to get married?"

"Well, it's a damn nice house." He laughed before his voice grew more serious, "I guess it sounds pretty shallow. It's just… hard to give up your home, you know?"

Braley nodded. "Yes, I do."

"And besides," he went on, "my brother, he's the oldest, he's arrogant… *You know?* Kind of thinks everything should be his, 'cause he was firstborn. I guess I'd like to come out ahead for once."

"I understand about brothers and leaving home, but have you thought about the poor woman? Someone who has her hopes up to build a life with someone she could care about, not knowing she would be used to settle a rivalry? That's hardly fair, and it doesn't make for a good marriage. Marriage should mean so much more than that. And home has a lot more to do with who is there than what is there."

There was another long pause. *How must she feel, separated from her little girl?* "What would you think of a bargain?"

"A bargain?"

"Yes. I was on my way to buy some cattle to start my own herd, and I was going to look for a wife. But you're right, I don't want to marry for the wrong reasons. It seems like there should be something more to it, and you don't want to be married at all. I've already told you the truth, and it will be cold soon. Winters are harsh out here. You'll have to find a place to stay. What if I help you find your daughter, and you stay with me at the ranch through the winter? Pretend we're married. I'll leave you alone, I promise, and you can leave in the spring."

"I have no intention of ever being married again, fake or not. Not in a million years."

It must have been worse than he thought. "I'm sorry," he said. "It was a stupid idea. I'd still like to help you, though."

"Why?" She asked.

"Why?" *Jeez, she was as thorny as a prickly pear.*

Braley nodded, "Why do you want to help me?"

"*Because you need help?* You helped me. You probably saved my life, you know. I'd like to see you find your daughter. I'd like to see that you get home safe." She didn't look convinced. "I have some friends up by Fort Laramie. I could at least see you that far. That is, if you have to go that far." *He didn't know why he offered. The whole thing was too darn sad.*

Braley weighed the consequences. If he knew the area, his help could mean getting to Eliza faster. That was all that mattered, and she didn't love being alone. She had to admit these past days had been much better. *Dog liked him. Of course, he could kill her in her sleep. He didn't seem the type, but she had made that mistake before.*

"You can think about it." He pulled something from his saddlebag and lit a lantern.

"What's that?" She asked.

He held up a book, "The Three Musketeers. Frenchmen with swords who guard the king. Have you read it? I'm sorry, can you read?"

"I can. But no, I haven't." She didn't know why, but the idea that he had brought a book out of all the things one needed on the trail touched her heart. "Do you read a lot?"

"Whenever I can. I like learning about different things, different times and places, you know? I can start over, if you like," he offered. "I've barely begun. I could read it out loud." He smiled and shrugged.

Braley moved cautiously closer for what would become an evening ritual, a comforting voice in the night, and a much-needed escape from the harsh realities of the days.

Chapter 7

He had found her. He was here. A dark shape leaned over her, holding her fists as she struggled and fought, trying to get away, her heart pounding, until the words reached her.

"…a nightmare. Braley, it's me. It's all right now. You were having a nightmare."

It wasn't Jacob, it was Laith. She stopped fighting and nodded.

"I'm sorry. You were crying out in your sleep. I'm going to let you go now. It's all right. I thought you were going to punch me. Try to sleep. I'll be here," he said, as he pulled his bedroll over and lay down closer to her.

Braley reached out in the dark and placed her hand on his arm.

Three more days of hard travel, on a trail she would never have found, brought them to a tent city settlement near Fort Laramie. She checked the outdated newspapers brought on the stage and searched for flyers and placement committee members. Braley was not fond of busy towns or crowds, but in this case, it lifted her spirits to see people walking down the street doing everyday things, women in dresses and bonnets, coming and going, and children playing. There were shops and what passed for a hotel, and even a bank being built. She was surrounded by life, and it gave her hope.

A woman who volunteered with a local children's home looked at her with sympathy when she had told her story. "We don't get children out here. Not from the Society." She lowered her voice, "Some children came through on the stage line recently."

"I didn't know they traveled by stage." Braley half questioned.

The woman looked around and shot her a warning look. "They don't. *Not usually.* Two older boys is all and one young'un that continued on..."

Braley's heart began to pound. A girl Eliza's age with dark hair, but no recorded name, had been sent by stage to Idaho Territory near Soda Springs. She tried to ignore the tingle that ran down her spine. *She would not dare to hope. She would not. She could not.* She went to the post office to mail a letter to Constance, knowing she could very well be back before it ever reached her. Careful to stretch her money, she washed her clothes and bought a new wool shirt and some extra stockings. They were now in Wyoming Territory, and the nights were getting cooler as summer's end drew near.

They could not take a train. It would be months before the railroad extended this far west, and even then, the tracks would run far to the south of where they needed to travel. At this point, the speed and relative comfort of a passenger car would have been heavenly, and the thought of hitting the trail again was daunting. *But if Eliza waited at the other end...*

Laith did indeed have friends who lived near the settlement. Mr. and Mrs. Saunders would take the extra animals temporarily. It hurt her heart to leave Dog behind, but it was too far for the poor animal to have to run. They set off, Braley's heart leading the way down the road, but she could not help but feel there was a small piece left behind.

The days, marked by miles of dust, prairie grass, and rocky trails blending together, her calendar stick running out of room for the notches she carved, they traveled on. Several smaller settlements that had sprung up along the trail had little to offer, and they didn't stay long. They would take the well-traveled South Pass through the mountains, and Laith set a daunting pace when possible. He had to admire her spirit. Most of the women, and plenty of the men he knew, would probably complain at the hardship. It was surprising to him that she kept up without a word and was always ready to go some more. But, then again, she had more reason than most.

Due to the speed of travel, they spoke little, unless it was at night around their camp, or when they rested the horses, and at one such stop, he decided to tell her his thoughts. "You're some kind of woman, Braley Stuart."

Braley, dressed as she was, wiping at the dirt on her face and feeling the grit of trail dust in her teeth, was not feeling especially womanly. She shot him a sideways glance. "There's no need to be mean."

"I wasn't." *Jeez, she was always looking for insults. Thank Heaven she had turned down his proposals. Talk about dodging a bullet!*

She watched the smile fade from his eyes. *Laith had been good to her. He was kind and considerate, doing all the heavy lifting, caring for the stock, saddling and unsaddling the horses, setting up camp, and doing a lot of the cooking. He stopped whenever she asked without getting angry and had never made her feel uncomfortable. He still read to her at night. When they had finished the book, they had started it over, neither willing to give up the comfortable bond. Why then would he be mean to her out of the blue? It was possible he hadn't meant it that way.* "I'm sorry. I guess I'm used to…"

"Forget it. Let's go."

She studied his back as he rode ahead. *Had he meant to compliment her then? Why? And why was it so confusing?*

As expected, it was yet another hot and dusty day. Midway through the morning, they came upon a young couple struggling with a broken wheel. Braley slowed, trying to decide how best to ask Laith if they could help, or to tell him she was going to. She searched for words, not yet making eye contact with the stranded travelers in case he passed them by.

He pulled up ahead of her. "Hold on," he said, before she could speak, "I'm going to give them a hand." For the first time, he saw her smile. Really smile, and he stopped to study her before nudging his horse forward.

Pleased and relieved, Braley chatted with the wife and looked on as Laith not only offered to help, but did most of the work, straightening the jack and greasing the hub and axle before switching out the wheel. She watched him wiping his hands on a cloth, talking with the young man, saying something that made him laugh. It was strange to feel a certain amount of pride for being with someone who was friendly and kind. She found she much preferred it to being embarrassed and making excuses. The men shook hands, and they continued on their way.

"That was nice." She said, further down the trail, not able to explain that she was proud of him. *What would he think of her?*

"What's that?"

"You, stopping to help."

"Well, sure. That's how it works. Wouldn't anybody?" *Jeez, what kind of people did she know?*

No, she thought to herself, *no, they wouldn't.* But she nodded in agreement.

The towns were fewer now, and smaller. After Kansas, without the trains, not many orphans had been sent this far. There were fewer, if any, newspapers in the smaller towns, and when there were, there were no advertisements for children. Much of the communication was by word of mouth, and Braley, in her desperation, was not above going person to person and stopping people on the street.

Laith watched as she stood there now, searching up and down for someone she hadn't yet asked. He saw the moment her shoulders dropped as hope faded, and his heart went out to her. He stepped up and took her by the elbow.

Braley, defeated and near tears for the first time in a long time, felt herself being grabbed from behind, and snatched her arm away. She spun around, ready to fight back.

"No, Braley. It's me."

His eyes were soft and kind, and full of something she couldn't quite name. She collapsed against him, wrapping her arms around his waist, and he held her.

"We'll find her. We still have Soda Springs," he comforted, holding her loosely at first, unsure what she would want, and then tightening his embrace when she didn't move away. "It's all right."

"But the stage passes through here. Someone should have seen her…" She pulled herself together, hating the momentary lapse in her resolve. She could feel his warmth and his compassion, but she didn't want his pity. She straightened and stepped back. "I'm sorry."

He nodded, and they walked in silence to get the horses. Hours later and miles down the road, he could still feel her arms around him.

It was late in the day when they reached their destination. They had pushed the horses hard and long on the last stretch, and when Braley dismounted she wasn't sure if her knees were shaking from the ride or fear of what she was about to find out. She did her best to ignore the thought that Eliza could be anywhere by now. *Anywhere in the world.*

Laith, who had been extra solicitous of late, was there to steady her when she slid from the horse. "You okay?"

"I think so. If she's not here, I don't know…"

Laith wasn't sure when or why finding her child had become the most important thing in his life. Maybe it was watching her carry on, day after day, knowing how she suffered inside, or realizing that such sheer cruelty could exist in the world. He put his hands on her shoulders and looked into her eyes. "Listen to me, Braley, we're not giving up. We'll go all the way to Oregon and back if we have to, and China after that."

They stopped to send a telegram to Constance to let her know they had arrived, knowing a letter could take weeks or even months without a connecting railroad. Braley held her breath when they went in to see the sheriff.

"Oh yes, I got a telegram about you, from a sheriff back east. Murphy, I think…" He searched his desk. "Yep. I'm sorry about your little girl. I have three girls of my own. It seems they think she may be out this way." He directed them to a home in town. "If she were signed into their care, it's between you and the home, but if you have any trouble, you come back and see me. Good luck."

Braley grabbed Laith's arm as soon as they left the office and held tightly as they walked along. "Did you hear what he said?"

"Yes. So, your friends back east heard the same thing you did? There's a chance this might be your daughter?"

Braley didn't speak, but she hugged his arm tighter.

It was a neat clapboard building on the edge of town, with only a small sign above the door that proclaimed it a '*Home For Children*' in neat lettering. Laith stood with his arms crossed and let Braley do the talking.

"I'm Braley Stuart," she said to the woman behind the desk, her voice wavering, "I'm searching for my daughter who may have come on the stage."

Something flashed in her eyes before the woman answered. "Well, this is unusual," the woman said, not unkindly, but eyeing Braley up and down, her eyes coming to rest several times on the gun strapped to her waist. "So, you surrendered her, and now you want her back?"

"No, that is not what happened."

"Then how did she get here?"

Braley took a deep breath. "She was stolen from me. We were kidnapped from a friend's home at night, and she was taken to the train while I was locked in a room with the windows boarded up."

Laith listened, her words hitting like a punch to his gut, the blood roaring in his veins, and took a step toward her, his arm encircling her shoulders of its own accord.

Braley's stomach churned as the woman's expression turned doubtful. She hurried to explain, "I came as soon as I could. I have followed her all the way across the country… Her name is Eliza. She is almost eight months, with dark hair…"

"What makes you think she would be here? These are mostly local children. We are not part of the Children's Aid Society; we obviously have no trains and…"

"But I was told she may have been sent here on the stage…"

"Children are not sent by stage."

Braley leaned over the desk and grabbed the woman by the wrist.

"But that's what I was told."

The woman glanced around the room. "Not unless…"

"You'd better tell me."

"If she came by stage, someone paid for it." Her voice lowered to a whisper. "Someone who ordered her, or someone who sent her."

Braley accepted the first and raged inside at the second. "But how… how would she start out in the care of the Society and end up here?"

The woman looked down at the desk. "If enough money changes hands, the shadows grow deep. I suggest you stay out of them."

"Like you do?"

"You can't tell anyone. It is best you do not mention the stage."

Braley stared into her eyes for a long moment and released her wrist.

"We have two little girls of that description, and one a little older. I don't think there's an Eliza on record, but one came with no name, just a number, as I recall. I think she may have a claim pending, but there are others, as I said. If it helps, we prefer to place with couples rather than single people, so that is in your favor. And you should know, there may be a fee."

*Something was wrong. Why all the secrecy? And she had never heard of a fee, not that she wouldn't pay any price…*Braley's heart was nearly thudding out of her chest, "But she's mine."

Laith placed his arm around her shoulders again, tighter this time.

"I am unsure of the protocol for that. I don't know if it has ever happened before. Mrs. Clark would know better, but she has gone for the day. You'll have to come back tomorrow."

"But you may have my daughter."

"There's nothing we can do tonight." The woman glanced up at Braley and, seeing the look on her face, seemed to soften. "Don't take this the wrong way, dear, but are you sure you would even know which was yours? I mean, being so young at the time, you said it's been a while, and they do change quickly, you know."

"I'll know," Braley ground out.

Laith slid his arm to her waist to urge her toward the door. "Come on," he whispered, "We don't want to make them angry." *He prayed she wouldn't lose the temper he could sense boiling just below the surface.*

"But I've come all this way and we're so close. It's not fair. It's not fair to be this close and not know."

His heart ached at the anguish in her voice.

"Wait." The woman rose from her chair. "I'm sorry. I see so many children come and go that I…" she sighed. "I suppose we could at least look, so you'll know one way or the other. Mind you, I still can't do anything tonight without the proper paperwork, and as I said, there may be a claim. But if you promise only to check…"

Braley did promise, and the woman motioned for them to follow her up the stairs to a room at the back of the house. There was a line of beds against the wall and four cribs in the corner. An aide sitting in the room watched in curiosity.

Braley reached for the woman's arm, and she stopped. "She has a scar on the back of her neck," she said, raising her arm to touch the back of her own neck in indication. "It's a curved line with a small burn at the bottom."

The woman stared at Braley before nodding her head. "Then it's her." She indicated the bed at the end of the row.

The room grew cold around her while heat burned in her chest and down her arms. Certain her heart had burst, she leaned on Laith's arm and fell more than walked forward.

Braley braced herself… *Her hair…* Her hair was longer, and she had grown, of course, but there was no question in Braley's mind or heart that this was her Eliza. *She's not terribly bigger*, she tried to convince herself, as she bent over the crib. *You didn't miss that much.* She brushed a hand over the dark head and leaned in to check the scar to be sure she wasn't dreaming, wasn't fooling herself out of desperation, because she so needed this to be real.

The mark was smaller than she remembered, and it had faded, but it was there. *Eliza.* She sank to her knees beside the crib, staring through the bars and through the tears that came at last. Tears of joy, and relief, and exhaustion, for prayers answered and time lost, but most of all, for love found. Laith placed a hand on her shoulder.

"Do you want to hold her?" The woman asked, her own voice sounding not the same.

"Let her sleep," Braley whispered, her eyes never leaving the child, remembering her promise, and knowing once she held her, she would never let her go. She touched the tiny hand. "It is enough for now to know where she is. I'll be back tomorrow."

Outside, they embraced, because there were no words, and he kept his arm around her all the way back to the hotel and to the door of her room.

"I'm as happy as I can be for you, Braley Stuart," he said, his voice breaking despite his best efforts. "That little scar was almost a good thing in a way."

"I'd like to think—*I do think*— I would have known it was her without it. I could feel it. I could feel that it was her," Braley said, thinking there was nothing good about that awful night.

"I don't doubt that," Laith explained, "but you knowing it was there, for sure convinced that woman. Of course, she does look just like you."

"Oh, do you think so?"

"Definitely. Same eyes, same hair, same pretty face with that stubborn little chin." He grinned.

Her heart soared.

He asked about the scar, and she told him there had been a fire, inviting him into her room so they could talk a little longer. She told him how her friends had helped her put it out and how they had discovered the wound on the baby afterward. "That's when I got this," she said, touching the mark on her cheek, "and I have a scar on my shoulder." She didn't know why she told him that; she didn't have to, except that she was caught up in the moment, in the terror, and the truth.

She hadn't slept after he left, and she was ready extra early. She had bathed and washed her hair and put it up, and paid the maid at the hotel to find her a skirt and blouse. Although not new, they were clean and neat, and she didn't question where they came from.

Laith did a double-take when she opened the door. She wore a pale blue walking skirt and a white shirtwaist. "Jeez, Braley." *She was all girly and soft-looking. Should he tell her? Would she get angry?* He had spent most of the night thinking about what she had said about the fire, being kidnapped, and her baby being stolen. *Stolen!* And when he thought about her being locked in… He hadn't known, and he could only imagine how awful that must have been. He had never hated someone he had never met before. No wonder she was more ornery than a bull in summer, and jumpy all the time. "Jeez," he said again, taking off his hat and searching for the right thing to say. She was beautiful. But she was always beautiful. She was… *Different.* "You look different." *Jeez, that wasn't it.*

Had she hoped for something more? No. She knew better, and besides, she had more important things on her mind, but she had thought for a second when his eyes widened, he might say she looked nice. "I thought it might help. I'm not sure that woman was impressed with my attire. I miss wearing my gun, though," she said, brushing her hand across her middle. "I feel naked without it."

Their eyes met. There was a moment of silence where she blushed, and his eyes swept down the front of her before he forced them away.

"I've got mine." He stated the obvious, "and if you need yours, we'll come back and get it."

She didn't think he was joking, but she couldn't think why she would need it.

"Let's go get your daughter." Laith swept his hat in an arc, inviting her to lead the way.

"Wait!" The maid hurried down the hall. "I found this for you," she said, holding up a soft woolen shawl. "I thought you might need it."

"Thank you." Braley smiled, and wrapping the shawl around her shoulders, left with a happy heart.

Mrs. Clark was an imposing woman with her graying dark hair worn in a fierce bun. The woman from the night before hovered in the background while Braley told her story.

"And now you want the child back."

"Of course," Braley said, chills prickling the skin on the back of her neck. She glanced at the other woman, but she shook her head, moving back into the shadows. She would clearly be of no help.

"Most unusual," the woman muttered to herself, reading over a file on her desk. She glanced up at both of them. "Number forty-seven. This child has been placed out. Claimed before you came, so I would think that takes precedence."

Placed out? Claimed? The words might as well have been foreign for all the sense they made to her mind. "But I'm her mother."

"That may be, but she was signed away by her father." She held up a single page with a scribble at the bottom. "Where were you then?"

"I told you…"

The woman shot an impatient look to Laith. "Are you the father?"

Laith stepped to Braley's side.

"Her father is dead," Braley said, wishing it were true.

"I see." The woman looked undecided as to what she should do. She didn't want any trouble, and this woman reeked of nothing but.

Braley waved a hand to indicate Laith. "You would give her to him, and not me?" She wished she *had* brought her gun. She would gladly release the woman from the discomfit of her hideous hairdo. She might yet, she thought… with her bare hands.

"Well, we do prefer couples, but the only reason the child is still here is because the claimant had to go out of town. He'll be back tomorrow. He's a farmer and he…"

"He?" Braley was near to losing all semblance of control. *"He!? A single man?"*

"Yes, but he has a farm, and you must know, a single male is considered a better prospect than a single female."

All those miles, all that time, she had at least hoped that if she didn't find her, Eliza would have a mother to love her. Braley had done fine with, and considered herself blessed to have had Papa Joe. He had loved her mother, and he had loved her, but how often did that happen? And this… *this stranger* had claimed her daughter? A single farmer with so much work to do? *What kind of care would she get? What did he want with her?* She closed her mind to answers beyond consideration.

She straightened her spine and tried to force breath into her lungs. "I want my child. Give her to me, or I will go to every court in the country and expose you for what you truly are. I know about the stage, I know about the fees you charge. I will scream the truth from the rooftops. I will knock on every door, and I will never stop. I will tell everyone how you steal children from the streets and give them away to anyone, anywhere, just to be rid of them. How you tear siblings apart from one another. How you fill orders! How they most likely work and slave for the privilege of a roof over their heads, no more than servants." She stepped closer to the desk and felt Laith follow, as her voice rose, "I have read every newspaper between here and Ohio, and *I know.* I know all the stories, and I will never forget them. I have seen it with my own eyes! Not only will I shut you down, but I will make you pay for every mistreatment, every disservice to every single one of them."

Laith took hold of her arm with one hand and held his other hand in the space between the women. He tried to hold Braley back as she leaned across the desk, screaming into the woman's face.

"How many have been discarded? How many are turned out with no place to go when they don't fit in? How about the ones who have disappeared? Where are they? If you don't give me my child, I will have nothing else to do with the rest of my life but come after you. *Do you understand? Nothing!*"

Mrs. Clark sat speechless. They could not afford that kind of trouble, nor the publicity it would garner. There were already too many rumors and questions about what good the society was really doing, and she could not risk anyone looking too closely at her own operations. *And it was one child. Was not one child much like the next? The farmer could choose another. He couldn't possibly be as much trouble as this little bitch. But what about the legalities? She already had his money.*

The lengthy silence was too much for Braley. *"I'm her mother!"* She tried again. *"She belongs with me!"*

The woman shook her head and held up the page that said otherwise. "There is still the contract." She added that page to the other, waving them in the air as if to torment the young mother.

Laith had seen enough. With one quick movement, he snatched the pages from the woman's hand and stepped away.

Her jaw dropped, and she struggled to her feet to charge around the desk toward him as he crumpled the papers in his fist.

When she reached him, he stuffed the whole mess down the front of his pants. "Problem solved." He stepped closer and looked her in the eye. "Get the child ready, and whatever paperwork you think you need. We'll be back in an hour, and there will be no excuses. And she better be here."

He grabbed a shocked Braley by the arm to usher her out the door.

"But where are you going?" The woman demanded, wondering what had happened and whether she would need an attorney.

He stopped only long enough to glare at her. "We're getting married."

Chapter 8

"Are you out of your mind?" They were halfway down the block before Braley recovered enough to find her tongue. "I'm not getting married."

"You want your kid?"

"Yes."

"You wanna' get her out of there?"

"Of course."

"You wanna' go get your guns and take her by force?"

Yes, she thought.

"You want them comin' after us and maybe taking her away, and we end up in jail?" He asked, as though he read her mind.

"No."

"Then we get married."

"No!"

"Look, I don't want to get married either. You're right. It should mean something. It should mean everything. It doesn't have to last. I'll let you go, I promise. But you heard her, that farmer is coming back tomorrow. I'm thinking we'd better be long gone. He stopped in front of the church. "Okay. Same deal as before. You'll come home with me for the winter. I won't touch you. You won't tell. We both get what we want, and you leave in the spring."

"But even if I wanted to, which I don't, we would need a license."

"Not here."

"And witnesses."

"Not in Idaho. All we have to do is walk in here and get married." He held out his hand. "You comin'?"

The horses and the mule were packed and waiting. Laith was by her side, the sheriff was following behind, and Braley's heart was in her throat. She had changed her clothes and wore her holster, and Mrs. Clark's eyes widened at the sight of her.

"Is there a problem here, Hester?" The sheriff asked.

"Not at all, sheriff. A little mix-up in the paperwork is all. I have everything ready. We merely need to fill in the names and sign the papers." She did not mention a fee.

Braley watched as Laith showed the hastily written proof from the minister and listened as he spelled out his name, *her name,* for the woman, "Demoranville, D-e-m…" Her heart was hammering. *Had she done the right thing?* She signed her name. The first woman they had dealt with entered the room carrying a baby—*her baby*—and placed her in her arms, and nothing else mattered. She would deal with anything else as it came. She sank to the nearest chair, pushing off the blanket and kissing the soft cheek, holding her to her heart. *"Hello, my baby. Eliza. Hello Eliza. Mama's here. Mama's here."* She alternated between holding her close and placing her on her lap to look her over, inspecting and adoring her tiny nose and rosebud lips, until it was time to go. Laith shook hands with the sheriff and held out his arm like a sheltering wing, "Ready?"

Braley nodded to the first woman and did not so much as glance at the other. They were on their way out the door when she heard the sheriff. "I'd like to talk with you, Hester."

Traveling with a baby was different, to say the least. Carrying her on horseback proved to be a challenge. She grew heavy after a few hours, and they took turns. Braley was always reluctant to give her up, thinking Laith might be resentful. She waited on the edge of her nerves and took note of his every expression, but he never complained. Everything took twice as long. There were no skipped meals and no eating on the move. The frequent stops slowed their pace, but Braley didn't care. She had her child, and she would be forever grateful. There was no hurry now, no urgency, and no wondering where she was. She was here and certainly made her presence known, calling for changes and feedings, which made her mother smile. *But how did he feel?*

"I'm sorry," she said to Laith one morning, handing him his breakfast.

He scowled, which made her nervous. "What for?"

"You know, it's taking so long, with all the stops. You would have been back home a long time ago without us."

"Are you crazy? This is great." He stretched his long legs across the ground and grinned up at her. "Look, breakfast in bed."

It was true that more frequent fires to cook the cornmeal or porridge for the baby meant more hot meals for all of them, and no more skipping coffee in the mornings.

They stopped to buy or barter what they needed and made their way back to Fort Laramie. Braley, noticing for the first time the admiring glances directed at Laith by the women who passed, and finding she didn't care for it. There was a letter from Constance waiting, and Braley splurged on another telegram of few words, *I have her,* announcing the joyous news, and sent a follow-up letter telling most of the story, and explaining that she would be staying for the winter. She did not tell her she was married, because by the time she got back, she would not be.

Of course, she could not go back, *not to stay.* As much as she would like to be near Constance, she couldn't take that chance. But she did want to see her and Warren, and at least thank them. *Maybe she could arrange to meet them somewhere out of town.* She also had to decide where she would go. Perhaps back to New Bedford. She missed the ocean and the salt air, but she had plenty of time to think about it.

Laith bought a buckboard to carry everything and they made a stop to pick up the animals.

Mrs. Saunders invited Braley inside to feed the baby while the men readied the wagon and hooked up the team.

"Thank you so much. I'm worried that she doesn't eat enough," Braley said. *The woman had seven children. If anyone would know…*

"If you don't mind my asking, why do you not feed her as God intended?" She watched as Braley made a mixture of cornmeal with cow's milk and water. "It's so much easier when you're traveling and better for her."

Braley, struggling to get Eliza to take some of the mixture, did not meet the woman's eyes. "We were separated for a long time. By the time I got her back…"

"Oh, that won't matter. Lots of women have interruptions for many reasons. You can start again. She should fatten up in no time."

Braley studied the woman, wide-eyed and open-mouthed. *Could it be true? "Really?" What else did she not know about motherhood? The possibilities were endless and overwhelming.*

"Sure, you keep on like usual, at regular times. It may take a while, but it will come back. It will comfort her, too. Of course, at this age, you can add the cornmeal and porridge, squash and carrots… I'll get you some from the root cellar before you go. She'll do fine, lovey."

They set off for the last leg of their journey with Braley more confident in her abilities and looking forward to having a home. *Well, home for now,* she corrected, but after all her travels, staying in one place, even temporarily, would be nice.

The lone sad note was that Dog was not with them. The family said he had run off shortly after they had left for the pass and had not returned. Braley was heartsick. She had missed him. Somehow, in their time together, she felt they had formed a bond and would always care for one another. She had looked forward to having him around again. She only hoped he had not tried to follow them and gotten lost somewhere out on the trail.

She usually drove the wagon with her horse, the mule, and the cow, tied behind, and Laith rode his horse beside her, or scouted ahead. Sometimes they would switch, and other times they rode in the wagon together. He would drive, and she could tend to the baby. On this day, the path was narrow and rocky, and Laith scouted ahead, making sure the wagon could make it through.

Braley pulled up the horses and listened. It was not the first time she had imagined she heard a familiar bark. Over and over in her mind, the scenario played out… She would turn around, and Dog would be there. She knew she was being foolish. He had been gone for months and was not coming back, but she couldn't help it. *Stop torturing yourself. It was the wind, a noise from the horses, a jingle of the harness; it could be anything.* She lifted the reins, but before she slapped them down, one of the horses snorted and lifted its head. Their ears were up and alert. Braley eyed the woods on either side of the path, her heart beginning to pound. The cow lowed, and when Braley turned around, Pappy and the mule were also alerted, ears up and tails swishing. She sat very still, her eyes on Eliza sleeping peacefully in her basket, and the sound came again. *That was a bark.* She wasn't crazy. She stood.

Far behind them, there appeared a speck on the horizon moving at a lope, and then faster. She jumped from the wagon and ran partway down the road. Conscious of leaving Eliza too far behind, she waited, calling encouragement as Dog came into view. Thin and dirty, tongue lolling, he jumped into her waiting arms. Braley went to her knees in tears, but he didn't stay long. He pulled away and ran circles around her, returning to lick her face and bark in excitement. She followed him back to the wagon, where he renewed acquaintance with his old friends, the horses tossing and prancing in place. He then gave Eliza a thorough inspection and plopped down beside her in the wagon.

Laith returned to check on her, to find her feeding the dog her lunch and giving him the last of the water. He did not escape his turn at an exuberant greeting before the dog settled down again and went to sleep. He liked the dog, but he was most pleased for Braley, and his heart swelled at her smile. He had seen the sadness in her eyes and the way she alerted to every far-off sound, the wind in the trees and the wolves at night, and the hopelessness that followed. She'd had enough sadness in her life.

"His feet are so worn," she said. "Do you think he followed us all the way?"

"I guess we'll never know, but I wouldn't doubt it."

They kept moving, with Dog sometimes running ahead to check on Laith, or riding in the seat next to Braley, but most often settling next to the baby as her self-appointed guardian. They traveled as far as they could each day, stretching the daylight, until they reached more familiar territory, and Laith led her to a campsite where the water was clean and the fishing was good, and they could rest for a few days. "It's still a little rocky, but it's one of the best spots around."

"It's beautiful here," she said, as they unloaded the wagon and set up camp. "Except for those," she gave wide berth to a patch of prickly pear cactus spread across the ground. "I hate those things."

"Do you? I like them."

She made a face. "Why? What in God's name is good about them? They're miserable."

"Well, they grow in spite of everything. I mean, look how they have to live. Look what life has thrown at them. They grow in the brutal heat and survive the cold of winter, and they still bloom to guide the way with pretty yellow flowers. Yeah, they're prickly," he stopped to look at her, "but maybe they've had to be defensive to survive, to keep things that would hurt them away. Look here…" He held out his hand and led her to a spot that overlooked the trail where it curved out and around a massive patch of the flat-looking plants she found so offensive. "Their sharpness protects them from being trampled into the earth." He stood beside her, his voice soft so close to her ear, "*Stay away*, they say, and who can blame them? In spite of everything, they survive and they blossom because they have a purpose. Beneath all their defenses and their toughness, they are really quite beautiful."

Braley felt his eyes on her, but did not dare to look at him, struggling with the thought that he had stopped talking about the cactus some time ago, and wondering what to reply. Fortunately, at that moment, her *purpose* began to cry for her dinner.

He remained behind, staring down at the cactus, considering its sharp points and nearly invisible bristles, and how once they were under your skin, they were almost impossible to get rid of.

Laith was pleased with their progress in more ways than one. Braley was less shy with him now and would feed the baby with him nearby, as long as she had a diaper or her shawl to cover herself. At least he no longer had to leave the campground. She talked more, and no longer ducked whenever he raised his arm, which was definitely a step in the right direction.

Braley had begun to think Mrs. Saunders had played a mean trick on her; it had taken so long, but then the tiniest drop of milk dribbled down Eliza's chin, and within the next few days, she began to see and feel a difference. Her heart soared. At least this was something she could do for the child she had missed so much time with.

"What are you so happy about?"

She froze, her heart shredded by the talons of the past, but his posture was relaxed, and he was smiling back at her, nothing but kindness in his golden eyes. "It's working." She smiled harder, putting her head down, hiding behind her hair as a blush rose in her cheeks. She had told him what she was doing; there was no way to hide it, and he gave her what space he could. There was little privacy to be had on the trail, where one ate, slept, bathed, and did whatever one had to do pretty much in the open. He wished now he had gotten her a covered wagon, but he had chosen the lighter buckboard for better speed in hopes of reaching home sooner. They managed fairly well by being careful and considerate of one another.

This day, Braley had gone down to the small creek to bathe and do some washing while Eliza napped in the back of the wagon. With the baby there was more laundry than the usual few items for Laith and herself, *and it smelled decidedly worse.* She decided to do the clothes and the diapers downstream, and laid them out on the bushes to dry. She smiled to herself when the tiny things seemed to take much more time than the others. Back upstream, the sun was hot, the creek calm and smooth, and she couldn't resist a short swim before washing up.

Laith finished gathering firewood and setting up the camp for the night while keeping an eye on the baby. Braley had been gone longer than usual. He called out, but there was no answer. Ten more minutes and he began to worry. Five more and he would check on her.

Braley finished her bath and dried off. She had put on her trousers, but as she picked up her shirt, she wrinkled her nose. It had been clean that morning, but it now smelled of stale milk. She would wash this shirt and wear the other, which should be at least partially dry by now. She walked back upstream to get it.

Instructing Dog to stay by the baby, Laith took the path with long strides, only to find she was not there at the water's edge. *No need to panic*, he told himself, but he did, and seeing the footprints in the sand, he began to run along the bank.

Braley had wrung out her shirt and stood shaking it out, to lay it on the nearby bushes, when she heard him behind her.

"Braley?!" He burst into the clearing.

She hugged the wet cloth to the front of her and spun away from him, her arms crossed.

Laith came to a halt. She was back to him, naked to the waist, her hair clinging to her in wet spirals. His breath caught, and he reached out a hand to touch her.

Braley closed her eyes.

"Your shoulder," he said, placing his palm over the scarring that covered the upper left portion of her back, and noting the lash marks only partially hidden by her hair.

She didn't breathe. He had touched her before. He had put his arm around her, taken her elbow, and held her hand to help her from the wagon. He had even hugged her on occasion, but there was something far too intimate about this touch.

Maybe it was his compassion, instinctive and raw, or maybe it was the exposure of her most personal secrets, part of her that no one had seen before. Though she was well covered, she felt naked to his gaze, as though all her wounds, physical and otherwise, were laid bare, and she could no longer hide from him.

"I'm sorry," he whispered, placing a hand on each shoulder. She didn't pull away, and he rested his chin against the side of her head. *"Oh my God, I'm so sorry."* And then he left her.

Braley took her time getting dressed and folding the clothes before she returned. She felt strangely isolated, as though she had lost her only friend. It would be different between them now. She didn't want to go back. He had seen her scars, her ugliness, and the history of failure that she carried, and he had turned away. She didn't want to see pity in his eyes, or worse, *disappointment.* She didn't want to answer the questions. *Why had she stayed? Why had she let those things happen? Why hadn't she done something?* She was sick to death of the questions. She asked them every day.

Chapter 9

Downhill. It was not a good direction for friendship or travel if one were traveling by wagon. They emerged from the tree line and sat at the top of a steep rise.

Braley looked at Laith, "Well, this can't be right."

Laith pointed into the valley, "Yep, that's home, we'll be there by nightfall."

She could barely make out some buildings in the distance. "Maybe on horseback, but we can't go this way with the wagon."

He dismounted, "We'll be all right, I've done it before." He untied the animals from the back and reached under the seat for the metal shoes that would keep the wheels from turning.

Braley scrambled down and retrieved Eliza from the back.

"We'll walk the other animals down," he said, and I'll come back to drive it down alone.

It wasn't as bad as it looked at first. They had walked in a zig-zag pattern to make the descent easier.

"I'll be right back," he said when they had reached the bottom.

Braley grabbed his arm, and his eyes swung to hers. "Be careful," she said, the words terribly inadequate for the emotion that flooded her chest, but she couldn't find the right words, and said nothing more.

She had plenty of time to think while she watched him climb the hill. *What was it that had her panicked at the thought of him getting hurt? Intuition?* She didn't think so. *Fear?* Maybe. Their friendship had not changed after their encounter at the creek in the way she had feared. When she had gotten back to the camp, he had supper started and offered her a cup of coffee and a smile. He had boiled carrots and cornmeal for Eliza. He thanked her for washing his clothes and did not avoid looking her in the eye. He talked about the plans for the next day, and the weather, and kept up the inconsequential conversation until she began to join in. He didn't ask any questions. The only difference was that night he had placed his bedroll next to where she slept with the baby, and gone to sleep with his arm around them both.

She watched the horses prance and toss their heads as Laith forced them over the bank. He stood in front of the seat, working the reins as they slid and lurched, and bumped their way down the grassy slope. At one point, she would have sworn the wagon left the ground entirely, only to land hard on all four wheels. She winced, the words that had escaped her earlier coming easily to mind. *What would she do without him?*

He skidded to a halt beside her and jumped from the wagon, checking it over. "Boy, she's rugged some, ain't she? That was great!"

"The horses didn't think so." She stroked them and checked their legs and feet.

"Well, we made it, so what does that tell you?"

"That they're smarter than you are."

He laughed and pushed his hat back on his head.

The light mood carried them forward until the last miles of their journey, when Braley began to grow nervous. "What if they don't like me?"

"You only need to be yourself and they won't have any choice." He said, as he rode beside her in the wagon, handling the reins, with Eliza and Dog in the back.

Braley looked at him out of the corner of her eye. His sneaky compliments always seemed to leave her tongue-tied. She shifted on the seat. "Are you still going to tell them we're married?"

"I thought I would, unless you really don't want me to."

"I guess it's all right."

He nodded.

"What about Eliza?"

"What do you think?" He asked.

Braley didn't have to think about it. She had been thinking about it for weeks. "I'd rather say I was a widow than not married. I really don't want to explain all of it. Is that terrible?"

"I think it's fine. That way, there'll probably be fewer questions. Not that they'll ask a lot," he added, at the look of concern on her face.

"I'm not sure I can do this," she said.

"Just pretend we're married."

"We are."

"Oh, yeah. Then pretend you like me." He smiled.

He had a nice smile, and that part wouldn't be all that hard, she thought. He had helped her so much, and she would always be grateful.

"I'll do most of the talking," he offered. "Not that you can't. *Talk,* I mean. Just play along." Laith hadn't thought he would be nervous. He hadn't really thought too far ahead. Now he wondered if they could pull it off.

"Maybe I should kiss you."

Her eyes widened. "What!?"

"Once in a while, you know, to make it look good."

"Oh." Her pulse jumped to alert, and she wished she hadn't come.

"That is, if it's all right. I'm thinking, if we *were* married, I would probably hold your hand and put my arm around you sometimes."

"We are," she reminded him again.

"Oh yeah." He pulled back on the reins to stop the horses. "I think we should practice."

"What?"

"I think we should do a practice kiss so it doesn't look awkward. You know, like we've never kissed before. It should look natural, like we're used to it."

Braley swallowed with difficulty. *It was true.* When they had gotten married, he had kissed her cheek. "I guess," she said.

He pushed his hat back and leaned close, placing his hand along her jaw.

Braley drew back and braced for the cold unpleasant pain she remembered.

Laith scowled. *Did she find him that repulsive?* "Jeez, you look like you're about to be bitten by a rattlesnake. Are you sure it's all right?"

She nodded and appeared no less tense as he leaned closer.

To her shock, his mouth was soft and warm, and opened slightly, molding to fit to hers like a missing puzzle piece fitting into place. She felt something inside. Something she had never felt before. *Things she didn't understand.* She leaned closer, not wanting it to end until she could discover what it all meant. He lifted his head.

Too soon, she thought. "What was that?"

"It was just a kiss." He picked up the reins and slapped the horses into motion, not meeting her eyes.

Just a kiss? If that was a kiss, then she had never truly been kissed before. "Wait." She placed a hand on his arm, and he pulled up the horses.

"Kiss me again," she said, "I need to see something."

Laith smiled. He hadn't meant to kiss her that way. Not for the first time. He only wanted to break the ice so things would appear natural between them. It had gotten out of hand, but he wasn't about to turn her down. He had wanted to kiss her when he showed her the cactus flowers, and that day at the creek. *All over.* To wrap his arms around her. To hold her and heal her. He hadn't trusted himself to stop, so he had walked away.

"Okay," he said.

It was the same. She had not thought it would be. *That it could be.* It was as though he caressed her lips with his, gentle and strong at the same time. *The same melting feelings. Irresistibly warm and inviting. Inviting to what? Oh, that's why it was so wonderful… To tempt her to that other thing that was supposed to follow. That horrible, painful act that left her feeling used and broken and… No, she was never doing that again, but this…*

His arms tightened around her, and he pulled her across his lap, deepening the kiss, his tongue coaxing and playing, sweeping her into ecstasy.

What the hell was this? Braley copied his movements, her tongue parrying his. When he moaned and kissed her deeper still, she thought she might turn inside out, maybe even die. *And it might be worth it. But she was still never doing that other thing again. Unless… The kiss that led up to that first time had been awful, and this was certainly different. Did that mean…*

Laith lifted his head, breathing heavily, "Jeez, Braley," he said after a minute, staring into eyes dark with desire. "We'd better go." He picked up the reins.

She nodded. "Do you think it will look natural?"

Chapter 10

Braley needn't have worried about her entrance into Riverdale, as the ranch was called, at least for the first few minutes. Laith's father, a barrel-chested man with blue eyes and white hair, was overjoyed to see his son, nearly crushing him in a bear hug. "We almost gave up on you, boy! What happened?"

A woman, her pretty silver hair held up with a comb, was next, with an embrace almost as big, in spite of her frail-looking frame. "Oh, Laithram! We were worried near to death!"

"I was ambushed about thirty miles out," Laith explained. "They took my money, so there was no point in going on to get the cattle. They took a shot at me and grazed me, but I fell and hit my head. They must have known I wasn't dead, but instead of finishing me off, they tied me up and left me. Braley here, came by and saved me, and we got a little sidetracked." He held out an arm, and Braley took shelter against his side to accept their greetings and much appreciation.

"Did they break your arm?" His father asked.

"No." Laith looked confused, and Braley tensed.

"And you couldn't write a letter?"

Both men burst into laughter, and she relaxed.

"And who is this?" The woman asked, her bright blue gaze caressing the baby. "May I?" At the mother's nod, she took the child and cuddled her close. "Oh, my!" She grinned at Laith, "Is there something you

want to tell us?"

"Well, as a matter of fact, there is," Laith answered. "This is Eliza, and Braley is my wife. We got married last month.

"Ye haw!" The father stepped forward, and Braley found herself the recipient of the same enthusiastic hug as Laith, and it did not seem to be the embrace of a sickly man.

"Braley, my pa, Beaumont Demoranville, and Mrs. Hewes, Cousin Ella, my father's cousin. She's our… She's our everything."

The woman beamed at the compliment, gave Braley a hardy handshake, and then drew her in for a hug. "Please, call me Ella."

"And call me Monty." He turned his attention back to Laith, "Now, I might be old, but I can still count, and you've been gone three months, and while it's a long time to go missing, it's not long enough for this." He held his forefinger out to Eliza, inviting her to grasp it in a tiny fist.

Braley held her breath. *Would her baby be accepted?*

"Yep, got me a bonus. Official papers and everything." Laith patted his pocket and put his arm around Braley again, giving her shoulder a squeeze in support.

"Well, I'll be damned," Monty said.

Braley was still nervous until Monty Demoranville broke out in another huge grin, coaxing the baby from his cousin.

"What you got here, son, is a head start, and a beautiful one at that." He smiled at Braley, "About damn time we had some little boots running around this place. Welcome to Riverdale."

The door opened, and two men entered and paused as one, disbelief painting their expressions. The larger of the two seemed to wrestle with a tremulous smile. *"Laith?"*

Laith went immediately to embrace his brother. "Lee!" The big man who took after his father in build and looks, with the exception of his light brown hair, hugged his brother and then looked him over. "Ain't you a sight for sore eyes. We thought for sure you were a gonner, isn't that right, Trotter? Where the hell you been?"

The other man, tall, dark, and pleasant-looking, smiled as he pumped Laith's hand and patted him on the back.

"I had a little trouble, but it turned out for the best. I want you to meet my wife, Braley, and our daughter, Eliza. Braley, this is my brother, Leland, and our foreman, Trotter."

Leland's eyes met Braley's and passed quickly to Eliza, and then to his father. Braley read no welcome there. *"Your wife?"* He turned back to Laith, "Less than three months? And you expect us to believe she's yours?" He gestured toward the baby.

"She is now." Laith smiled, but Braley felt the tension in the air.

Leland was conscious of his father's watchful eye. "Well, what do you know, I'm an uncle." He slapped his brother on the back. "Welcome," he said to Braley, but this time he did not meet her eyes.

Riverdale was impressive. The main part was built of once towering trees, but it was no cabin. It was a sprawling two-story home with furnishings and paintings as fine as any she had seen back East. There was a huge stone fireplace, and thick carpets covering the floors. *Laith was right, it was 'a damn nice house'.* To a weary traveler, it was heaven.

Braley thought she might be uncomfortable staying in the same house as Laith's father and brother, but their rooms were far enough apart that it was quite private, and Mrs. Hewes had her own room downstairs, so she was not the only female.

The woman had ensconced her in what she said had always been Laith's room, on the back of the house, and Eliza was now asleep in a cradle that had been brought down from the attic. Braley admired the beautiful brass bed and looked over the impressive collection of books, the pictures of maps and woodlands on the walls, and wondered about this new side of her *temporary husband.* "Thank you, Mrs. Hewes."

"Ella, please." Ella turned in the doorway. "I'm so glad you're here, and I'm over the moon for you and Laith. He's a wonderful boy. If there is anything you need, don't hesitate to come to me. We women stick together out here." She paused and returned to place a hand on Braley's arm. Her kind blue eyes grew serious, and her smile faded. She lowered her voice. "Don't take this the wrong way, dear—don't be frightened—but do watch out for Leland."

Braley had washed and changed to her clean underclothes to sleep in. It was the best she could do for now. She was in need of some new things and wondered if Laith would take her into town. There had been no need for a nightgown and robe on the trail. The very idea of it made her smile as she settled into the lovely feather bed to think over the evening. There had been a delicious dinner, with lively conversation as the men traded stories and caught up on the past months. She had excused herself to give them time alone and get Eliza to bed, and they had retired to the study for brandy and cigars.

Laith yawned behind his hand. It wasn't terribly late, but it had been a long day of travel and an emotional reunion. Braley had retired over an hour ago. His back still stung where his brother had slapped him overly hard, the wretched cigar smoke was burning his eyes, and all the coffee in the world was not enough to keep him awake much longer.

"You look tired, little brother," Leland said, for the third time. "Maybe you outta get to bed."

"I'm okay."

"If I had a pretty little wife waitin' for me, I wouldn't be sittin' here yakkin'. Unless, of course, there's some reason you can't go upstairs."

Laith grinned, "What are you trying to say?" He asked, although he was pretty sure he already knew. Leland had been full of questions about where and when he had gotten married.

"I'm sayin' it wouldn't be too much of a stretch to think you're bluffing your way into a nice inheritance. You could be paying her. How much would that cost, I wonder. Maybe about the same as you took with you to buy those cows you supposedly went after. I bet you didn't even go after cattle."

"You're drunk, Lee. I am going to go to bed, and you should too. And that goes to show those were your thoughts, not mine. It's a wonder you didn't have a wife here waiting when I got back. You had plenty of time.

"All right, boys, that's enough." Monty looked from one to the other. It was not that it hadn't occurred to him that his proposal to split the ranch might cause some hard feelings, but he thought it was a fair deal, as the smaller house came with more land than the main house. "All right, boys. We'll talk about all that tomorrow with clearer heads."

Braley pulled the covers up to her chin. Laith had been guarded at dinner about what parts of their story he shared, for which she was grateful. What he did share made it sound more like they had met and fallen in love, *like a real romance*. Earlier, he had claimed Eliza as his own, and called her his daughter, and he had said when his plans for his future had changed, things had *'turned out for the best'*. He sounded very convincing. *Was he that good of an actor?* She could hardly keep her eyes open and was about to turn down the lamp, when there was a quick knock on the door.

"Yes?" She called uncertainly.

Laith stepped into the room, closing the door behind him. "Sorry," he said, with a strange look on his face.

"For what?"

He lowered his voice, "I didn't think about this."

"About…?"

"I have no place to sleep."

"What?"

"I stayed up as long as I could, thinking they would go to bed, but I'm so tired I was falling asleep. Then I said I was going to bed, hoping they would copy me, but they didn't leave, so I did. Then they followed me up, and Leland was watching from down the hall, so I had to come in here."

Braley was exhausted to the point where she was not sure she understood. "I'm sorry? Do you mean you don't have a room?"

"This *is* my room."

"Oh." *Of course. It had always been his, and it still was. Why would he have a different one?*

"It would look strange if I used a guest room, and Leland is already suspicious. I can sleep on the floor. Is that all right?"

It hardly seemed fair after all that time on the trail, and her in a comfortable bed. *His comfortable bed.* He had only been a day's ride from home when he decided to go with her. He could have been sleeping here the whole time. They had already slept side by side, and he *was* her husband—*her temporary husband*—and she didn't really care for Leland.

"No," she said.

"All right, I guess I'll…"

"No, that's not fair. You can sleep here." She indicated the bed beside her. "But you know…" she searched his eyes, hoping he understood, "*Just sleep.*"

Oh, thank God, because he didn't really know what else he would do. Laith took the extra quilt from the foot of the bed and stretched out on top of the covers. "Thanks, Braley."

She turned on her side, facing away from him, and turned out the lamp. It really didn't feel that awkward. The blankets made a barrier between them. She was used to having him near; she felt safe, and his sigh as his head hit the pillow was worth it.

For the first time in months, they slept in. Even Eliza, having been up extra late, was off schedule. By the time they dressed and descended the stairs, it was nearly seven o'clock. Laith shot his brother a huge grin as he entered the dining room with Braley, dressed in her skirt and blouse, on his arm. "Sorry we're late," he said, pulling out her chair. "Did we miss anything?"

"I've already been out to the south pasture and back," Leland answered. "You can't expect to run a ranch if you're going to be gone for months and then sleep all day."

"Sorry, being a married man comes with certain *obligations*. You know, helping a lady downstairs, and all."

Braley kept her head down and spooned some eggs onto a plate for herself and Eliza while Mrs. Hewes greeted her with coffee and cooed to the child.

Monty, who had stood when she entered, eyed both sons with a warning glare. "Good morning, Braley, you look lovely. I hope you slept well."

She blushed, unused to compliments. "I did, thank you. I'd almost forgotten what it was like to sleep in a real bed."

"Or with a real man," Leland muttered.

"That's enough!" Monty put his napkin on the table, consulted his gold pocket watch, and excused himself to Braley. "Leland, come with me. We'll be in my study. Laith, join us when you've finished."

Laith never made the meeting. Before he had finished his breakfast, they heard the door to his father's study open and slam shut. Leland left the house, and the front door suffered in much the same manner. Laith exchanged looks with Braley and went to see his father.

Monty was seated behind his desk when Laith entered and questioned with a look.

"Well, you know he's not going to be happy," Monty answered.

"He had as much time as I did to find a wife."

"I guess he didn't think you would really do it," his father said. "He still has doubts that you did. And I'm wondering…"

"I have proof, but I wouldn't lie to you."

"That's not what I was going to say." Monty heaved a deep sigh. "I'm wondering if I've done the right thing."

"Does the deal still stand?"

"Yes. I meant what I said. But I'm not dead yet, I hope you're not too anxious." He grinned and then turned serious. "I didn't want to cause trouble between the two of you. I hoped that you would find someone you cared for. Someone to love like I loved each of your mothers. I only meant to hurry it along a little. To get you to start looking. I never meant for either of you to marry only to get the ranch."

Laith sat in the nearest chair and crossed his booted feet on the leather ottoman. "I wasn't looking. It crossed my mind I might meet someone on my trip, but that was all. I did get ambushed, and I did meet Braley when she stopped to help me." Saying only that there was a mix-up, after Braley had lost her husband, he told the story of chasing the orphan train and searching for Eliza, and how they had helped each other along the way. He was careful not to say too much, protecting Braley's privacy.

"So, you didn't marry her to get the ranch?"

"No. She needed me, and I…" *He, what? Saw an opportunity that had little to do with owning the ranch? A chance to be with her? To hold on? To spend more time in her company because he couldn't bear to give her up? What was he doing?* "I guess I needed her, too."

"So, you do care about her?"

He looked his father in the eye, "Yes, I do."

"I'm glad to hear it." Now, we'd better get to work."

Laith followed his father out, feeling a bit confused, but not the least bit guilty. *He hadn't lied.* Neither had he confided his other concerns. Not yet.

Chapter 11

It was apparent that appetite trumped anger, because however angry Leland might get, he always returned by suppertime. He often monopolized the conversation, and each day had been much the same. Today, the topic was the annual autumn fair that was coming up in town with prizes for horse pulling, produce and livestock judging, shooting contests, and games for the children. "I'm going to enter our greys in the horse pulling, and I think we should enter that new heifer. I've been talking to Bill Henley. He's on the planning committee, and we've got a damn good chance. Another blue ribbon would be a credit to the ranch."

Without the least bit of subtlety or shame, he somehow turned this into the topic of affection between couples. Braley was certain most of it was for her benefit, but not a word was directed at her. *It was almost as if she wasn't there.* In fact, she was acutely aware that he never so much as looked at her, and she was quite sure everyone else noticed as well. *That was fine.* She had played this game before. Before, when she was alone and vulnerable. Since then, she had camped by herself in the wilderness, learned to protect herself, and fought for what was hers. She listened as he continued.

"…I'm just sayin', It's only natural to see some affection between a couple *supposedly* in love. I was over to Henley's place today, and he can't keep his hands off his new wife."

Laith countered his brother, "I thought you always said public affection was disgusting?"

Leland glared at his brother and glanced at his father. *He had said that—many times.* "Well… yeah, but it's still natural. Don't you think so?"

"Instead of all these insinuations, why don't you come out and say what you want?" Laith challenged. "What are you trying to say?"

"Nothing. Nothing at all. I was just asking."

"That's enough, boys," Monty interrupted. "I'm sure we have bigger questions to answer, such as who would have ambushed Laith and taken his money. I saw the marshal, and I've been thinking it over. It had to be someone who knew you were traveling with a good amount of money, possibly someone in the area, or even on the ranch, someone who doesn't care about you, at least when it comes to money, and thankfully someone who is a poor shot."

Laith laughed uncomfortably, "That's true. All good points."

"Can you shoot, Leland?"

The table fell silent. It was Braley.

Leland's face flushed with rage. He could hardly ignore her now. "Yes. But I don't miss," he ground out. "And what are you trying to say?"

"Nothing. Nothing at all," she answered. "I was just asking. With the fair coming up, I wondered if you would enter the contest. I'm a bit rusty myself, not having practiced lately while traveling. It scared the baby. I was hoping there would be someplace to practice around here."

Laith was caught speechless for the moment. First, because she had spoken to his brother at all, doubly so by what she had said, and how she had neatly tied it with a bow to make it sound so innocent. Never mind that she had hinted at his deepest thoughts out loud. *Thoughts he was ashamed of.* "We can practice if you want," he covered. "We have a setup out behind the barn. Don't we, Lee?"

"Speaking of town," Mrs. Hewes did her best to help ease the moment, "I'll be needing the buggy tomorrow after breakfast. I need a few things. Would you like to come, Braley?" She smiled, her blue eyes warm with admiration. "I would love the company, and we can get to know each other."

Braley shifted her eyes to Laith, who looked at her expectantly but said nothing. The silence grew long, and she was aware of everyone's eyes on her. Her heart began to pound, but still, he did not speak. "I would love to," she said, trying not to make it sound like a question, watching his eyes, and trying to decipher what it meant when he smiled.

Braley waited in the bedroom. She had rocked Eliza an extra-long time, reluctant to put her down for the night. Now she paced the floor in her chemise and drawers and the wool shirt she used as a robe. She was waiting for Laith. Each night, he had come an hour or so after she retired and slept on top of the covers. They had kept up their habit of reading from the books in his collection, discussing Hawthorne, Dickens, Twain, and Harriet Beecher Stowe. She told him about Coleridge and tried to explain the albatross in The Rime of the Ancient Mariner, which he had never read. She enjoyed these quiet times. She had even grown comfortable enough to tell him about her books that Jacob had burned. But this night she waited up, not wanting to be caught lying down if he were angry. She nearly jumped when he knocked, and she spun to face him when he entered.

Laith eyed her up and down, and his pulse quickened, a problem he'd had of late. He was used to catching glimpses of her in varying stages of dress on the trail, but not standing in her unmentionables in the middle of his bedroom. "What's wrong?"

Her eyes darted over his face and his stance looking for the signs. His eyes, his mouth, his shoulders, his fists, were all relaxed. *"Nothing?"*

He scowled. "Then why you standin' there all in a lather? You look like you're gonna give me a thrashin' the likes of which I haven't had since I was five and ran off to the creek by myself."

"You're not angry?"

He glanced around the room. "At what?"

"About me going."

His stomach felt like he had taken a punch after all. *Was she leaving? Were Leland's comments too much for her?* "Going where?" He asked, his throat dry.

"Into town."

"Into town?"

"With Mrs. Hewes. Ella."

Was she serious? He saw the apprehension in her eyes and remembered her hesitation at the dinner table. "Oh, Braley. *Is that how it was?*" She didn't move, and he put his arms around her. "Of course not. You can go anywhere you want. Anytime you want. You're free of all that. I'm sorry if you thought otherwise. If you want me to go with you, I will. If you want me to watch Eliza, I will. You only have to say what you want."

It was a few moments before she relaxed against him, letting his warmth and kindness reach her. Still, she wasn't sure she could quite believe that she was perfectly free. *After all, she was going with Mrs. Hewes and not by herself.*

Why hadn't he thought of taking her into town? He usually went more often, but he had been so busy catching up on the ranch. It only stood to reason she would need things now that she didn't need on the trail... Bonnets and dresses, and all those girly things that went underneath. Laith stepped back and cleared his throat. He didn't want to let go of her, but a promise was a promise. "Meanwhile," he walked to his closet, "you can use anything you want in here, and there are nightshirts and things in the bureau. I don't usually wear them. Help yourself, I'm going to wash up across the hall."

When he returned, she was under the covers, but he could see she wore one of his nightshirts, the long flannel sleeve rolled to her wrist. It would be much warmer than her sleeveless chemise, but it did not stop the vision of slender arms twining about his neck.

He sighed and stripped down to his underwear and settled on the bed.

She turned down the lamp. "Do you have any idea who might have shot at you?" She asked, brave in the darkness.

"I don't know, but it couldn't be my brother."

"It's hard to think it was a random stranger. Why would they shoot at someone out of the blue? It is more likely to have been someone who knew where you were going and that you were carrying cash."

"I guess."

"How many people knew? Who knew where you were going and what for? Someone on the ranch?"

"Unless someone flapped their gums in town. Then it could be almost anyone."

"But still, who knew? Who knew to *flap* it? It would still narrow it down, and you could find out who they told, even if it was accidental. How many people knew?"

Laith knew the answer, but he had managed to avoid it so far. Now he found he resented being forced to confront the truth. "Two," he said. "Three, if you count Ella, and I don't."

"Well, I don't think it was your father." Braley dared to push to expose the truth, even as she wondered if she was stepping where she didn't belong. "What about Mister Trotter? Although he seems to like you."

Laith laughed, "I guess he knew, and either he or Leland goes into town often to get the mail, but his name isn't *Mister Trotter*, it's Alan Winslow. Trotter is a nickname. A long time ago, he was sick and kept trotting to the outhouse. Leland called him Trotter, and it stuck."

"Oh." She smiled, "I'm glad I didn't call him that to his face."

He was quiet for a long time. "It couldn't be Leland, he's my brother. He loves me."

"That may be, but he also loves the ranch."

Laith nodded.

She took his hand and held it on top of the covers. "Promise me you'll be careful."

It was true. All Mrs. Hewes had done was say she wanted the buggy, and it was waiting outside the door with Trotter waiting to assist. Braley had dressed in her best, wearing her skirt again, and put her hair up for the occasion. Laith stood admiring her as she came down the stairs with Eliza. She wasn't willing to leave her behind yet, but did surrender her to Mrs. Hewes, who took her out to the buggy.

"Wait!" Laith called, and Braley turned, framed in the doorway. "Pretty as a picture," he said, catching up to her.

Her brows rose in question.

"Here, take this." He handed her some bills.

"Thank you, but I have enough," she assured him.

"I want you to have it. I feel bad I didn't think to take you sooner. Get whatever you want. Go crazy. And get Eliza whatever she needs. If that's not enough, put it on my account. Tell them you're my wife." He grinned, seeing the excitement in her eyes, and liking the sound of his own words.

Braley, who was already brimming with anticipation, laughed out loud. "I've never *gone crazy* shopping in my life. I will get what I need."

"But I want you to…"

In one motion, she took the bills and pressed herself against him, pulling his head down.

Her intent was clear, and he was more than willing to meet her halfway. He had no time to wonder why when her hand cradled his jaw and she kissed him the way he had kissed her in the wagon. Her lips parted, and her tongue sought his, teasing and tempting. He didn't care why. His arms tightened around her, one sliding down around her hips to pull her against him. He was about to pick her up and carry her off to the nearest level surface, when she brought it to an end, looking into his eyes.

"I'm going to miss you," she said, touching her forehead to his.

The kiss left him breathless, and before he could speak, she rushed out to the buggy, her skirts billowing in the breeze. Laith had almost forgotten she was leaving. He stood with his heart pounding, not sure why she had changed her mind about the money, or why she had kissed him, until his brother stepped from the hallway and walked up beside him to watch the carriage drive off.

"Jeez," Leland said, letting out a long breath.

Trotter had handed them in and wished them a good day. Ella took the reins, and Braley felt like she was riding away with her fairy godmother. She had half-expected something to happen at the last minute... That something would go wrong and there would be a change in plans, but there was nothing. They drove off on their own as if it were perfectly normal. It had to be her imagination that the sun was warmer and the air sweeter.

Perhaps she did go a little crazy, but there seemed to be so many things she needed. She purchased two dresses, underclothes, a nightgown and a robe, and some slippers, scented soaps, and a few odds and ends, but between herself and Ella, they bought even more for the baby, including a small rag doll. Braley hadn't shopped for enjoyment in years and spent more time looking and admiring than buying, and Ella was touched by her appreciation for everything, including the lunch they had shared. It was an easy bond, these two women in the wilderness. Ella was nowhere near as frail as Braley had first thought. She handled the reins like she was born to it and climbed in and out of the buggy without a problem. She had lived out here for years doing all the household chores of the ranch after her husband had died. She didn't say any more than that about him, and Braley did not ask.

"Well, this certainly was a lot more fun than a boring trip to town by myself," the older woman said on the way back.

"I enjoyed it so much, Ella, thank you for inviting me."

"Anytime, dear. We'll go again. Maybe next week."

Anytime. How good it felt, and how odd, Braley thought. Not that she could now go anytime she wanted, but that there had been a time when she couldn't. How did that happen? And who was really to blame?

Chapter 12

Jacob Turner pulled himself from his bed and stood holding onto the bedpost and then the dresser. In this manner, he made his way into what was left of the kitchen. Maybe it would be better if it had all burned that night, he thought. *No, no. Ephesians 4:31, 'Let all bitterness be put away'.*

It was raining now as it had then, and the water was streaming into the collapsed side of the house, soaking the charred debris. The rain had come too late to save the church. It had been reduced to charred rubble with only the steeple left standing, its blackened carcass a scarred and shriveled reminder. It didn't matter now. He had a new mission.

The fire had been smothered, but only after a section of the roof had fallen in and carried the floor beneath it into the downstairs. He had foolishly gone up to survey the damage and fallen through the weakened boards. His broken leg had caused him a lot of pain and much too much time.

The neighbors he had refused to let Braley help had come to his aid, having seen the billowing smoke in the morning light. They were relieved to learn Braley and the baby were away—*visiting*—at the time of the fire. The doctor was summoned to set the leg, but aside from that good man who continued his visits, and those same neighbors who had brought offerings of food until he told them to stop, he had been on his own for months. He couldn't wait. He had things to do. He had to claim his wife to save his soul and hers in the process, undeserving as she was. He would get her to marry him again. He would convince her he had changed. He would make her see.

His determination not to be dependent on others had caused him to use the leg too soon, and it had not healed properly. "Proverbs, 16:18," he mumbled to himself, as he poured his coffee and hobbled to the table, *'Pride goeth before destruction.'*

Constance had finished sweeping and put the broom away. Warren had healed enough back at the sheriff's office a few doors away, and the boys were in school. She was leaving on a trip in a few days, and was about to start packing when there was a knock on the door. She opened it without a thought.

"Where is she?"

She saw a haggard stranger with an untamed beard echoing the dark shadows under his eyes. Her pulse quickened as recognition dawned. *"Jacob?"*

In that moment of hesitation, he pushed his way in, the buggy whip still in his hand.

"Warren!" She screamed, turning her head toward the back of the house.

"He's not home. Do you think I'm stupid? He's back to work. Now where is she?"

"Who?"

His eyes locked on hers. "You're going to tell me anyway, so you may as well save us both some trouble."

He took a limping step forward and she moved toward the back room.

"It had to be you," he said, advancing.

Constance retreated, wondering what he knew.

"She had to have help, and it had to be you."

Her pulse raced as she mentally ran through her options.

"You were her only friend. Did she come to you for help when she escaped? How did she get here? Did you give her money for the train?"

He didn't know she had been there… Constance looked at him defiantly. *Keep him talking.* "I haven't seen her since that night when we went to bed. Are you saying you took her? You took her from under my roof? You had no right!" She was almost to the back room.

"She burned my church and destroyed my house!"

"She did?" Constance had heard about the house fire, but she didn't know what had happened. She only knew it couldn't possibly have been Braley. "You don't know that. Anything could have happened. It could have been lightning."

"The fire was started with ether! I found the empty cans."

"Was it really?" She stepped into the room and slammed and locked the door.

Jacob cursed and grabbed a steel pen to jam the double-sided lock when something on the desk caught his eye. *Constance wasn't going anywhere. He would get to her in a minute.* He returned to search the papers on the desk. It was only a few seconds before she tried the door, and he smiled in satisfaction when she could not open it.

The smile was short-lived when a blast splintered the wood and the door swung open. He looked up to see a shotgun leveled at his chest.

"Get out," she said. "Get out and don't come back."

Having heard the blast, Warren was there minutes later to find her still holding the shotgun. "It's all right now, love." He took the gun from her trembling hands. "Don't be scared," he soothed, as she poured the story out into his shoulder.

"I'm not scared. I'm angry with myself because I didn't stop him." She shook her closed fists in frustration. "I had the chance and I didn't do it, and now he's gone after Braley."

"But you don't know that, and she's safe. He'll never find her."

She looked at her loving husband, "He's got a hell of a good start. He stole her telegram."

Chapter 13

"You're good," Laith complimented, as she hit three bottles in a row. They were practicing at the makeshift shooting range behind the barn.

It had been an adjustment getting used to wearing dresses, except when she went riding or shooting. Braley was much more comfortable wearing her trail clothes as she did now. "I'm more rusty than I thought," she admitted.

"But you got them all."

"My aim is decent, but my speed is off."

Laith pushed his hat back and raised a brow at her. *"Really?"*

She nodded before taking up a stance and trying again.

"Why do you shoot three at a time?" He asked, joining her at the table to reload.

He was delighted when she laughed and told him about Herkules, and how they had met and made their bargain, and the things he had taught her. It wasn't often she opened up about her past. He loved her smile and watching her expression as she told her story, so different from the times when he could read the sadness in her eyes.

"Your turn," she said, and he stepped up and shot three targets as she had.

He smiled. "I like that, three shots, but you're faster than I am."

She put her hand on his arm. "I don't think so."

"I have an idea." He walked out and replaced the targets while she watched. "There, we'll go at the same time, three each. I'll do the left. Ready?"

Braley nodded.

"Now!" He yelled, and they fired. "You see?"

"I'm sure it was luck," she consoled, watching out of the corner of her eye to see if he was upset.

After three more challenges, he finally got her to admit she was quicker. "Maybe a little, but my gun is lighter and the barrel is shorter."

Laith shook his head as he carefully measured out more powder. "Why can't you say you're better at something? It doesn't make me feel bad. It makes me proud of you." He put his arm around her shoulders.

"Thank you," she said, thinking over his words, finding herself staring into eyes full of sincerity and kindness, and something that scared her more than a little. She wanted to fall against him and feel his arms around her, and she wished he would kiss her like he had before. But they, too, had a bargain. "I'm not very good with a rifle, though."

Laith shook his head at yet another attempt to appease him and reluctantly let her go. He had almost kissed her, but he remembered his promise and how she had kissed him in the house. If she had wanted to kiss him, she would have. "Let's try that then. Maybe I can give you some pointers."

Yes, it was best if he did not kiss her like he had before. The memory of it still warmed her. She felt herself blush, raised the rifle to hide her burning cheek, braced for the recoil, and shot. "See?" She said, having missed high, the butt of the gun pounding into her shoulder.

"You're afraid."

Her heart beat harder, still thinking of that kiss. *Was she?* At her questioning frown, he stepped closer.

"You're afraid it's going to hurt, so you're backing away."

"It does hurt." *His words were truer than he knew.*

He nodded. "Yes, but if you hold it away from you, it's going to kick back and hit you harder. You've got to cradle it against your shoulder… *like Eliza*."

The look she gave clearly said he was out of his mind.

"Line up your sight." He put one arm around her and gently placed the rifle into the curve of her shoulder. "If it's already touching you, it won't hit so hard. "Now square up your feet. A little further apart." Without thinking, he placed a hand on her inner thigh and moved her leg outward.

Her breath caught, but he didn't seem to notice, as he enclosed her front hand to slide it along the barrel. "Hold it firmly, but not too tight. Relax."

Her pulse quickened, and she found it hard to breathe when he slid one arm low around her hips and placed a hand flat against her abdomen. "Straighten a little." The arm around her hip slid to her back in support, and the other gently touched her jaw to guide her closer to the stock. He leaned in to peer down the barrel. "Easy now," he coaxed, in the same voice he used when he was trying to soothe the horses. "Easy, hold it like a baby, gentle but firm. Use the far sight and pull gently, don't jerk it."

The timber of his voice tickled something deep within her breast. She could feel his arm around her, and his breath warm against her cheek. The other arm dropped to her waist again, in an attempt to hold her steady. Braley drew a breath. Her heart hammered and her hands shook. She missed.

Neither moved. He turned his head to see her reaction, and his cheek brushed her hair. He breathed in the flowery scent of her mixed with gun smoke and closed his eyes. "Close," he whispered.

She could only nod.

He cleared his throat and stepped back. "That's all right. Try again."

She cocked the lever, took aim, shot, and missed again.

This time, he placed both arms around her, his hands on hers as she held the gun, sighting down the barrel. "Nice and level. Easy, girl. Don't let it rise up," he whispered in her ear, his breath hot on her neck. "Now squeeze…"

She squeezed the trigger, and the bottle shattered.

"Ha! There you go!" Laith picked her up and spun her around before placing her back on her feet. Her cheeks were flushed, and her lips were parted in surprise. His head lowered, and with all the willpower he possessed, he stopped, staring into her eyes.

Braley thought she would melt in the heat of his gaze. She wanted him to kiss her, and something more. But she didn't want to want it. *It meant marriage. The sealing of a commitment and the breaking of a bargain, and she'd be right back where she started.*

He felt her mood change and released her, taking some deep breaths and searching for something to say. It was getting harder to think straight around her, and harder to let her go. "It will be suppertime soon. We can try again tomorrow. Come on." He held out his hand. "That was a great shot."

She took his hand and followed on trembling legs. "Thank you," she said. She didn't tell him she had closed her eyes.

Braley had washed up, fed Eliza, and set the table before helping Ella in the kitchen. Laith was quiet at dinner, while Leland droned on about the fair that was fast approaching, and Monty was talking about the ranch. Braley was only half listening, wondering what was wrong with Laith. Every time she looked up, he seemed to be watching her to the point where she grew uncomfortable. She chatted with Ella and sipped her coffee. This time, when she glanced at him, their eyes locked, and he scowled. *What had she done?*

Laith ate his dinner in silence, wondering what he was going to do.

He had promised Braley he wouldn't touch her, and now he was sorry. *Why did he make such a stupid promise?* It wasn't like he wasn't attracted to her at the time. He had thought she was pretty from the first, and over their time spent together, he had seen how the ornery attitude was her protection. She had every right to be angry and suspicious. Life had not treated her fairly. He had wanted to make it better. To help her get her daughter back and get back home. Yes, it might have helped him in the bargain, but it was no longer about the ranch. Now he just wanted to be with her. To continue to take away her suspicions and win her trust, and show her the love and kindness she deserved. The problem was, trust was part of the bargain. How could he go back on his word and expect her to have faith in him? He watched as she chatted with Ella. He had almost kissed her earlier, and he wanted to kiss her now. It was getting more and more difficult to lie beside her at night and not reach out to hold her and love her. He scowled. *Why did he make that damn promise, and how could he keep it?*

Monty addressed his sons, "It's time for one of you to take some men and bring the herds down from the north pastures, whose turn is it?"

"Aw shucks," Leland protested, giving himself away. "Do I have to? I'm busy getting that team ready. I would miss too much time practicing."

Maybe that was it. He should get away. Stay away from her. It would be safer for both of them. "I'll go," Laith said.

Monty looked at him with surprise, and Leland with suspicion.

Braley looked from one of them to the other and then at Laith. "You're going away?" *Clearly, he did not have to go; he was leaving voluntarily. Why? What could she have done this time? Everything had seemed fine between them.*

The look in her eyes, wide and dark, hit like a blow to his chest. He wasn't sure if it was shock or fear mingled with uncertainty. It was almost the same as the first time he had seen her. *What had he done?*

"How long will you be gone?" She asked when he finally came upstairs.

He had hoped she would be asleep. Dog greeted him, and he bent to say hello. "Not that long. A week or so. I'm sorry if I disappointed you."

"I didn't expect it, that's all."

She was lying. He could hear the hurt in her voice. *He had done the wrong thing.*

"Of course, you're free to go. It's not like we're…"

"Married?"

"Committed," she answered.

Laith frowned and held up a hand to stop her.

She didn't understand until he opened the door and looked up and down the hall.

"Never mind," he said, "I thought I heard something."

"Well, even if we were committed, you would certainly leave at times. It's only that we've been together every day for months. It's going to seem strange, and I'll be here with your father and Leland. I'm sure everything will be fine." She didn't like the idea at all, but she smiled, "I thought you might be leaving because of something I had done." *Maybe she was being foolish, but why? Why would he want to leave if it wasn't because of her? They had traveled so much already, and he was so happy to get home. Would he be honest? Would he tell her?* "Have I? Have I done something? Is that why you're leaving?"

What could he say? It wasn't something she had done; it was everything she did. The way she smiled and laughed, and the way she looked at him, the things she said—and God—the way she kissed him. He wanted to be with her, but he couldn't tell her that; she would think he had lied when he made the bargain. Laith shook his head, not meeting her eyes.

He couldn't tell her why he was leaving, and she wouldn't beg.

Chapter 14

Three days. Memories of silence and days of isolation plagued her. It wasn't the same, of course; she had Ella to talk to during the day and Eliza to keep her busy, and if she felt closed out of the men's conversation at the dinner table, it wasn't Monty's fault. She made an extra effort at first to join in and comment, but Leland either ignored her or talked over her. It didn't bother her that much. She didn't care if he ever spoke to her. What bothered her was that he was getting away with such blatant rudeness in front of his father. That, and the snide comments he made whenever the opportunity arose.

It was the nights that bothered her the most. She missed Laith more than she would have thought possible. She missed reading together and their discussions at the end of the day. She missed the way he laughed, and teased, and encouraged her. She missed him being there. She loved how considerate he was, and she loved listening to him breathe on the nights he fell asleep first, and how she slept better knowing he was there. *If she missed him this much now, how would she leave him in the spring? But she would.*

She spent a lot of time with Ella and avoided Leland whenever she could. She was dismayed this morning to find him in the kitchen when

she came down with Eliza. *Damn, she hadn't waited long enough,* she thought, when Dog stopped to growl a warning at the doorway, but she could hardly turn around.

"Good morning," she addressed the room in general, placing Eliza in her play corner and pouring her coffee.

Ella answered her in kind, but Leland only grinned.

Feeling like a gnat that had flown into a spider's web, she waited patiently. There was nothing else to be done, and he was nothing if not predictable.

"I bet you miss your *husband.*"

As usual, it wasn't what he said, it was how he said it. "Yes, I do," she answered, "but I imagine some people are more likely to be missed than others. Are you leaving anytime soon?"

Leland scowled, not sure of her meaning, but he heard Ella's smothered laugh, so he was pretty sure it wasn't good. "Kind of funny that a new *husband* would be so eager to leave his new *wife.* Unless, of course, he wasn't missin' anything."

"He wasn't all that eager to go, judging by the night before he left." She was bluffing, thinking of Constance and some of the things she had told her. "And did you forget he is doing you a favor?"

"Maybe he wouldn't have gone at all if you were a little more *committed.*"

"And what would you know about marriage, exactly?" Braley laughed off his comment, but she was certain he knew something. *His choice of words could not be a coincidence. Had he been listening outside their door? And if so, how often, and what else had they said?*

Ella watched over Eliza as she napped, and Braley changed into her trail clothes to take Pappy out for some much-needed exercise. She rode the beautiful meadowlands and rolling hills with Pappy stepping lively in the cool fall air, but she could not get Leland out of her thoughts. *If his words carried a deeper meaning, what was it? He couldn't know anything for certain, and what could he do if he did? Plead his case to Monty? Try to prove that she and Laith had some kind of arrangement... which they did?* She hoped Laith would be home soon.

Returning to the barn, she had unsaddled her horse and was brushing him down when Dog growled low, and Leland stepped into the shadows from outside.

"Well, hello, *Mrs.* Demoranville."

Braley swallowed her apprehension and tried to keep her voice steady. "What's your point? Are we to be formal now? Shall I call you Mister?"

"I'd like to know one thing."

"Only one? It seems to me there are a lot of things you don't know, like how it's not a good idea to sneak up on people."

"What?" He shrugged and spread his hands wide. "I was only out for some fresh air."

"In the barn?"

He laughed, but the mood did not lighten. "I'd like to know how long you're going to keep up this farce."

"What farce is that?"

"This farce of pretending to be married to my brother. I know you're faking, and I know it's to get the ranch. You saw me in the hallway that time you kissed him goodbye, didn't you? I want you to admit it to my father. I want you to leave."

Braley finished up and led the horse into the stall as he spoke. Her heart pounding, she stepped out to face him. "You're wrong. I *am* married to your brother. He has proof and has shown it to your father. You can ask him."

"You're not. I heard you say you're not committed." He stepped closer, blocking her path to the door.

Dog crouched and bared his teeth, the hair on the back of his neck raised like a warning banner. "Like I said, ask your father. And stop lurking at people's bedroom doors. And just so you know, I am committed to Laith. I love him. Now get out of my way."

He didn't move. She opened her coat to display the colt strapped to her waist, and waited, having no idea what she would do next. *Shoot him three times? Of course not.* She smiled at the absurdity.

He was unarmed. *She wouldn't. But that grin… was she crazy?* He had watched her practicing behind the barn with Laith and stepped aside. "I'm not done! I'm going to find out the truth!"

Braley, Dog at her side, kept walking, as tall and straight as she was able on trembling knees, unsure whether she was shaken because of his words, or hers.

That night at dinner, the sullen silence from the end of the table was enough to let her know her brother-in-law had indeed spoken with his father and was not at all happy with the answer he received. She only wondered what he intended to do about it.

She didn't have to wonder long. She was awake extra late, trying to finish a chapter, only to find herself reading the same page for the fourth time, when Dog got up from his spot on the floor, hackles raised. Moving like a ghost in Laith's oversized nightshirt, she slipped out of bed and checked on Eliza, who slept peacefully. She stood listening and watched the doorknob as it turned with painstaking slowness. She edged closer, holding her breath. *It couldn't be Laith. It was too soon, and he had no reason to be that careful.* The lock held, and the knob turned carefully back into place. All she could hear now was her own heart pounding in her ears. *Dammit! She knew who it was, and she wasn't going to cower.* "Who's there?" She called, before throwing the door wide, holding the colt behind her back.

There was no one there, and she closed the door, not wanting Dog to go after them. She would wait for Laith. She locked the door again and moved an armchair in front of it. She had only started locking it since Laith had left. She was never afraid when he was there, and he always came up later than she did. As she gripped the gun still in its holster, she remembered the words of Herkules. *Never draw your gun unless you mean to use it.*

She wondered if she would have.

"You're sure?" Braley questioned Ella for the third time, watching Eliza sit like a reigning queen on the woman's lap.

"Of course. You know I love our time together, now go take your ride. We'll be fine."

"And you won't leave her?" Braley asked, not sure how much she should say.

Ella gave her a look that spoke much more than her words. "I understand."

It wasn't about Eliza, Braley thought, when she went to saddle her horse and noticed the cinch cut partway through. *It was her he hated. It had to be Leland. Did he think she wouldn't notice? Did he think she was stupid?* She knotted the cinch anyway and climbed on the stall rail to mount, putting no pressure on the damaged strap. Setting off at a walk, she took the pathway that led past the barns and out to the woods, pretty sure he would be watching. When she reached the stream, instead of crossing, she circled back, careful to travel on rocky ground to hide her tracks, and hid in the brush to wait.

Not long after, Leland passed by as she expected. *Leland and Trotter.* "We'll find her," Leland said. "*It's got to look like an accident.*" "And what about when your brother gets back?" The other man asked.

"*Well, then he won't be married no more.*"

Braley rode back to the barn, deep in thought. *Did he mean it? If so, her life was at stake, and what would become of Eliza? Where could she turn for help? Would Monty believe her? He loved his sons.* She finished putting Pappy up and pulled her knife from her boot.

Hours later, when Leland burst in, late to dinner, sweaty and dirty from the trail and scraped from the brush, she sat calm, coiffed, and innocent, in her new gray dress, holding Eliza on her knee.

He did not hide his surprise at seeing her there, nor his anger. "Somebody cut my cinches!" He complained to Monty, as he slid into his chair.

"Mine too!" Braley said to her father-in-law, "Who would do such a thing?"

Monty was appalled, *"We'll get to the bottom of this!"* He stood and threw his napkin on the table.

Leland glared at Braley. "She did it! I know she did."

Braley stood and handed the baby to Ella. "Why would I cut my own saddle?"

Monty glanced at her and scowled at his son. *"Don't be a fool. Come on."*

Braley followed them out.

"What the heck?" Monty sighed in exasperation and pushed his hat back on his head, reminding her of Laith. It was true. Someone had cut the cinches on two of Leland's prized saddles and one of Laith's, and Braley's was cut too. "Why would anyone do this, and who could it be? I'm sure no one wandered out from town to cut them. Nothing's missing, and my saddles are fine." He looked at Braley. "Don't you worry, sweetheart, I'll send these in to be repaired tomorrow, and there'll be a guard out here day and night. I'll post guards everywhere until this is sorted out. I'm going to talk to the sheriff, and I would prefer you not ride out alone."

It had turned out much better than she had thought. Braley took the arm he offered and walked back to the house feeling much safer, but not quite safe enough to let Leland see her grin.

"I'm telling you they're not really married." Leland sat with Monty in the study after dinner.

"And I've told you they are," Monty answered. "I saw the papers. Why can't you leave it alone?"

"Because it's not real. He's pretending so he can take over the ranch, and she's in it for whatever she can get. Look around, who wouldn't want to live here? She and her little brat have it made. It's all fake. I bet they don't even sleep together."

"You're wrong. I see the way they look at each other. He's crazy about her, and he's as happy as I've ever seen him. And that child is as sweet as can be, leave her out of this! Maybe you should stop envying other people and try to find your own happiness."

"Think what you want, Pa. You're fooling yourself. I know it, and I'm going to prove it."

Chapter 15

Laith put aside his book and turned out the lantern. There was no point in trying to read when he couldn't think about anything but Braley. He shouldn't have come. He knew as soon as he left, he had made a mistake. He was in trouble. He thought distance would help. He had feelings for her. Feelings he promised he wouldn't have, and being away from her only made things worse. He missed her. He missed everything about her, her strength and her counsel, and her endearing, uncertain smile, as if she wasn't sure she deserved to be happy. More than anything in the world, he wanted to change that. To see her genuinely happy. To hold her and show her the love she deserved… *that love could be good.* Should he tell her? *Tell her he loved her? Would she be angry?* He missed Eliza, too. He had fallen in love with the child the minute he had watched Braley touch her hand, and he knew it was his job to protect them. Now, as he thought back over his suspicions, he wondered if he had left them in danger. Surely not. Surely his brother would never go that far. But someone had shot at him, and he didn't think it was meant to be a miss. But then they had tied him up when they could have killed him. Why?

He put his hands behind his head and stared up at the stars, praying mother and child were safe. He was almost there. Just a few more days. *It would be the fastest drive on record.*

First came the shouting, and then the cows. Braley, waiting on the porch, had never seen so many cows. They were everywhere, streaming down the hills, flooding the pastures. *Cattle,* she corrected. If she were going to live on a ranch, she was going to have to learn… *Where did that thought come from? Oh, who cares,* she thought. *It was the riders that mattered, and that one in particular.* They came from the rear of the herd, emerging from the cloud of dust as the cattle entered the corrals. Her eyes darted from one to the other, trying to make out who was who, until one rider separated from the others and rode straight for the house on a horse of gold.

Laith threw himself from the saddle, and she ran into his arms. "Laith!" She wrapped her arms around his neck, knocking his hat off.

He picked her up and spun her around, both astounded and pleased at her greeting. "I missed you so much, I'm sorry I left, I…"

Her lips claimed his.

She was kissing him like he dreamt about, with all the passion and the heat that usually woke him from his dreams, leaving him breathless and wanting, and he wasn't about to argue. *She was very convincing. His brother must be watching.* Laith wasn't about to waste the opportunity. He set her down to return the favor, bending her over his arm, taking all she gave and giving more in return, plunging her mouth with apologies and forbidden promises, trying to tell her how he had thought of her. *How much he missed her… Everything.*

Braley hadn't planned to kiss him. She was overjoyed to see him and ran to greet him, and it naturally followed. When her lips met his, she forgot everything else. How there was no commitment, and how this—whatever this was, between them—wasn't real, and now she was somehow wrapped in his arms, lost in the heat of his kiss, and it only seemed right.

This was his chance. A chance to tell her all the things he was never supposed to say, how much he needed her, how much he loved her. *He loved her.* He straightened up to stare into her eyes, and then he kissed her again, long, and sweet, and loving, and she wondered at the change in him. He held her close and whispered in her ear, "Where is he?"

"Where is who?"

"My brother, where is he? I didn't see him."

"I have no idea. Down by the barn, I think, I…" *Oh.* She pulled back, averting her eyes. *He thought his brother was watching.* The very air around them seemed to change. "You must want to get cleaned up," she said, ignoring the crushing weight in her chest and the tears that rushed to burn behind her eyes. She continued, sounding overly cheerful to her own ears, "You must be tired. I'll see to your bath." She quickly took herself off to the kitchen.

Laith followed her into the house, deep in thought. His brother was nowhere in sight.

Braley was quiet at dinner while the men discussed the drive and made plans for the winter. Laith answered the best he could, trying not to stare openly at Braley.

Leland glared at them both.

Laith stole another glance at his wife, looking exceptionally pretty in one of her new dresses. *Why had she kissed him if not to dissuade Leland from his accusations? Could she have missed him that much? Did she still want to leave come spring, and if so, what was he going to do without her?*

"Laithram?"

"I'm sorry?" Laith turned to his father.

"What do you think?" Monty asked.

"What was that? I'm sorry, I guess I'm tired."

"You haven't heard a word I said. Where's your mind wandering, boy? As if I didn't know." He glanced at Braley and grinned at his son before repeating the story of the damage done to the saddles.

Was Braley in danger? His father now had his full attention. He had so many questions the conversation continued until after dinner, when the men retired to the study.

"And you have no idea what happened?" Laith asked for the third time. His blood boiled to think Braley had been in danger, and he was angry at himself for not being there to protect her.

"Not yet. Like I said, we notified the sheriff and set guards, but we haven't seen anyone around, and there was only that one incident. I know it's odd, but I'm sure the truth will out. It usually does."

Leland had nothing to say, and it was extra late when the men headed to bed.

He wasn't coming. Braley put her unread book aside and tried to ignore the voice in her head. Laith should have come upstairs by now. *Had things changed between them? Did it have to do with her greeting? Perhaps she had scared him into thinking that she wanted more. She didn't. They had a bargain and she would stick to it. Even if it killed her.*

Laith crept into the room and greeted the dog. Unbuttoning his shirt, he turned to speak to Braley. She slept; her face turned to the side, her hair spread across the pillow, one slender arm outstretched, bared to his gaze where the sleeve had ridden up. It looked feminine and fragile, but he knew its power and could almost feel its silken softness slide around his neck.

How he had missed her, and the thought of her being in danger made him want to hold her. He swallowed hard as he fought back his growing desire and stretched himself out on the bed, careful not to wake her. He studied her face, relaxed in sleep, the arching brows that could be so expressive, the small scar that made her unique, the beckoning lips that had welcomed him but a few hours ago. Drawn by a power beyond his own reason, he placed a gentle kiss at the corner of her mouth.

Far from the response his arduous mind had conjured, that silken limb that had so inspired him swung around, the hand balled into a fist that he caught just in time. Her eyes flew open, and he felt the power surge in her shoulders as she struggled to sit up, full of fight.

He stopped the other fist by catching her wrist. Holding her arms on either side of her head, he moved over her, pinning her down with his weight, afraid she would hurt herself *or him.* "It's me, Braley, it's me!" He whispered, trying to calm her, sorry—*almost*—that he had kissed her. *What the hell kind of reaction was that?* "I'm sorry, I'm sorry! I won't hurt you. I'll never hurt you."

The words penetrated, and she stopped struggling as she came awake. *It was Laith. Not Jacob. He was back. He was lying on top of her, and he was sorry.* She stared into his eyes, inches from her own, and tried to fathom the reason and all that she was becoming aware of. Her heart was still pounding, she could hardly breathe, and those strange feelings were stirring deep inside. She felt his breath hot against her skin, the weight of his body pressing against her, his long legs matched against the length of her own, seemed to sear her through the blanket.

Laith watched her eyes widen, as dark as the night sky. His gaze dropped to where her breasts heaved against his chest, and his gaze moved back to capture hers. "There's no need to fight. I'm going to let you go now."

"Don't," she whispered.

Laith wasn't sure what she wanted. *"Don't?"*

"Don't let me go." For once in her life, she wanted to be loved. Her gaze moved from his eyes to his mouth, giving him the encouragement he needed, and he moved his lips to hers.

He let go of her hands and felt the resistance melt away. She made a soft sound as he slanted his mouth across hers.

Her breath caught when he kissed her throat and her neck, whispering and coaxing until her fever matched his own.

At last, he felt her arms around his neck, pulling him closer. He closed his eyes, savoring the feeling, and slid one hand down her body to rest on her hip as he moved to his side to caress her.

Braley felt a moment of panic when his hands moved over her, but it faded with the next kiss. This wasn't Jacob. This wasn't the painful, insulting grabbing meant to bruise body and spirit. This was a gentle, loving caress, almost worshipful in its tender touch. This was soft, and loving, and wonderful. *This was Laith.* Her arms moved over his shoulders as he finished the kiss, and broke away to whisper her name against her throat. He kissed her neck and spread his warmth lower across her collarbone into the open neck of her nightshirt.

Yes, this was different. This was right. She wanted this. She ran her hands into his hair and gave herself up to the liquid fire as his mouth closed over her breast, and her heart soared.

The door opened, and then came the belated knock.

Laith jumped to his feet, her protector, blocking her with his body, and Braley pulled up her gown and the covers in one quick motion while Dog stood growling, waiting for an order.

"What do you want?!" Laith demanded.

"Trouble with the herd," Leland spoke with a smirk, and Monty averted his eyes.

Both men had already taken in the scene. Laith's tousled hair and angry scowl, Braley's furtive movement in the bed behind him.

Monty's glance at Leland was triumphant as the two men headed for the stairs with Laith following behind.

A dozen steers were out and easily herded back through the gate. "You didn't need me for that," Laith said angrily.

"No reason you can't do your share, little brother." Leland retorted.

"*My share?* I just got back from taking your drive, you ungrateful ass! Why couldn't you leave me to sleep?"

"Didn't look like you were sleepin' to me. You're just mad because you didn't get any…"

Leland's words on the way out, met Laithram's fist on the way in, with all his pent-up suspicion and frustration behind it, landing the big man on his backside in the dust. He scrambled to his feet. "You little…"

Monty stepped between them, "That's enough, you two!" He wrestled with Leland, holding him, until he gasped and fell against him, reversing their roles.

"Help me!" Leland shouted to Laith, who took his father's other arm to help him to the house.

"He should be fine for now," the doctor said when he emerged from Monty's room. "But he has to be careful. He has a weak heart. Keep him quiet. No hard work and no unnecessary excitement."

Laith walked over to Braley, who had come down in her robe to wait with them. He hugged her.

She could feel the relief washing over him as he let go of the fear that his father would die. "Come on," she said, "It's almost dawn, you should try to rest."

The doctor declined their invitation to stay but promised to return soon. Leland stayed behind while they walked him out to his buggy.

When he had driven away, two men approached. "We have to speak with you, Mr. Laith."

"What is it, Wes?"

"Alone, sir."

"It's all right, this is my wife." He made the introductions.

"Well, sir," he glanced at Braley, "just between us…"

Braley nodded her greeting and her reassurance.

"I was guarding the barn tonight, and Cory here was out watching the back pasture, and those critters didn't get out on their own."

"What do you mean?"

"There weren't no busted fence or nothin'. They was let out."

Laith glanced at Braley, remembering what he had seen. "You're right. The gate was open."

"Yes, sir."

"Did you see anything?"

"Yes, sir."

"Well?"

The men exchanged looks, and Cory nodded encouragement to his friend. "It was Mister Leland, sir. He opened the gate and shooed 'em out and ran back to the house. There were a lot more, but we got most of 'em back before you came out. It was kinda' strange, so we thought you should know."

"And you're sure it was my brother."

"Yes, sir. Ain't no mistakin' Mr. Leland, the way he runs, but we don't want no trouble. We're just doing our job."

"And an excellent job. Thank you. There'll be some *appreciation* added to your pay this month."

"Why would he do that?" Laith wondered aloud when they were back upstairs. He stripped to his underwear.

"For an excuse to come to our room," Braley said, making a point of locking the door. "He doesn't believe we are truly a married couple. It's not the first time he's come here."

Laith sent her a questioning scowl.

"I think he was trying to prove a point to your father. If he could have caught you sleeping on the floor or in the chair… As it was…" She blushed, feeling a rush of heat at the memory of what they had been doing.

He went to her and took her in his arms.

"As it was, he defeated his own cause and proved to your father we at least appear to be husband and wife."

"When did he come here?"

"Remember when you heard a noise outside the door?"

"Yes."

"I think it was him, listening. After you left, he teased me about *being committed,* which is what I said that night. And another night, when you were gone, Dog was growling…" Dog lifted his head at the sound of his name. "Good boy," she whispered, and he thumped his tail on the floor a few times before going back to sleep. "I got out of bed and saw the doorknob turn, but I had locked the door. I opened it anyway."

Laith raised his brow at her.

"With my gun," she added, "but he was gone. I'm sure it was him."

"Thank God you were smart enough to lock the door. I'm sorry I left."

"There's more," she said, wincing, feeling like a tattling child.

"Tell me everything."

"My feet are cold."

He laughed, "What?"

She nodded toward the bed and led the way, walking around to her side and climbing in. When he went around to his side, she held the covers wide in invitation.

He looked at her, his heart thudding.

"It's a long story," she said.

Laith thought he had never had a more welcome invitation until she placed her cold feet against his legs. "Jeez. You weren't kidding."

She grinned and pulled her feet back, wrapping them in the bottom of her nightshirt.

"Tell me the rest."

"Are you sure you want to know?" She asked, growing serious. "I don't want to come between you and your brother."

"I think we are long past that. I need to know." He put his arm out and she curled against his warmth.

"I cut the saddles."

"*What?! Why?*"

"First of all, he cornered me in the barn." She told him about the comments and the threats, and how she discovered the cut cinch on her saddle but rode out anyway, and what she had heard.

Laith was quiet, his lips pressed together in anger.

Then she told him how she got Monty on her side, and the whole ranch on alert. "I cut your saddle to make it seem less obvious. I'm sorry. But it's fixed now," she added.

Laith let out a long breath when she finished. "That was some plan."

"To be honest, it worked out much better than I had hoped when your father ordered the guards, but I know a few things about deception," she confessed. "I learned from the best."

"Do you realize, if it hadn't been for the guards, we wouldn't know what happened tonight?"

She nodded, much more aware of his shirtless chest beneath her cheek, now that she had finished her story.

"I'm sorry. I'm so sorry I left. I had to get away, or I thought I had to because…" He paused, unsure whether he should cross the line.

"I would like to know," she said, staring past him toward the dark side of the room, "Was it something I did?"

"Yes, it was."

Braley held her breath.

"It was the way you smiled at me, and the way you helped me when I needed advice. The way you listen, and the way you kissed me." He turned to look at her. "I had to leave or I was going to kiss you again."

Her eyes met his. "But now you're back."

"Yes," he whispered, barely able to find his voice.

"Will you kiss me now?"

"Just so you know, I may not be able to stop," he warned, his eyes never leaving hers.

She nodded, placing her palm on his chest, and he leaned to comply, his mouth covering hers, the spark renewed, the connection immediate. He paused, giving her time to change her mind, and she slid her arm behind his neck to urge him back to her.

He claimed her again, his tongue seeking and finding hers in a remembered pattern of courting, teasing, and demanding, fanning a flame that threatened to burst in his veins and consume him.

Braley melted in the heat of his kisses and knew the moment when he gave up his restraint. She welcomed it. The raw honesty of feeling, of unbridled passions set free. He kissed her neck and whispered in her ear, feeding her desire. He unfastened the ties at the neck of the nightshirt she wore, which was large enough to slip down over her shoulders. He followed its path downward with his mouth, claiming her breasts each in turn, stopping to conquer and surrender, worship and praise, paying homage with his tongue and teeth, all the while watching for her reaction or resistance, but in this moment, she was his, giving herself up completely, her head back in surrender. Smoothing his hands over her ribs, his mouth trespassing across her stomach and the hollow of her hip, he continued his gentle assault on her past, stopping to coax her to turn over, sensing her reluctance. Brushing her hair aside, he teased her ear with his mouth and kissed the back of her neck before moving to her shoulder.

Braley, immersed in a flood of feelings, came suddenly to the surface, and would have shied away to hide her scars, but he straddled her, the naked contact shocking her to her core. *When had he removed his clothing? How could she hide now? And then he was kissing her shoulder. All over. And over again, and the lash marks across her back. Her horrible, ugly scars. And he was telling her she was beautiful. Her! Beautiful!* He massaged her shoulders and her arms, and lifted her to her knees, caressing her breasts from behind, teasing her to ecstasy with his calloused palms until she forgot her shyness and her shame. And still, he bathed her scars, healing her with his love, and telling her she was beautiful, until in that moment in time, she became what he told her she was.

She had never felt beautiful before, and she spread her arms with the power as though she would soar. His hands slid down her body to claim her center, and she caught her breath, putting her head back on his shoulder, moaning against his neck, reaching for him, pleading without words.

Laith caught his breath when she enclosed him, her touch gentle and unsure. He placed his hand over hers, guiding her harder and stronger, teaching, until they turned together and he came to her.

This was a part of herself she had never known, a part that not only wanted him, but needed him. *How could she want this?*

Even now, he paused to make sure she was ready and still willing, and she urged him on, dreading but welcoming the joining, and there was no pain, no horror of invasion, only the revelation, the fulfilment of long-lost expectations. Another piece of the puzzle that fit so well. *She hadn't been wrong after all.*

He filled her, and she held her breath in wonder, somehow more complete than she had ever been. "I didn't know…" she whispered, "I didn't know it could be like this."

"Oh no, love," he answered above her in the darkness, "this is only the beginning." He moved and waited and moved again, until she matched with him, catching his rhythm, beginning a new journey, losing herself in a maze of sensation, following him to the end of everything she thought she knew. To the end of time and space, in a search for something she hadn't known existed, and yet needed desperately to find. On and on he led her, out of her valley of despair and disappointment, bringing her to the highest peaks, bathed in the light and warmth of his love, where she discovered a completion so full of wonder that she was sure it could never come again.

Laith dropped beside her, pulling the covers over both of them, holding her now like he had imagined so many times before.

"Something happened," she whispered breathlessly into his shoulder.

He smiled. "I should hope so."

"But, is that… expected? Is that normal?"

He took a deep breath, "That was a bit more than expected, but one could hope."

"Every time?"

"When it's right, yes." He wanted to ask her about her marriage. *She had a child, surely, she had known…* But this did not seem the time to stir those memories.

"Well, it never happened before. Of course, there was only the one time."

One time? Again, he did not know if he should ask. Now or ever.

She settled beside him, closing her eyes, floating on a cloud of satisfaction from one dream into another. *Papa Joe and the old neighbor lady had certainly never told her about that. Constance had tried, but she hadn't really believed her. Perhaps it was something one had to find out for oneself.* Braley was almost asleep when the thought occurred to her… *No wonder Constance was so happy.*

Chapter 16

Jacob Turner stepped onto the train platform and cursed the day he was born. It was the end of the line as far as traveling by train, and he still had a long way to go. *How did she do it, a woman alone, out here in this God-forsaken country?* He ran his fingers over the worn telegram in his pocket with its pitifully short message sent from the office in Soda Springs. He couldn't possibly travel that far on horseback with his bad leg. He would have to wait for the stage.

The frequent stops for fresh horses and overnight rests took extra time; he found the tent cities and relay stations less than adequate, and by the time he reached Soda Springs, he was filthy, tired, and more angry than when he had left. The Children's Aid Society was not difficult to find.

He took a deep breath and concentrated on his smile. "How do you do, ma'am. I'm here about my daughter," he said to the harsh-looking woman behind the desk with her graying hair worn in a tight bun.

"And what makes you think she is here?" Mrs. Clark asked, barely looking up from her paperwork.

"Because I sent her," he said. "We had run into some hard times, my wife and I, and we couldn't care for her. I believe my wife has already picked her up." He smiled again, "We were traveling separately. I had an accident and had to stay behind, and there's been some kind of mix-up. She was supposed to meet me. I need to know where she went."

Mrs. Clark squinted up at him. "We don't always keep those kinds of records, and people move around all the time, but I suppose I could check. What is your wife's name?"

"Turner. Braley Turner." Jacob waited while she checked her files.

"I'm sorry, I don't have anyone by that name."

"What about the child? Her name is Eliza."

"I have no Turner at all."

"But you must have! Less than a year old, dark hair?"

She sat back at her desk. "Do you have any idea how many children have gone through this office? I couldn't possibly remember them all."

"But you must!" His smile faltered, and his voice rose. And then he remembered, "She had a scar on her neck, on the back, a burn. An accident when she was younger."

The woman frowned in thought, "I do remember a child with a scar like that, but she was taken by a young married couple; I don't recall the name." She rose from her seat again and began to search the files.

Jacob was losing patience, and his leg was beginning to ache from standing too long. "That couldn't be her, she…"

"Oh, here it is," Mrs. Clark cut him off, "Demoranville. That's it. I remember now. We had a bit of a *misunderstanding* with them, but it all worked out in the end."

"That can't be right. She is my wife. You must be mistaken."

"No, I don't think so. *Braley* is a very unusual name. I know *I've* never heard it before. What are the chances of two of them coming here looking for a baby with the same scar?" She shot him a piercing look, her lips pursed.

Jacob put a hand to his temple. "Tell me where they went."

"Well, I don't know, our records are usually confidential. I only told you what I did because you seemed to know the child."

"Do you not see, woman? They lied to you, and now they have

my daughter!" His voice rose again. "You will tell me where they went!"

Mrs. Clark stared at the rage in his dark eyes and made her decision. Whatever happened would work itself out far away from her. "All it says here is Riverdale Ranch." She kept reading. "It says it's south of Crow Creek, and that's all I have."

Jacob closed his eyes for a moment and then turned and left without a word. He was not feeling thankful. He had passed her and traveled more than a month out of his way.

Constance hustled down the wooden sidewalk and burst into Warren's office.

"Hello, darl… what's wrong?" He asked, moving around the desk to meet her, when he saw the look on her face.

"I got a letter from Braley."

"Isn't that good?"

She shook her head, "There is no mention of the telegram we sent warning her about Jacob, and she wants to know why I haven't written."

"What…"

"I've written three times!"

"Well, you know how the mails can be, darlin', it doesn't mean…"

She met his eyes, "She's not getting my letters."

"Now, sweetheart," he comforted, wrapping his arms around her.

She rested her forehead on his shoulder a moment before pulling away, "Something's wrong. I know it. I can feel it."

Warren put his hands up in surrender. "Far be it from me to argue with your intuition, my dear, but it is possible the mails are just…" he stopped at the mix of fear and determination in her eyes. "All right, all right, and what shall we be doin' about it then?"

Chapter 17

The long-awaited day of the fair dawned crisp and clear with a beautiful October sky. Braley came awake to find herself alone and Eliza crying in her cradle. She had overslept. *Maybe it was for the best that Laith wasn't there. What would she have said? I'm sorry I broke my promise?* She thought it over as she gathered up the baby to comfort her. *What would he have said?* She remembered her own words earlier, telling him not to let her go, and groaned at the memory. Then, too, she had not missed the fact that he had called her *love. Was that why he left? Had he been caught up in the moment as she was? Could he have meant it? And where did that leave them?* She couldn't stay in the room forever and began to dress.

Laith waited in the dining room, nearly jumping up every time he heard a noise that might be Braley. *What would she think? Would she be angry that he had broken his promise not to touch her? He shouldn't have left her this morning like a coward. He had to face her sometime.*

Carrying Eliza on her hip, she entered the room in her blue walking skirt and white shirtwaist, reminding him of the first time he had seen her in her feminine attire. The front of her hair was tied back, leaving the rest to fall around her shoulders and Laith thought she looked perfect. He jumped to his feet, and their eyes met and held before she lowered her chin in a nod of acknowledgement. He went to meet her, taking her elbow and leading her to the table as usual, but something had changed. It was in her eyes and in her manner. He could feel it through the hand he placed at her waist, a current traveling up his arm and swirling through his insides. He only wished he knew what it meant. *Was it the unsurety of where they now stood? Was it fear he saw in her eyes?*

Braley entered the room holding her breath. *Was it her imagination, or did Laith look exceptionally handsome this morning in his white shirt with a ribbon bow tie and dark trousers?* She had never seen him dressed up before, but it was the look in his eyes that held her attention. She had been afraid she would see regret, or even disgust in his regard, but it was something else. Something that she had never thought to see. Something that told her she was beautiful in his eyes. She took a deep breath and stood taller as he escorted her to the table, his hand burning a brand into her side. He seated her and dropped a kiss on the back of her shoulder, causing her to blush.

She busied herself trying to spread her napkin on her lap with one hand. "Good morning," she managed to say to Monty, who had watched the whole exchange with a satisfied smile.

Leland kept his head down and his eyes focused on the last of his pancakes while syrup ran down his chin. "Thought we were going to be late," he mumbled, getting to his feet. "I'm going to get ready now. I want to get the team there early."

"Here, I'll feed her," Laith offered, taking the child around the table to his seat. "Take your time. You can't be late for the fair."

"Will you be going?" Braley asked Monty to cover the awkward silence while she ate alone.

"I think I'll go along with Ella in our own buggy, in case we want to leave early. The fair doesn't change much year to year. If you've seen one, you've seen 'em all. Hate to miss it though." He winked at her and grinned before checking his watch.

"He doesn't like the crowds," Ella chimed in, "and to be honest, neither do I when it gets later and folks get to drinking. I like to see the quilting and the baking. After that, I will be happy to watch Eliza while you young folks have your fun, if you like."

Leland left early, Monty and Ella were up ahead, and Laith, with Braley and Eliza, brought up the rear in their own buggy, the tension still humming between them.

"Do you suppose the post office will be open?" She asked, desperate for something to talk about.

"It's usually open 'til one to give folks a chance to do what they need to, and then they close for the fair. We'll be there in plenty of time. Did you need something?"

"I thought I'd check for a letter from Constance. She hasn't written for weeks, and I'm worried about her."

"We can check," Laith answered, but he couldn't think of anything else to say. *Should he apologize? Was now the right time? His hands tightened on the reins,* "Braley, I…"

"I wonder if I should send her a telegram," she spoke at the same time. "I'm sorry, you were saying?"

"Nothing," he said, holding back the horses so the dust from the carriage ahead wouldn't be as bad. *How could he apologize when he wasn't sorry?* He tipped his hat back on his head, his hair glinting like polished gold in the sunlight. "Well, about last night…"

Braley averted her eyes to the passing pines, her pulse quickening. *Here it was, the regret and the humiliation…*

"I want you to know, it was the best night of my life."

Her heart skipped.

"But I feel I should apologize for breaking my promise. I mean, I'm…" *No, he wasn't sorry about the night they spent together, and he couldn't bring himself to say the words.* "To be clear, I'll keep my promise. When the time comes, I'll let you go."

Braley watched the scenery and nodded, thinking she was not at all sure that was what she wanted to hear, and if it was, why was she struggling to hold back tears?

"In the meantime," he continued bravely, hoping his voice didn't waver, "there's no reason we can't make the best of today and have a good time."

"Of course," she agreed. "No reason at all."

There was no letter from Constance, and Braley turned away, disappointed for the second time that day.

"I do have a package, though. Came through yesterday."

"Oh," she said, opening a copy of *The Rime of the Ancient Mariner* that had come all the way from New York. "I ordered this for Laith. It took so long I had forgotten."

"It's been a while. For a while there, you were one of my best customers. Really putting us on the map." He laughed at his own humor.

"I beg your pardon?" She paused, and Laith stopped beside her, holding Eliza.

"A letter three weeks in a row and a telegram... don't see that very often. I remember noticing because your name was new at the Riverdale address and it's different, *Braley,* pretty name, and I thought don't tell me... and sure as shootin', Mr. Laith got himself married."

"A telegram?"

"Sure, Mr. Leland picked it up for you. Nice man, Mr. Leland."

A chill ran down her arms. "Three letters?" Braley exchanged a glance with Laith, and at his nod, she moved back to the window with him right behind. "When was this? I don't recall a telegram. Perhaps Mr. Leland misplaced it."

"Can we get a copy?" Laith asked.

"Oh, sure, sure, unlikely both of you would forget, though, him having a note from you and all." The kind man pulled out his pocket watch. "I'm about to close up today, and it will take some time. It was a month or more ago, as I recall, and I'll have to look back. Why don't you check back, say, the middle of next week?"

"I understand," Braley said.

She took Laith's arm, but turned back again. "From now on, I would prefer to get my own mail. Would you hold it for me until I pick it up? Is that possible? Telegrams as well? Also, it may be best if they were not sent to the house until further notice."

"Oh, sure, sure. Sign here for no delivery." The man looked to Laith as Braley signed. "Is there a problem, Mr. Laith?"

"The lady is not certain. I am sure she will let you know as it is her mail."

The man bobbed his head to Braley, "Of course, I apologize, missus. I hope I haven't done wrong. I'm sure I still have the note on file. I'm sure there's an explanation. We shall have to get to the bottom of this."

"Yes, we shall," Braley answered.

Outside, she seethed as Laith handed her into the buggy and passed Eliza up to her. "He took my letters!"

"Well, we don't really know that…"

"Of course we do! He has stolen my mail and my telegram. I am sure that's a crime in the eyes of the law!"

"We'll get a copy."

"Of the telegram. But there are no copies of my letters! And what if it was something urgent? It's been over a month. It had to be from Constance! What if she needed me!" She buried her face in Eliza's blanket to calm herself. This was not something to cry over. "I should have sent Constance a telegram asking her what was wrong."

Laith placed a comforting hand on her back. "They're closed now, but we can come back. I'm sorry. If he has really done this, I'll… I don't know, but I'll make him answer for it."

"Why, though? Does he hate me just because I'm here? Is it the ranch?"

Laith shook his head. "I don't know. Maybe he's looking for the proof that we're not married."

"There isn't any." She smiled through her tears.

"Oh, yeah. I mean that we're…" He didn't know what they were. "Well, he doesn't believe that. Would you rather go home?"

Braley thought it over and dried her eyes. "No. What's done is done, and that won't change it. I won't let him take that from us. Let's go to the fair and deal with it tomorrow. I think it would be best if he doesn't know we know for now."

Everyone for miles around was at the fair. It was much larger than Braley expected, with booths and wares and food of every description. The aroma was heavenly, and she was reminded they hadn't eaten when her stomach growled in protest. They caught up with Monty and Ella and ate barbecue and corn on the cob, with Laith discussing the different varieties and how open pollination wasn't ideal, and joking about what he would do to make it better, until he had them all laughing. Braley watched his smile and the light in his eyes when he spoke of his dreams and wondered what the future held.

It was a time for dreams. Dreams and celebration, but there was something else in the air… The very spirit of a people who carried on against all odds. Who stood in defiance of the hardship and the threat of winter on the horizon. It was there in the giant pumpkins, tiny gourds, pies, pickles, and jams. Here was their hope, here in their offerings. There was joy in the games and contests, pride in every type of livestock, and the prize ribbons everywhere. The atmosphere was one of excitement, triumph, and strength, and Braley was soon feeling better.

She spent some time with Ella, admiring the many beautiful quilts and handiwork and choosing their favorites, while Laith and his father inspected the latest offerings in tools and farming equipment until it was time for the horse pulling event.

They migrated with the crowd to the open pasture and found seats in the shade for Monty and Ella. The heavy sleds, loaded with stone weights, sat waiting for the various teams to have their turn pulling along the marked stretch of bare earth. Leland's team of grays did well, and he advanced to the semi-final and then the final round. They waited at the break for more weights to be added, Eliza happy on Ella's lap and Monty beaming with pride. "He's got a good chance. Those horses aren't even struggling yet. They've got plenty of go left."

Braley smiled for Monty's sake, although she wasn't enjoying it as much as he. It was exciting at first, and awe inspiring to see the power of the beautiful beasts as they strained and pulled and somehow, when they seemed to have reached their limit, find the strength to go a little farther. But her excitement diminished as she began to wonder about the rightness of making the horses work so hard for nothing. It was true, they were born to it, and these were cherished animals. To be sure, many of the farms and, therefore, life, depended on them. In the field, it may be necessary, but here it seemed all for naught. She understood the pride in being the best, the most beautiful of the quilts and the tastiest of jams, but those were accomplished with loving hands and not at the suffering of a living thing. *Not with a whip*. It did not escape her notice that Leland was the only participant who used one.

The weight was added, the first team pulled and strained and pulled, until they had nothing left, and it was called to a halt, and then it was Leland's turn. The heavy draft horses seemed to have little trouble at first, but after the initial burst of power, as they moved down the track, they began to strain. Braley found herself leaning forward, pulling for them. Not for Leland, but for Monty, an old man's pride, and the horses themselves, valiantly fighting, inch by inch, as they neared the mark where the other sled had stopped. Pulling for them so they could be done with it, and in this case, she hoped, treated well afterward, because heaven help them if they failed. The whip cracked, the fingers of fire she remembered too well, touching down on the back of one and then the other. She turned her face into Laith's shoulder and he held her. The animals jumped forward as one and passed the mark. They had won.

The horses had won. Leland, of course, took the credit and basked in the glory of a five-inch blue ribbon. Braley stood back watching as he accepted the pats on the back and the praise, and thought about her telegram, her stomach turning. She made the effort for Monty's sake and managed not to choke on her forced *congratulations*.

Leland only nodded, eyeing her suspiciously, and then left to see to the horses. Some of the crowd began to dissipate, heading back to the heart of the fairgrounds when Ella spoke up, with Eliza now napping in her arms, and Monty dozing in his chair. "Why don't you young people go and enjoy yourselves while she's quiet, and when you come back, I think Monty and I will head for home.

"Are you sure?" Braley asked, running her hand over her baby's curls and kissing her on the forehead. "We could take her with us."

"Go. We'll be fine, I'm going to wait for Monty to finish his nap anyway," she whispered.

"I think it's a little chilly," Braley looked to Laith, "Maybe we could go to the buggy and get her sweater first?"

The buggy was parked on the other side of the pasture with all the others, and Braley and Laith wove through the milling crowd and across the field.

Laith wrestled with a grin as Braley dug through the many items she had brought, choosing not only the baby's sweater, but a woolen hat and a blanket as well.

"What?" She questioned as they made their way back.

"Nothing."

"Are you laughing at me?"

He looked at her, his lips pressed tightly together, and a smile in his eyes.

"What?!"

He pushed his hat back as the laugh burst past his best defenses, "Well, it's not winter."

She laughed too, stopping in the middle of the field to plead her case. "I know, I just like to make sure she has everything she needs, and it might get colder."

"I'm just teasing," he said. "I think it's adorable, and you're a great mo..."

"RUN AWAYS! RUN AWAY TEAM!" Someone screamed. Men were yelling, and stragglers ran for cover. Braley looked up to see the team of grays, still in harness, tearing down the field, heading straight at them. It was only for a moment, but she froze, hearing her heart thudding louder than the horses' hooves until, through the fog of confusion, she heard Laith's voice.

"Run! Braley, run!" Laith grabbed her wrist and they ran together, he with his long strides pulling her along, and then pushing her ahead of him, taking shelter behind a massive oak. He pressed her up against the trunk with his arms around her. The ground shook, and Braley closed her eyes and prayed, feeling the breeze on her cheek as the horses thundered past within a few feet of their questionable haven.

When the danger had passed, Braley opened her eyes, still catching her breath.

The horses outran their fear, and their panic spent, slowed at the end of the field and trotted off to one side, coming to a stop.

"Are you all right?!" Laith asked, turning her and holding her by the shoulders to look her over before hugging her tightly. His gaze turned down the field, searching the shadows of the barns where the horses had come from.

Braley nodded, shaken but unhurt. When he released her, she searched his face and then looked down at her hand. She still held the small sweater and the bonnet.

They found the blanket a few feet away, trampled into the earth.

Chapter 18

"Then how the hell did it happen?!" Braley was already upstairs in bed, but still, she could hear the brothers arguing in the study.

"I told you I don't know!" Leland said, "They just spooked, is all. You can't blame that on me."

She and Laith had left immediately after the incident, following Monty and Ella home, and any joy that might have been found in the rest of the day, overshadowed by their brush with death. Laith was quiet on the way home, and she let him be, knowing he was wrestling with the truth about his brother. She was sorry for his struggle.

She looked up as he entered the room and locked the door. "How did it go?"

"He won't admit to anything. But then, I didn't expect him to." He stopped to check on Eliza and stood staring down at her.

Braley's heart melted just a little.

"I don't want to upset my father, so I didn't push it any further. I mean, he's right, I can't have him arrested for aiming horses at us, but I don't think it was an accident," he said, as he stripped to his underclothes.

He hesitated at his side of the bed as if he didn't know which side of the blanket he should lie on, and she lifted the covers in invitation. When he slid into the bed, he held out his arm and she moved to his side. "I'm sorry about today," he said. "It didn't start well, and it ended worse."

"Not the day at the fair I expected." She smiled ruefully. "At least we're still alive. Thank you for that, and thank God we didn't have Eliza with us. I don't think I could have run with her."

"I was just thinking that." He thought for a moment more. "You probably would have," he decided.

"Or died trying."

His arm tightened around her. He wanted to kiss her and feel her warmth, a celebration of life, of their triumph, but she seemed still caught in the long shadow of the day.

"What are we going to do? We could have died. Do you realize we could have died today?" She spoke softly, but her voice rose with the question. "It's not you, he's after. He wants me gone. You just happened to be with me. I think the sooner I leave, the better off we'll both be." The severity of her own words hit her like a blow to the stomach. *Would she? Would she be better off? Could she really leave him?* She wished he would kiss her and lift the burden of the awful afternoon, but she guessed he wasn't going to. Lying beside him was nice, and it would have to do. At least he hadn't turned away and rejected her completely. She sighed and placed her hand on his chest, studying his profile in the lamplight.

Laith was quiet, knowing it was true they could easily have died or been terribly maimed, but it was the other part of her speech that scared him the most. He turned to read the look in her eyes, and his pulse quickened before he lowered his lips to hers.

Braley tensed out of habit, but then relaxed, melting into the kiss that was soft and sweet and full of questions. She felt the warmth spreading through her blood as she responded, pulling him closer.

Laith burned from the want in her gaze, and the kiss he gave built and changed in its midst, offering everything and demanding answers.

There was only one. *Yes.* Yes, to his deep kisses that twisted her heart and stole her breath. Yes, to his touch. To each caress that dimmed the atrocities of the past and worries of the present, and his loving words that made her feel like the most beautiful woman in the world.

Yes, to the heat he brought that cleansed her soul of the hatred and the insults she had known. Yes, to the moment when the ugliness of the world fell away, leaving only the brightest light and a different kind of flame that melded them together until she could think of nothing else.

He reveled in her response. *He loved her.* The welcoming warmth of her mouth, the scar on her cheek, her enticing breasts, and the curve of her hip made to fit his hand, her thoughts, her kindness, and her friendship, and her center where he longed to be, losing himself in her heat. He loved all of her, and he wanted her to know. He wanted her to stay, but he would not ask her. *He would show her.*

She met him kiss for kiss, her tongue shy at first, and then bold as it met his, making him crazy with desire. He touched her lovingly, worshiping her softness and her strength, and kissed her scars again before moving over her.

Braley held his head at her breast as he teased and tormented until her need was beyond anything she had known, and she reached for him, wanting him to feel the same. Coaxing him to her side, she touched and explored, noting his response, what he liked and what he loved… *Her.* He loved her. Or at least that was what it felt like when he moaned and pushed her gently onto her back, worshipping her with each thrust, slow and sweet and wonderful until neither could hold back, and she urged him on, letting him know it was all right. It was time. Time for… *something.* The pleasure increased, walling her in until it was all she knew. Her breath caught, and it happened again. *That thing the neighbor lady hadn't told her about. That thing that made no sound, but echoed around her, cradling her soul. That thing that took the giving of two to make each one whole. The thing she had thought too incredible to ever come again.* This time it came with a white light that surrounded her and carried her into her dreams as soon as Laith collapsed at her side with his arm around her and a whispered, *"Jeez, Braley."*

Laith was there when she woke this time, spooned against her back with his arm around her. His breath came even and warm against her neck, and she smiled and closed her eyes. It was a nice way to wake up, safe and warm, and *at least feeling loved.* It was early, and she was in no hurry, less so when he stirred, stretching out his long legs, and his hand began to wander, leading to a lovely morning interlude that brought her to two delightful conclusions. The second one being that Laith had been right; *that thing* was not as rare as she had initially suspected.

"You never told me about these." He said softly, passing his hand lovingly over her back, tracing the lines with his fingertip as though he would heal them with his touch.

She lay on her stomach, covered to the waist, still tentative in her enjoyment of the morning sun on her skin. "I thought no one should know that it was my shame. My responsibility to hide the evidence of such a terrible thing. I realize now that it wasn't. It wasn't me. I didn't do it. But I still don't want anyone to know."

He dropped a kiss on her spine.

She turned her head to look at him. "Why, though?"

"Hmm?"

"Why should I not? Why do we whisper about mean husbands and missing children? Why do we keep the secrets? Why do we hide the things that we should most shout to the world?"

They were late coming down to breakfast, and to Braley's relief, Leland was not there. Monty made no mention of the day before, asking only how they slept.

"We'll be going into town," Laith informed them, "if anybody needs anything."

"Leland left for town earlier." Ella said, "Odd, because we were just there yesterday."

"We have business at the post office. They closed early."

"I was hoping you'd ride the fences on the south pasture. We seem to keep missing a few head around there somewhere. Leland won't be back for a while, and I gave the men the day off after the fair." Monty grinned at Braley, "There's always a little too much celebrating."

"How about Trotter?" Laith asked.

"He went with Lee."

"I can do it when I come back. I promised Braley, and we won't be that long."

"I can wait until tomorrow if it's a problem." Braley volunteered, looking at Laith and glancing at Monty. "I don't want to cause a problem."

"Are you sure?" It was Laith, and he was scowling across the table. The south pasture really should be Leland's responsibility now, since it was included in the property with the cabin, but he chose not to argue with his father.

Braley wondered if she had said something to upset him. "Really, it's fine. They won't have the… other things I need yet, anyway, and one day won't make any difference." She gave Laith a long look, hoping he would understand her meaning, and he nodded.

"Well, all right then." Laith finished his coffee and poured a second cup, "I guess I'll do that. It's probably better to get an early start anyway; it could take a while."

"Why don't you go?" Ella suggested, seeing the look of disappointment on Braley's face. "I'll be happy to watch Eliza. We'll both be here." She shot a glance to Monty, who nodded.

"Sure, why not? Misery loves company. I'm sure it will make the job a lot more pleasant." He grinned at Laith.

Braley watched Laith closely, looking for his reaction, searching his face for a sign of disapproval. His eyes lit with happiness.

Laith *was* happy. Instead of a boring job, he had Braley to himself for most of the day, he thought, as he saddled the horses and waited for her to change. He pulled up his collar against the slight wind and eyed the clouds overhead.

She appeared looking much like the day he had met her, pants and boots, canvas coat, her pistol worn across her waist, and her wide-brimmed hat. She was beautiful now as she was then, but there was something different about her. It was the way she walked with her shoulders squared, no longer slumped in defeat, the spark of joy in her eye, and the smile she flashed him as she reached the barn.

They rode south for what seemed like hours, checking the perimeters, stopping now and then to rest the horses much like they had on the trail. Braley was lost in memory. It was easy to let her mind wander back to that time. The endless miles they had ridden together and the days she had spent alone, the constant battle of hope and despair. Her thoughts turned to Constance, and she hoped she was all right.

"There we go," Laith called from up ahead, spotting a breach in the fence where the wire was downed by a fallen tree branch.

Braley set out the lunch Ella had packed for them while Laith mended the fence. By the time he was done, more clouds had rolled in, and before they had finished eating, the first drops of rain had started to fall and thunder rumbled in the distance.

"Come on." Laith gave her a hand up. "We'll make a run for the cabin."

"That's your idea of a cabin?" Braley asked, as they topped a rise and their destination came into view.

Laith laughed and urged his horse forward in the steady rain.

The building, made of huge logs, was much like the main house and almost as large, with the exception of a second floor. They settled the horses in the barn and made it to the house as the rain turned to a downpour.

Braley looked around in appreciation. The furniture, the rugs, and the stone fireplace were all similar. "I don't understand," she said, when they had removed their coats and boots and set them to dry. "This is a fine house. Who would be unhappy about living here?"

Laith shrugged, as if seeing it from new eyes. "It's pretty nice, I guess, but it's not the big house."

"But surely the difference is not worth fighting over. Not worth losing your only brother."

He shrugged again. "I don't know, maybe he… I don't know. Let's have coffee." He bypassed the overlarge pot they sometimes used on the trail and chose the smaller one left by the sink, filling it with water from the hand pump. "Then we'll look for some dry clothes. You're soaked."

"So are you," she said, not anxious to borrow anything of Leland's and not fooled by his changing of the subject.

Laith started a fire and looked around the kitchen. His brother had obviously been here more often of late, going by the mess, and he cleaned up a little before joining Braley in the front room.

"Come on, let's look around." He led her down the hall, where there were three bedrooms, two seemingly untouched and one obviously slept in, with clothes scattered around and the bed left unmade. "He must be using this one," Laith said, opening drawers and offering up a set of long underwear with several stains down the front as lightning flashed.

Braley wrinkled her nose and held up a halting hand. "No thanks," she spoke loudly over the answering crash of thunder. "I think I'd rather catch cold."

"Yeah, I guess." Laith laughed. "Let's check the other rooms. We kept supplies up here, because sometimes the hands used to stay over if they're working up this way, and got caught in the weather, like us."

"You check that one." He left her at the next bedroom, while he continued onto the third.

Braley entered the pleasant room, feeling like an intruder. There was a double bed, two bureaus, and a desk in the corner, with a dirty coffee cup left on the blotter. She found some wool socks and several smaller pairs of long underwear with separate shirts that seemed to be clean and in good condition, if not new. Gathering the clothing on her way to see how Laith was faring, she stopped to grab the coffee cup when something caught her eye. A corner of yellow paper showed from a partially open drawer.

"Hey, did you get lost in there? I found…" Laith entered the room to see a pile of clothing where it had been dropped on the floor and Braley sitting at the desk.

Her face was pale, her eyes wide and brimming with tears.

"What's wrong?" He asked, adrenaline punching him in the gut.

She stared.

"What is it? Braley, say something."

"He's coming."

He took the stolen telegram from her icy fingers and read the message from Constance. His blood ran cold. Not from the message, but from the implication of finding it here. "And your letters?" He asked, eyeing the envelopes on the desk.

She nodded.

"I'm sorry," she said. "I'm so very sorry."

He took a breath. "Well, we kinda' knew…"

She shook her head and pulled the drawer all the way open, her tears spilling over to run down her cheeks.

Laith swallowed hard. With a shaking hand, he reached for the leather pouch with his initials branded into the front. *"Son of a bitch."*

They had changed their clothes and sat on the sofa in front of the fire, drinking coffee and trying to decide what to do. *"He's coming,"* was all Braley kept going back to. "He's coming, and the telegram was sent weeks ago. He could be here now."

She had read the letters. One was dated before she had found Eliza, in response to when she had poured her heart out about the children who were separated. One was in answer to when she had found her baby. And one was in follow-up to the telegram, explaining how Jacob had gone to the house and threatened Constance with the buggy whip. How he thought Braley was responsible for burning the church and the house, and how he had stolen her telegram from the desk, giving him a hint to her whereabouts. *He was coming.* She took a deep breath. *And what of Laith? How must he feel knowing his brother tried to kill him or hired someone to have it done? There was no hiding from it now. Would he go to the sheriff? And what might that do to Monty?*

She put down her cup and turned to wrap her arms around him.

Laith felt bad for Braley. He would deal with his brother, but the look on her face when he had first seen her was downright near to shock. He had brought her out to the fire and got her to change, putting the heavy socks on her himself, and got her to drink some coffee, but would she be able to deal with this—*this whoever he was?* Startled from his thoughts, he did the same as she, placing down his cup and holding her, thankful for the lifeline she gave. They would deal with it together.

"I was thinking," he said, his cheek resting against the top of her head, "We should put everything back where it was, so no one knows we were here."

"You won't tell your father? Or the sheriff?"

"Not yet. I'm thinking it would be best if Leland doesn't know we know, until we see how this plays out."

"But, my letters…"

"Well, that's up to you of course, but you've read them…"

"…and the pouch is proof. What if it disappears? He has tried more than once to kill each of us, and this is your chance to stop him."

"It's most likely been here all this time, along with the letters and telegram he *stole*, which isn't smart, and I don't expect he'll suddenly get any smarter. I don't want to hurt my father if I don't have to. At least until I know for sure where this is going. Anyway, we know about the ambush, and we know about your mail. What else could he possibly do?"

"He could try again."

Chapter 19

Damn the holdups! Coaches needed new wheels, horses had to be rested. There was the weather to be dealt with. Jacob now traveled west to east, backtracking his previous route, having gone straight to the relay station on the telegram, only to find out his *wife* was no longer there.

He closed his eyes and tried to summon patience for the constant rocking of the coach and for the diabolical journey itself. *None of this was necessary. None of it!* He slammed his palm down on his knee, startling the other passengers who looked at him sideways. But he mustn't get upset. He must show her that he had changed.

He would get there. He would get there, and she would be there. He was getting closer now. She would probably be glad to see him. The woman at the orphanage must be mistaken about this marriage nonsense. That was not possible. She was married to him, and she would be again. She probably didn't understand. That was all. He would help her. She would see. And if not, he would have to put an end to it all. It may be the only way. *They had sinned, purposely or not.* He would wait and see. *Yes. Patience. Ecclesiastes 7:8—'Better is the end of a thing than the beginning thereof.'*

Chapter 20

Braley sat in the living room of the main house, conversing with Monty and Ella, and watching Laith play on the floor with Eliza. It would have been a cozy evening at home if she weren't constantly on alert for any sign of Jacob, and the thought that Leland might make an appearance.

The man had made himself scarce as of late, at times even missing dinner, and spending more nights away from home. She couldn't help but wonder if he were staying at the 'cabin' and whether or not he suspected that she and Laith knew what they knew.

They had been careful to leave everything as they had found it. After their clothes had dried and the storm had passed, Braley washed the cups they had used while Laith restocked the kindling and the firewood, and together they tucked the clothes back where they belonged and replaced the dirty dishes in the kitchen. Braley took extra care with the desk, placing things exactly as she had discovered them, including the dirty coffee cup and the corner of the telegram, barely visible in the partially open drawer. She frowned. *Could he have wanted them to find it?* She dismissed the thought. As far as she knew, Laith seldom went there, and it was only by chance that she went with him. Leland wouldn't know about their discovery at the post office unless he had tried to get her mail recently. No, the whole cabin was in disarray, with things scattered everywhere and drawers left open. Leland was just a slob. She had hated to leave the letters behind. They were hers, and they were personal, and the resentment she felt was equal to the loss, but she didn't want to go against Laith… There was a knock on the front door.

The little party exchanged glances. It was late in the day, and they seldom had visitors. Laith handed Eliza to her mother and went to answer.

It was one of the hands who still guarded the house and the property, "You've got a visitor, Mr. Laith, A man in a hired buggy from town, asking if Miz Braley lives here."

Braley, listening from the other room, tensed with intuition and apprehension. She rose from the sofa and moved to where she had a better view of the goings-on, hugging the baby close. Her pulse quickened as she waited, her eyes locked on the front door.

Laith exchanged a few words with the hand, taking possession of a suitcase, and opened the door wide to reveal the driver who stepped aside.

"Constance!" Tears sprang to Braley's eyes as she ran to greet her friend, handing the child back to Laith to better embrace her.

The women hugged and cried, and cried and hugged, until Laith glanced at his father with a grin and a shrug. Monty and Ella moved closer and waited for introductions, and waited some more.

At last, Braley gathered herself long enough to speak, "But how did you… Why are you here?"

"You didn't answer my letters."

Laith liked her immediately.

Constance put her arms out for the baby, "May I?" Her eyes pleaded with him, and he complied. Rocking her on her shoulder as she used to, the woman closed her eyes. *"Oh, my. Oh, praise the Lord! And look how you've grown!"* She wasn't about to give up the baby, but turned her attention back to Braley. "I sent a telegram, and I wrote, and I could tell by your last letter that you didn't get mine. I came to see if you were all right. I have a lot to tell you."

"You are right, I didn't get them on time, but I have them now.

We'll talk later." Braley gave her a look, saying more with her eyes than her words. She made the introductions, her voice wavering. "This is my friend, my very best friend, Constance Murphy. Constance, this is Ella and her cousin Monty, father of... This is my husband, Laith."

Constance straightened, her eyes wide as she looked from Braley to Laith and back to Braley again. "Well," she smiled. "Con... grat...u... lations."

Braley's eyes still spoke volumes.

Constance's eyes also held volumes—volumes of questions. "Oh, yes, as you *told me in your letters,*" she said to Braley, before she nodded to Ella and Monty and turned to Laith, "How do you do?"

"You must be exhausted," Ella spoke up. You'll be staying, of course. "Braley can get you settled. I'll put on the coffee, and we can talk over supper."

They did talk politely over supper, with both women near to bursting with questions until Braley could put Eliza to bed and join Constance in her room. "What do you mean, *your husband,* and why didn't you tell me?" Constance reached for both of her hands as Braley sat beside her on the bed.

"It's not what it seems," Braley said sadly. "We have a secret agreement." She proceeded to tell her the story of how they met, robbery and all, Monty's proclamation for dividing the ranch, how Laith helped her find Eliza, and how they ended up getting married and why. She continued with Leland's resentment, the threatening incidents, and the missing letters, and finished with finding them in the cabin, along with the warning telegram and the stolen money pouch. "So, there you have it. Laith is my husband, but only until I leave in the spring."

"But you love him."

"No, I..." She blushed under her friend's knowing look. "Maybe. How do you..."

"Psh, it's all over your face every time you speak his name. Why wouldn't you stay?"

"Because I promised, and he promised. That was the agreement. He said he didn't want to be married either. He promised not to touch me, and he would let me go in the spring. Did I mention Monty has a heart problem and cannot be upset? And I wrote you about Mrs. Clark at the children's home. She still haunts me." Braley attempted to change the subject.

"Look at me."

Braley met her eyes.

"You're happy with him. And he's done more than touch you."

She blushed deeper.

"You're sleeping with him! And he makes you feel loved."

Braley nodded reluctantly. "It's everything you said, and more. I never knew there could be such a connection between two people."

"Of course not, married to that… I don't even know what to call him."

"We were never married." Braley took satisfaction in speaking the words.

"Right, and wasn't that a blessing. Have you seen him?" Constance broached the subject they had been avoiding.

"No." I only discovered the telegram last week, and I've been holding my breath ever since. Do you suppose he went all the way to Idaho?"

"I would think so. It was all he had to go by."

Braley was desperate to change the subject again. "I'm sorry, how are Warren and the boys?"

Constance colored in the other half of the picture. She spoke of her family and Jacob's visit, and how she had chased him off. How she had burned the church. "God forgive me, but the place had an evilness about it. It was not God's glory it was built for, and it was the best diversion I could think of, and God only knows what Jacob had in mind for all that ether. I don't know how the house burned, though. It must have been something he did. He was the only one there. It started in your room.

The bad thing is, he doesn't know I was there. He thinks you escaped and burned the church, and at the moment, I didn't think it wise to tell him the truth, him threatening me with his damn buggy whip."

Braley hugged her, remembering all too well. "I'm sorry. That's not a bad thing. It's a good thing. Let him blame me. I wish I *had* done it. I would have if I had thought of it. I let the horses go. I went down and set them free. I was afraid with none of the men around, they wouldn't be cared for." She smiled, "I think that stallion was halfway to Kansas before I got past town."

"Good." Constance said, "I wish I'd thought of *that*."

They were quiet for a moment before Braley said, "I guess he'll be good and mad when he gets here."

"There's something else you should know. Warren did some checking. He wrote some letters. Jacob was thrown out of seminary school. They've been looking for him. He beat a man to death."

Braley let herself quietly into their room, locking the door behind her. She looked in on Eliza, sleeping peacefully, and turned to speak to Laith. He sat up against the pillows, his book abandoned on his chest, his eyes closed.

She walked around to his side of the bed, carefully lifted the book, marked it with the ribbon, and placed it on the bedside table. She stood looking down at him, his long lashes, and the curve of his mouth, wondering if what Constance said was true. *Did it show on her face?* She leaned down and kissed him, unable to resist, and he opened his eyes.

"What was that for?"

She shrugged. She rarely kissed him first, like she had that day at the front door to fool Leland. "Is it all right?"

He stared up at her and crooked a finger, beckoning her back. "Yes, it's all right," he whispered before his lips covered hers.

"Are you liking the book?" She asked, brushing a lock of hair off of his forehead.

He made a face. "Around his neck, though?"

She smiled at his expression and nodded.

"But it's a dead bird! And it's huge!"

"It's symbolic," she whispered, leaning to kiss him again.

He embraced her, rolling her over him into the bed.

Braley laughed before their lips met again, and she forgot everything she was going to say.

Afterward, she lay exalted and exhausted, while Laith rested on his elbow to talk to her. "I like your friend. She must really care about you to come all this way."

"Constance has always been good to me, her husband Warren too. He is a sheriff, you remember, he sent the telegram to the sheriff in Soda Springs. They helped me so much." Her voice was soft in the darkness. "They were the ones who told me about Reverend Keats. They came to the house that night."

"The night of the fire?"

Braley nodded. "Constance was burned on her arm and her head, and Warren had terrible burns on his hands and his knees. My skirt caught and he put it out. I probably wouldn't be here now if he hadn't."

Laith frowned. She had never told him what happened. Not all of it. All he knew was that there was a fire and that was how Eliza was scarred, but there was a cut also. He had only bits and pieces of the tale, and he had wondered, but he didn't want to intrude. She rarely spoke of it, and when she did, there were very few details. But tonight was different. Perhaps because Constance was near, and it became raw again, or perhaps she was braver for her presence, but she kept talking.

"Jacob was angry, of course. He was never not angry, but this was different. This was his perceived downfall in his perceived life of devotion. Because we had Eliza, and then found we were not married, he said we were *'Condemned to hell for our sin'*. There was a lantern burning on the table. He went into a rage and overturned the table and the lantern smashed against the wall behind us. The kerosene went everywhere."

She grew silent, and he put his arms around her before she continued. "I tried to shield Eliza."

He held her tighter, "I've got you now."

"But he's coming. He's coming to force me to marry him so he will be saved from his biggest sin."

"That was not his biggest sin." Laith's voice was dry in the darkness. "And he'll have to get through me first."

"Constance rescued me."

Laith barely breathed, afraid to distract her.

"After the fire, Eliza and I stayed with them, but he broke in. Everyone was sleeping. I woke up and felt something over my face, ether, I guess. That's all… and I think I woke up in the wagon, and then I was back at the house, and Eliza was gone. I couldn't get out. I tried to use the grate from the fireplace to break the boards, but it didn't work. Then Constance came."

She was silent, and he realized she had fallen asleep, cuddled against his side. Some of what she said was difficult to hear as she drifted off, but he was sure of the last thing, and the warmth in her words, *Constance came.*

Constance was not only her friend, but the closest thing she had to a mother and a sister. They were family. He understood about family, *at least he had thought he did. No wonder she wanted to go home to be near her. They had fought that monster together. And where was he now?*

Braley slept, but Laith did not.

Chapter 21

"What should we do today?" Braley asked at breakfast. Monty and Ella had finished earlier, and she and Laith sat with their guest.

Laith felt alarm grip his chest. "You're not going anywhere."

Her eyes shot to his and her cheeks flushed.

Constance drank her coffee in silence.

Laith realized what he had done. "I mean, are you? Do you think it is safe? Until we know about… *him*. And there's Leland," he whispered, and word is there's trouble with the Sioux brewing up around Fort Kearny."

"You're stretching," Braley challenged. "That is not near us," she said aside to Constance.

Granted, it's pretty far, but there will be trouble. Mark my words."

"Should we really be worried about that too?" Constance asked.

Laith shrugged, uncomfortable now and sorry he had broached the subject. "I would say it's to be expected if the government keeps breaking its treaties. They have every right to be angry. I would be. The problem is the people breaking the treaties are over there," he said, pointing presumably east, "and the people dying are over here."

"All right," Braley conceded unnecessarily, "we won't go to the fort today." She shot him a small scowl. "I was only looking to show Constance some of the countryside around the ranch. There are still guards, and we won't go very far."

"All right," Laith answered, "But I'm going…" He stopped to look at each woman in turn and grinned, "to hope you invite me along."

"I know the perfect place for our outing," Laith said when he had brought up the horses, and the ladies came out ready to go. "I was going to take Braley, I just haven't gotten around to it."

"Ella is watching Eliza; I told her we wouldn't be too long."

"Don't worry," he said, "You're going to love it."

They toured the immediate grounds, with Dog padding around and running ahead, and took the trail along the river until Laith veered off to the east on a pathway Braley had never seen before. The small path widened to an overgrown road and soon Laith stopped on a bluff overlooking a small town.

The women pulled up beside him. "Oh, what a quaint little…" Constance stopped mid-sentence, noting the overgrown vines covering everything and the multitude of tumbleweeds that seemed to be the only inhabitants. "There's no one there."

"Is it really abandoned?" Braley asked.

Laith nodded, "Lime Rock Bluff. It was built around an old lime mine that operated before the war, mostly for the making of mortar, and then during the war, it was used for lighting and hospitals, too, and the demand pretty much wiped it out. Everyone's gone now."

They tied the horses at the hitching post and walked down the street, peeking into some of the abandoned buildings. The dog bounded up and down the street, stopping often to gaze back the way they had come. While Constance explored further into the sheriff's office, Braley pulled Laith aside. "I think someone followed us. I don't want to alarm Constance unless I have to, but I'm pretty sure I saw someone behind us in the trees, and I feel like we're being watched. It's obvious Dog hears something."

"It's all right," he assured her, "I had Wes follow behind us just to be safe."

She nodded as Constance joined them. "How is it?" Braley asked."

"Come see, everything is still there, the desk and chair, even the posters on the wall."

Braley went with her to look.

"It does have an eerie feel to it, doesn't it, with everything left the way it was?" Constance said when they came out again. She stood staring off into the hills, and Braley glanced at Laith.

"Come on, I'll show you the best part." He led the way to the end of the town and rounded the corner, where there stood a brick building and a much-deteriorated courtyard where one of the brick walls had fallen. "Ladies, I give you the Lime Rock Bluff Institute of Higher Learning."

Braley caught her breath. *"Eww!"*

Laith laughed, while Constance looked on in wonder at the courtyard that was now a mass of prickly pear cactus. The plants had multiplied over the seasons to grow and entwine upon themselves, not expanding beyond the patch of brick and concrete.

"It looks like a bunch of flat snakes," Braley said.

Laith was still laughing. "I think it's the added heat. They don't want to leave."

Her eyes met his.

He stopped laughing. "From the… bricks," he finished before he turned and walked away.

"What a shame," Constance commented, looking at her friend out of the corner of her eye. "To build something so perfect and then leave it behind. I wonder what they were thinking."

"Maybe they promised," Braley mumbled to herself.

Ella met them at the porch with Eliza wrapped in a blanket. "Laith! Your father went down to the main barn in the buggy, and he hasn't come back yet. Leland said they needed him. I'm a little worried because he went alone and he said he'd be right back."

"I'll have a look," he said aside to Braley.

"I'm going with you."

"No, I'm sure it's fine, you and Constance go ahead in and get settled."

Braley looked from him to Constance, apprehension coursing through her. "All right. I'll put up the horses."

"I'll help." Constance offered.

They walked the horses down to the barn and took the long way around by the corral to cool them. "I don't know," Braley said, "I'm worried." She paused as she spotted the two hands, Wes and Cody, coming in from the road to town.

"What's wrong?" Constance asked, at her friend's frown.

Braley shook her head as she waited for them to reach the barn. "Hello."

"Howdy, ma'am. Can I help you?" Wes spoke as they both tipped their hats.

"I wanted to thank you for following us out to Lime Rock."

The men glanced at each other. "We didn't."

"You didn't?"

"No, ma'am. We went down to the barn to get our horses, and Mr. Leland asked us where we were going. He said there was a change of plans, and you weren't going. He sent us to town instead. There wasn't any trouble, was there?"

"No. No trouble."

"There must have been some mix-up. I'll be sure to check with Mr. Laith, Ma'am. I mean, from now on, if there's a change of plans." The look in his eyes spoke what he dare not say out loud, and Cody nodded.

"Are you going to tell me what that was about?" Constance asked, when they had finished up with the horses and walked back to the house, and Braley had been silent for too long.

"Laith asked those two men to back us up today to make sure we weren't followed, you know, to be safe."

"And they weren't there," Constance said, as they went through the front door.

'Right." Braley wondered how much she should say.

"Well, somebody was."

"You knew?" Braley lifted Eliza to her shoulder.

Constance rolled her eyes as she washed her hands and then began to set the table, "Of course I knew. I sensed it, and so did the dog."

Ella turned from the oven, and at her questioning look, Braley started to fill her in on the story. "Wes and Cody…" she spun to stare at Constance, the hair standing on the back of her neck and cold creeping down her arms.

"What is it?"

Braley handed her the baby without a word.

"Braley, what is it?" Constance persisted, as Braley reached the door.

"Dog."

She began to run. The last time she had seen him, he had trotted off toward the barn when they arrived, but she hadn't seen him in the barn, and he had never followed them to the house. *Unless he had followed Laith… He never followed Laith.*

She heard him yelp and then whimper, her stomach lurching as she entered the side door and willed her eyes to adjust to the shadows. She forced one foot in front of the other until she saw him. He was tied in one of the large box stalls at the back, with Leland standing over him. Her hand went immediately to her side, but she had taken her gun off when she entered the house and, in her haste, had left without it.

Dog cowered, shifting from left to right on the short lead, unable to escape. Leland drew back his booted foot for another kick.

"Untie him."

Each prong of the pitchfork made its presence known, the sharp points pricking the flesh of his back, threatening to pierce deeper. "Okay, okay! Stop!" He tried to arch away. "I was just teaching him some discipline. It don't hurt none."

She pressed harder, shaking with anger, "Now."

Leland bent awkwardly to untie the rope, feeling the trickle of blood wet his shirt, his own movement tweaking the pain. He dropped to his knees.

Dog slunk to her side, and Braley shifted the pitchfork to hover over Leland's throat as he lay in the hay, whimpering. "If you ever touch my dog again, I'll kill you. Do you understand? Come after me, if you have the guts, but you leave my dog alone." She threw the pitchfork against the wall and kicked him as hard as she could, feeling nothing at his grunt of pain. "Glad to know it *don't hurt none.*"

Constance met her at the door of the barn, toting a shotgun, and followed her across the yard as she struggled to carry the large dog, her tears falling into his fur. "I guess you're mine now, boy."

Laith returned with Monty, none the worse for a damaged wheel on the buggy that the men had almost finished changing by the time his son had arrived. They found the women in the kitchen, Dog in the corner by the hearth, and Braley with tears in her eyes. She sat on the floor next to him, staring at the wall, her arms wrapped around one knee.

Ella did her best to distract Monty with a late lunch.

Laith looked questioningly to Constance, who pulled him aside and told what she knew, before he approached his wife. "I'm sorry." He said quietly. "Is he going to be all right?"

"I think his ribs are broken." Her blank stare frightened him. "I stuck him with a pitchfork."

Laith looked over the dog, who appeared at least outwardly unharmed, and back to Braley in confusion.

"Your brother. I stuck him with a pitchfork. I can't stay here."

His eyes widened. "What?"

"He's in the barn."

"Just a little misunderstanding. I'll be right back," Laith told Monty on his way out the door. He found his brother sitting slumped over on a haybale, talking to Trotter.

Leland struggled to get to his feet when he saw Laith. "She overreacted. I didn't hurt the stupid dog."

"You did. Get up. *Get up!*"

"I can't! I think she broke my ribs." Trotter tried to hold Laith back while Leland got unsteadily to his feet, holding his side. "And look." He held up his bloodied shirt and turned his back, showing a line of perfectly spaced small wounds.

Laith stopped wrestling to get past Trotter. "This isn't over. Do you hear me?"

"You're damn right it's not over. She's going to pay for this!"

"You stay away from me and mine, and stay away from the house, or I'll break your face."

"It's not your house yet!"

"No, but she's my wife. Don't let me catch you near her. Or her daughter, or her friend, or her dog, or her saddle, or anything else."

"She's a spoiled little bitch."

"She's not. You have no idea what you're dealing with."

"Look what she did to me! I should get the sheriff out here."

"You do that. And make sure you tell him everything. While you're at it, let's have him take a look at the wheel on Pa's buggy, shall we? That was no normal wear on those spokes, and nobody down at the barn sent for him. I don't know what the hell you're thinking, Leland, but it's not going to end well."

Trotter stood silent when Laith's eyes locked on his before he turned and left.

"He knows," Trotter said.

"Don't be stupid. He knows nothing."

Chapter 22

"We both knew this day would come."

Braley nodded, taking both of Constance's hands in hers as they sat up late into the night, saying their goodbyes. "I know, but it's almost harder than if you had never come at all."

"I promised Warren I'd be home for Christmas, and I plan to stop and see some family on the way. But I can hardly stand to leave with things so unsettled. Are you sure you don't want to come with me? I mean, I don't see how you would, with Laith, but I am worried about your safety."

Braley shook her head, holding back tears, "I promised too. He helped me find Eliza. I will stay until spring."

"And then?"

"I honestly don't know. I suppose it depends on how everything works out here. This whole mess with Leland wasn't part of the bargain. I don't think Laith could have foreseen it. It's breaking his heart."

"And what about the mess with Laith?"

"What do you mean?'

Constance gently lifted her chin to look into her eyes. "He's in love with you. Will that not break his heart also?"

"He has never said so."

"Oh, yes. *He promised.*" Constance smiled. "And you love him."

Braley looked away, but nodded her answer.

"And you promised to go."

"Yes."

"You'll stay."

"I don't think so."

"Oh?"

"We agreed I would go, and I don't belong here. I feel displaced, like my… my roots are elsewhere, and there's all this trouble and violence. I'm tired of fighting. I want to live a peaceful everyday life with…"

"Window boxes?"

Braley smiled sadly, "Yes, but…"

"But there's still Laith," her friend said, knowing she would have to work things out on her own.

"Yes. And there's Eliza. I don't see how this feuding and fighting over the land will end as long as they're alive. I feel we are in danger. In the middle. I don't think I could stay even if he asked me. And he won't."

"I guess that remains to be seen." Constance frowned and approached the chasm they had tried to skirt. "I hate to leave before he shows up. I feel like I'm leaving you to the lions."

"It's all right. I know you would do whatever you could. You've done a great deal just by coming. At least I know there's a possibility he will show up. You can't stay forever," Braley patted her hand, "and he may never come." She looked across the room as she spoke the words she did not believe. "Anything can happen out there on the trail."

Constance stared, "You can't ask me to believe that, if you don't."

A ghost of a smile touched her lips, and Braley nodded, "That's fair. But it is true that anything could happen. I'll be all right. We have plenty of guards here, and I have Laith and Dog, when he's better, and I'm a fair shot if it comes to that. And if he doesn't show up before spring," she shrugged, "I may beat him back East."

They made a brave show of tucking in their problems for the night and setting off to sleep, each struggling with nightmare memories of Jacob Turner.

The goodbye in town was so much harder than Braley had imagined. Despite the cold, she and Laith had made the trip in the wagon with Eliza to see Constance safely on the stage. The roads were still clear, and if need be, they could stay in town. Any travel this time of year was taking a chance, but Braley could not bear to see her friend drive off from the ranch by herself. She chose not to think about her traveling clear across Nebraska territory before she could get a train home.

Constance did not bother to hide the quick tears that burned her eyes. "I hate to leave you, not knowing… But you'll be careful?"

Braley nodded, unable to hold back tears of her own. "I'll feel better knowing you are safe, and your family needs you."

"But you're my family too. And you'll let me know… You'll be careful with the mail?" *And with your life*—she wanted to say. "And you'll let me know where you're going?"

"I promise." Braley nodded and hugged her before handing her Eliza for a last goodbye, barely able to watch.

Laith, having said his farewell, let them be for as long as they needed, or as long as they had before the call of the driver would split their world into two different halves. It was clearly a deep and personal parting and he could only imagine… He did imagine, and that was why he could not trust his voice at the moment. He turned away, eyeing the crowd.

"You're going to miss her," he said to Braley in the wagon.

She could only nod.

"I guess you'll be seeing her soon enough." *It was not a question. Did he expect her to answer?* He chanced a glance at her, but she stared straight ahead.

Braley hugged Eliza even tighter, hiding her tears. *Did he expect her to answer? What did he want her to say?*

It was a long and very quiet ride home.

There had been several snowstorms already, but the roads were passable and Ella suggested another of their trips to town. It had become quite a regular outing for the two women, and with the bad weather closing in, she thought to take advantage of one of the last opportunities and perhaps lift Braley's mood. Christmas was only a week away, and they could do some shopping and stock up on staples. Soon enough, it would be too difficult, and they would be isolated for the winter months. Hopefully, the weather would hold for those attending the annual dance on Christmas Eve and, of course, church on Christmas Day.

Surprisingly, Laith was waiting when she went to their room to get ready. "I don't want you to go."

Her face grew hot and her back stiffened as she turned from the closet to face him.

"Now hold on. Don't go getting all righteous and uppity."

She crossed her arms. *"Uppity?"*

At the look on her face, Laith had second thoughts. "I meant riled up. You know, *touchy*."

"Touchy."

"Well, I mean…"

She took a deep breath and stood waiting. He had never once tried to deny her her freedom, and she would hear him out, but she was rather enjoying his discomfort as he searched for the right words.

"Look at you, you're all like a prickly pear, waiting for me to say the wrong thing."

"That is not better. Why do you insist on comparing me to those awful things?"

He smiled and took a step closer. "Because I like them. I like that they are tough, and the way they defend themselves and hold their own, and I like how if you're real careful…" he came closer and dared to take her in his arms, "you can get close enough to see the beauty under all those sharp edges." His kiss was long and sweet.

Braley was both relieved and disturbed. Relieved, because he had not touched her since the night Constance had arrived. She had felt rejected and disappointed, even though she had tried to convince herself it was for the best, and disturbed, because her reaction to him had not lessened in the meantime. If anything, it had grown stronger, blossoming immediately and spreading to dangerous ground. She gave herself up to the kiss, melting in his arms until common sense prevailed. "You're changing the subject."

He drew a deep breath, his eyes locked with hers. "Is that bad?"

She shook her head and dropped her gaze to his mouth, inviting him to kiss her again, until she remembered her mission and made a half-hearted attempt to leave his arms. "I mean, yes, because Ella is waiting. She will wonder what has become of me." Unknowingly, she glanced longingly toward the bed, bathed in the mid-morning sun, drawing his gaze as well.

He sighed, and let her go. "I would like to go with you. Please."

Braley shrugged. "Sure, if you want to, but I think we will be fine."

"Maybe I have some Christmas shopping to do myself."

"Then why didn't you say so?" The side look she gave let him know she was not convinced.

She felt vindicated in her suspicions when Laith waited by the buggy with a small army on horseback. She recognized Wes and Cody and some of the other half dozen men who were in high spirits, having been pulled from regular chores for an unexpected trip to town. Sadly, Dog still had to be left behind, comfortably ensconced on his blanket in the study in Monty's company.

The trip itself was uneventful, and once in town, the men were given free rein, but she noticed as she and Ella went about their usual stops, they always seemed to be in sight of one or more of the makeshift guard, in addition to her pesky, endearing, temporary husband, who rarely left her side.

After lunch, they left Ella resting with Eliza at the hotel restaurant, under the watchful eyes of Wes. "Don't you have some shopping to do?" Braley asked Laith, after several attempts to slip away long enough to pick up the gift she had ordered without him hovering over her.

"Nope. Did mine," he grinned. "Ordered yours last month and already picked it up." He leaned on the counter, drumming his fingers.

"And the rest of it?"

"Yep, Eliza, too."

"Your father? Ella?"

"Yep."

"How nice for you. What about your brother?"

His eyes were sad for a moment. "That was more difficult, I admit. But it is Christmas, and I thought he might come for dinner."

"Even knowing what you know?"

"I am torn," he said quietly, "but there's Pa, and at the very least I am keeping up appearances. He still doesn't know what we know."

"Then I shall need something too, I suppose. For your father's sake. What did you get him?"

He leaned close to whisper, "Long underwear. No stains."

Braley smiled. "Won't that give you away?"

"Nah. It's what I always give him."

"I see," she laughed. "I need to finish up." She tried once more to walk away and felt him step behind her. She turned, her arm outstretched, palm out, "Stay."

"But I…"

"I'll never finish if you won't let me be."

"Oh."

"Give me ten minutes. Then you may come with me to shop for your brother."

"Well, take…"

"I have this." She stepped closer, and in the pretense of kissing him goodbye, pulled his hand beneath her coat where he felt the colt hidden at her waist. He wasn't quite sure if it had been accidental that his palm also brushed her breast before she released it.

He adjusted the brim of his hat and watched her go. *Braley Stuart, what am I going to do with you? Or without you?*

He did join her soon enough, and she did shop for Leland, but only for Monty's sake. She had thought about a shirt to replace the one she had put the holes in. She had heard from Ella that the blood stains had not come out either, but no. Her blood nearly boiled at the memory. She didn't care that his shirt was ruined, and she didn't want to give him a gift. She closed her eyes and prayed for forgiveness and for the giving spirit. In the end, she decided on a bible and smiled to herself. Leland didn't like to read. She prayed for forgiveness again as she paid, and tucked it among her bundles—a beautiful woolen shawl for Ella, a fancy belt for Monty, and a copy of *A Christmas Carol* and other Christmas stories, for Laith.

On the way out, she eyed the poster for the Christmas dance with longing, knowing they would not attend.

"What's the matter?" Laith asked, seeing her shoulders drop as she read the advertisement. "Don't you have anything to wear?" He took her packages, with the exception of the one she would not surrender.

Braley gave him a glance as they neared the hotel, "What do you mean?"

"For the dance. Do you need something while we're here?"

"Do you mean you're going?"

Laith looked confused. "Of course I'm going. It's about all there is in these parts. It's the biggest celebration of the year, and I…" He turned to look at her, his mouth open, "I'm not going without you. Do you not want to go?"

She stared back, her pulse quickening. "Are you asking me?"

"Oh no! Yes. Yes, I'm asking you. I'm so sorry. I just assumed you would go with me. I never gave it much thought."

"Don't be sorry. I'm really quite flattered you assumed we would go together." She waited until a man passed between them and placed her free hand on his arm. "I assumed we would not be going at all."

"Why?"

She wasn't sure she could explain. "Well, because I've never been. I mean, he, my—Jacob—*She hated speaking his name out loud.* We never attended anything. Except church."

"But most times the dances benefit the church, so they can help people."

She nodded.

"No parties? No dancing?"

She shook her head and backed up against the storefront so people could pass.

"No barbeques?" He dodged another passerby and joined her against the building.

"No."

"No barn raisings to help the neighbors?"

"God helps those who help themselves," she repeated from some far-off memory, so softly that he had to bend close to hear her in the bustle of the busy street. The look of horror he gave caused her to smile sadly.

"And no dancing? Ever?"

She winced, "I don't know how. I used to stand on Papa Joe's feet and he would dance me around, but I never really learned. After my mother died, he didn't go out much either."

Laith grew serious, *at least she thought he did*, when he removed his hat and held it over his heart.

"Braley Stuart, will you do me the honor of accompanying me to the Christmas dance, where we shall dance the night away?"

"I would love to." Her eyes lit with excitement, "Can we really go?"

"Of course," he laughed, thrilled with her enthusiasm.

She didn't bother to correct him this time. She liked it when he called her *Braley Stuart*. She wasn't sure if he really forgot or was sending a subtle reminder. She preferred to think of it as a term of endearment, because it reminded her of the first time he said it, when he said he would not hurt her.

Chapter 23

It had snowed again, but not so much that they could not travel. Braley had been worried when she woke on the morning of Christmas Eve, but she and Laith were able to take the horses and a sled to gather greens with some of the men. She waited, stomping her feet in the cold while they cut down a good-sized tree for the house and another for the bunkhouse.

The house was decorated with extra candles and greens on the mantles and the banister. The tree in the corner proudly displayed popcorn garlands, a variety approved by Laith, and popped days before, so it would harden off for stringing, and some cherished ornaments Ella had collected over the years. Having not celebrated for the past years, Braley thought it the most beautiful Christmas since her early childhood. Some of the baking was done and everything was ready for tomorrow's dinner, but now it was time to get ready for the dance.

Laith was as handsome as ever with a white shirt and ribbon tie and a wool vest, and Braley chose her green dress with the fullest skirt. A light snow fell, and scant moonlight begrudgingly lit the way as two sleighs full of family and cowhands left the ranch, with several following on horseback. Bells jingled, the men, full of holiday spirit, joked and laughed, and Braley, caught up in the excitement, forgot all her worries, except for the fact that she didn't know how to dance. She grew more nervous the closer they got, and by the time they entered the community building, she was practically hiding behind Laith.

"Here now, what's this?" Laith asked, pulling her around to stand by his side. He lifted Eliza to his shoulder and set about meeting and greeting and making introductions.

It was easier with his arm around her, and Braley's trepidation with the townsfolk grew less as they made their way around the room. *Except for some of the young women.* She had grown used to the admiring glances her temporary husband received whenever they were in town, and she supposed she didn't blame them, but a few of these glances were downright flirtatious. *Laith didn't seem to notice, but the least they could do was...*

"Laithram Demoranville!"

They turned as one to face a beautiful dark-haired woman who tried to shoulder Braley out of the way and throw her arms around Laith. It was not easy with Eliza in the way. Braley didn't move and Laith's arm remained around her waist.

"Laithram, where have you been? I have not seen you since last summer. I missed the fair this year. We were traveling. Did you miss me? I assumed you would call on me to see why I was not there, after all we..."

"Braley, this is Niki Paterakis, an old friend. Niki, this is my wife, Braley, and our daughter, Eliza."

The woman froze with a half-smile on her face, and Braley prayed the awkward moment would end quickly. *Niki. An old friend.* The look on the woman's face clearly told her there was more to it. Braley may not have a lot of experience in these matters, but she didn't need a neighbor lady to explain this. *And why wouldn't Laith have old friends? He was a handsome man. But he was her husband. For now.*

That didn't go well. Laith thought, seeing the doubt in Braley's eyes and feeling a change in the air as they walked away. *Damn Niki. She had always been forward and overbearing and a pain in his backside since they were kids.*

Braley glanced at him, and he stopped to pull her close, his hand playfully feeling her waist, "You didn't bring your gun?" She laughed as he had hoped, and he searched the room for Ella, who had found a seat with the older ladies. He handed Eliza over to the admiring elders, but not before kissing her cheek, unknowingly touching Braley's heart.

He took her hand as the music changed. "Come on. We'll start slow. This is a waltz. It's easy," he said, showing her the steps. "We count, one, two, three… one, two, three. Just move with me…" His hand, low at the back of her waist, pulled her closer against him and he whispered in her ear, *"Like when we make love."*

She blushed and missed a step.

He grinned and they started over.

It was like making love, she thought, and it was easy with Laith, leaning against him, feeling and anticipating his movements. *No wonder people liked dancing.*

It was not as easy when she was claimed by other partners, when she did not lean into them, no matter how hard they tried. Some were nicer than others in respecting the distance she kept. *There was a lot to learn about dancing.* Thankfully, there were other dances besides the waltz. Square dances, reels, and polkas. She did love the polka, which reminded her of jumping and skipping like she had as a child, and the square dancing made her laugh once she got the hang of it, but nothing was like the waltz. Her first waltz with Laith. She would never forget it.

She waltzed with Wes, apologizing now and then for her inexperience.

"No matter, ma'am. I'm grateful to have a woman for a partner, and a pretty one at that."

Braley smiled and dismissed the compliment as part and parcel of these easy-going cowboys, with their ready charm, but the other part of his statement seemed to hold more water.

He gave a nod of his head to indicate the other side of the room, where some of the cowhands danced with each other, or alone. It was true, there were fewer women by far, but it was one of the rare festive occasions that bobbed to the surface in a sea of hard labor, and no one was about to let good music and good spirits go to waste.

The shortage of women, then, would cause one to wonder why Laith claimed the company of his *old friend* Niki, for the second time. Braley considered this, as she stole another glance at them. Laith, tall and blond, Niki with beautiful dark curly hair and a perfect complexion, both young and good-looking. She watched as the woman attempted time and again to move closer to Laith, and each time, he moved away. This made an odd configuration of a dance, not at all following the beat, and Braley frowned.

Wes turned to look at what had caught her attention, and with a knowing nod, waltzed her across the room and tapped Laith on the shoulder.

In one move, she found herself in the arms of her husband, while Wes danced away with Niki. "I didn't know you could do that," she whispered.

"Remind me to give that man a raise."

"Are you saying you didn't enjoy dancing with her?"

"Not really. Once was enough. Once is polite."

"Then why would you?"

He shrugged, "She asked me. I didn't want to embarrass her in front of everyone."

More of that cowboy cordiality, Braley thought, before he pulled her closer and she concentrated on the dance. It was a few minutes later when she looked up to see that Leland was there. He was standing by the wall, seemingly deep in conversation with Niki, and they were both staring in her direction.

The house was quiet, ready to burst with the once-a-year celebration. But not yet. Now was the time of indefinable anticipation. The time between the eve and the dawning, when the world held its breath, veiled by the holiest of nights.

"So, Niki…" Laith ventured, taking off his boots.

Braley turned from the window where she had been looking out at the mid-night sky and the moonlit landscape. The snow had stopped and the stars glittered in the clear cold air. "Now?"

"Well, I don't want you to be jealous."

"Hold your horses, cowboy. Did I say I was jealous?" *There was no need to tell him that it hurt her heart to think of him with someone else.*

"No, but…"

She tilted her head to study him. "Are you sure you don't want me to be?"

"No. I… the way she was acting and all… putting on airs, like there was something between us. I just want it to be clear."

"So, there wasn't?" *She guessed it was okay with the knots in her stomach if he wanted to clear the air.*

"Maybe when we were five. She lives miles away. Her father's ranch borders ours at the furthest outskirts of each, and their house is at the far end. I've seen her once a summer at the fair since we were kids, and at a few other gatherings. She might have taken some things for granted, but I never gave her any reason to."

"Not even at a dance?" She placed his hand at her waist and put her palm on his shoulder, and began to waltz with him around the room.

"A few dances," he mumbled. "But everybody dances."

"No kissing?" She slid both arms around his neck and pressed her lips to his. She had intended to play, to give him a quick kiss and carry on with her inquiries, but that one touch awakened the thirst that had grown all evening, taunted by the closeness of their bodies and the temptations of the waltz. With that one touch, she had gotten too close to the well and toppled over the edge.

His arms tightened around her, and he captured her mouth, molding her against him like he had wanted to do at the dance, confessing his need, and she was lost in the satiating abyss, falling into the darkness and the bed that held all the answers she needed for now.

"I love this bed," she said long afterward, reaching over her head to touch one of the brass bars as if in wonder. "It is the only place I have felt…" *Loved…* she thought. "Safe," she said, "in a very long time."

"Safe? Is that all?" He asked.

"*Desired,*" she confessed, feeling herself blush. "*And beautiful.*" She hid her face against his shoulder, knowing it was not the bed that made her feel so.

"So, Niki…" she ventured, a short while later, on the verge of sleep. "Now?"

Her laugh came softly in the darkness, and she turned on her side to face him. "I'm just curious."

"She's not my type."

"Why not? She's very pretty. And when you were looking for a wife, she was nearby."

"Pretty is nothing by itself," he said. "And exactly… If I had wanted her for a wife, I could have ridden in the other direction and called on her, but I didn't, and I don't, end of story."

"But why not?" She was genuinely interested. "If you were looking to make a bargain, like when you first asked me…"

"She would never have accepted the bargain, and I can't imagine being stuck with her."

Her heart lurched a little. *Did he feel stuck with her? Probably not, because he knew she was leaving. But, still.* "She does seem like a good match," she continued.

"Why do you say that?" He knew she wasn't being coy. It wasn't in her nature.

"Well, she's from here, she's tall, and pretty like you, and she's… *your kind.* Her family obviously has money, she likes you, and she knows ranching."

"Ha! She probably never got her hands dirty in her life. She's really not my type. It's the ranch she likes. Or rather, her father does. I once saw her cry because she got caught in the rain. Ruined her hair or something. I can't see her leaving home alone to make a life for herself, or traveling across the country to find her daughter, or taking the time to bury people she didn't know at the risk of endangering herself."

"But you weren't looking for a wife who would do those things."

"No, but I knew her when I found her."

They fell silent. Laith, thinking he had said too much, and Braley wishing he would say more.

"She's not prickly."

"What?"

"She's all sugar. Probably why she's afraid of the rain." He could barely see her in the moonlight, but he knew she smiled. "You're pretty, and she doesn't have your…"

She braced herself, her hand going immediately to her cheek. "What?"

His hand cupped the back of her neck and he raised on his elbow to lean over her. "Yes, that little scar right there, that looks like a dimple when you smile," he said, kissing her cheek. "Or your gumption, or your fight, or half your determination—the things that make you beautiful—or the most inviting lips." He moved his mouth over hers, lingering until he felt her respond with a passion that stirred his soul. "Or breasts like velvet," he said, nuzzling his face into the opening of her gown."

"How do you know?!" She sat up.

"What?"

"How do you know she doesn't, unless you…"

"No, no, that's not what I meant!" He tried to capture her softly pummeling fists, until they both collapsed in laughter.

"Well?" She asked, after a while.

"What?" He lay still, holding her wrists.

"What else does she not have?"

"You mean you forgive me?"

"I might, if the list is long enough."

"Really?" He asked, picking up where he left off, choosing his words with the utmost care.

They were late coming down Christmas morning, but Monty and Ella had also slept in. They exchanged gifts after breakfast. Laith gave Eliza a small toy rabbit that was an instant favorite, and found a quiet moment alone to give Braley a small gift wrapped in a silken scarf.

"But this is like two presents," she said, unwrapping the pretty material to find a gift that made her both laugh and cry. She placed the wide silver bracelet on her wrist and studied the raised image of a prickly pear cactus in full bloom. "I love it," she said. And she did. She loved the thoughtfulness and the planning it must have taken, and she had secretly come to love the comparisons he made. *And I love you,* she thought, all too aware that their time was running short.

Chapter 24

Laith had been right. The trouble had come. Their lovely Christmas was now overshadowed by the news of a horrible military disaster near Fort Phil Kearny. The Fetterman Massacre, as it was being called, after the commander, had happened days before; they just hadn't known. News took time out here. Three days before Christmas, eighty-one soldiers had died in an ambush. Laith was right. People could only take so much. Too many lies, too many broken promises, broken treaties. Braley knew as well as anyone that people had their boundaries and their breaking points. She didn't blame the tribes and their allies for fighting back. *Why would they not?* But it did bother her that so many had died, the bodies gathered and buried even as the people here had shopped and celebrated. Perhaps as they danced.

She felt a chill run down her spine as raw as the prairie wind, and she shivered. With the exception of Laith, this land held a coldness for her other than the harsh winter. The vast emptiness, the loneliness that hung like an echo in the air, the broken dreams of those who never reached their destinations, and the blood that had seeped into the very earth that had been *won,* to be farmed and built upon. Where was the pride in it? Working hard, yes, that was commendable, but fighting a people who had inferior weapons and were far outnumbered, and pretending they could live in peace, was nothing to be proud of.

She was homesick. Homesick for the ocean and the salt air that would somehow cleanse her mind and renew her soul. She would like to take Laith there, to share the sea and walk the shores of her home… Her thoughts were interrupted by Dog, who was much healed, pushing at her elbow over the arm of her chair. He wanted to go out. *That's odd,* she thought, he had been out just a short time ago… She opened the door to find Laith readying the sleigh with blankets.

"The roads aren't too bad. I'm going into town, and I thought you might want to go for the ride."

"I do. I want to check the mail, and I have a letter for Constance. Let me see if Ella will watch Eliza, it's awfully cold."

She was ready in ten minutes, leaving Dog behind because of the cold, also, and because he could not yet be let to run to warm up. The wind stung her cheeks and her eyes watered as she admired the snow-covered pines and wondered about the tracks ahead of them on the road.

"Leland," Laith answered when she voiced her question. "He left earlier."

Mention of her brother-in-law somewhat dampened her mood. He had come for Christmas dinner and cast a pall over any festive atmosphere that might have been. Conversation at the table was stilted, and he kept grinning at her, as though he held a secret. He had brought gifts only for his father and Ella. That was fine with Braley, who left his gift sitting under the tree and waited impatiently for him to leave.

Her mood brightened when a letter from Constance waited, wishing them all a Merry Christmas. She had some delays getting home, but made it for the holiday, and all was well. There was no mention or news of Jacob. She posted her letter as Leland entered the office.

"What are you doing?" He said to Laith, who instinctively stepped forward to shelter Braley.

"Picking up our mail."

The big man turned red in the face. "But that's my job. I always get the mail."

Laith shrugged. "We were here so… Any reason why we shouldn't?"

"Of course not." He frowned and turned to glare at the postmaster before making his exit.

Laith followed close behind with Braley. "Funny thing, Braley wasn't getting some of her letters. I wonder what could have happened." He adjusted the brim of his hat to stare at his brother.

"What are you looking at me for?"

"I'm wondering, because you always get the mail. You said so yourself."

"Aw, get out, why would I want your girlie letters?" He pushed past Laith and headed for the saloon.

"I never said who they were from."

Leland kept walking, and they watched him go.

"Now he knows we suspect him," Braley whispered, taking Laith's arm.

Laith glared at his brother's back and settled his hat back into place. He glanced at Braley, "I probably shouldn't have said anything. I couldn't help it."

"We should go get them now, before they disappear."

"Yes. I guess so."

The regret at having taken the unexpected step toward the inevitable showed in his eyes, and Braley held tighter to his arm. "If we hurry, we could go this afternoon."

Braley went to the general store to get the things on Ella's list, while Laith completed his errands. Standing at the counter to make her purchase, the accidental meeting weighed heavily on her mind. Except for Christmas dinner, which was uncomfortable at best, she had seen nothing of Leland since their fight in the barn. After today, she realized his very presence was so much more disturbing. There was an aura of hate that hung like a cloud around him. It had always been there, but, of course, had grown worse since their confrontation over Dog. Why she had ever agreed to sit down to dinner with him was beyond her now... *Monty. Yes, Monty and his weak heart. But how much did she owe the man who had purposely pitted one son against the other and refused to see the evil that was spreading because of it?* She closed off the thought and the guilt that went with it.

"Hello, Braley."

She froze at the voice close behind her. Her heart began to pound. *Jacob.* She had waited for this. She had expected it for weeks. Imagined it for months. But she wasn't ready. She turned.

He wasn't as tall as she remembered. He looked different with a full beard, and though he still dressed in the same type of suit and wore his collar, his clothes were worn and dirty from travel. *That was all.* The surge of fear in her chest subsided. *He was just a man. She owed him nothing. Had she built him up in her mind to be bigger and more powerful than he was? The power he held over her was what power she had given him, and she could take it back. Why had she given it to him in the first place?* She had feared his coming, was afraid to face him again, yet, standing here before her, he seemed no more than a distant memory. She moved to step around him.

He gripped her wrist. "Don't go."

She glanced at his hand and the people around them, and he released her, but she didn't move and she didn't flinch.

This was not the woman he remembered. It was not only the way she was dressed, which was unacceptable—no minister's wife could be seen to wear a gun belt—but it was something else. The look in her eyes was different. The way she looked at him... It would not be easy to persuade her he had changed. "I've come for you."

"You've wasted your time." She took another step.

"I can save you. I can save your soul. In spite of everything you've done, I'm willing to marry you again and set things right. I've changed. I'll prove it to you. We can make this right and both be saved."

Braley moved away from the counter so they would not be overheard. "It can never be made right, Jacob. You can't change the past."

"But I can. I have. I can change everything. You have to give me a chance before we are both condemned to hell."

"What can you change? Can you give me back the months away from my child? Can you take away the fear, the searching, and the anguish I lived with each day, not knowing if I would ever see her again? Can you change this? She lifted a hand to the scar on her cheek. Can you change the burn on my shoulder or the marks on my back? No, and you cannot change the scars on the soul of that poor young girl who came to you full of hopes and dreams. A girl who had nothing left in the world, but was willing to put her all into building a future, into building a life, and was naïve enough to trust a stranger to want the same. A girl who was foolish enough to wish for love from someone who didn't know how to give it. You stripped her of every hope, every joy, real or imagined. *That* was your chance, Jacob, and you crushed it into dust. Just like you crushed her. You can't marry her. She's gone. She no longer exists."

"We can go to dances. You should have told me you liked to dance. I would have taken you."

She felt the pitch in her stomach and her eyes searched his. *He was there. He was there at the dance. Watching her? How long? How long had he been here?* "That's a lie. You never cared what I wanted. Never. We are done."

"But we have a child. You have to marry me."

"I *am* married. This time it is real; there are records and papers to prove it. And you never wanted that child. *You gave her away.* Don't try to pretend you want her now. I am at peace with my God. Go make peace with yours. Ask for forgiveness. He may forgive you. I cannot." She moved toward the door and did not stop.

Her eyes had changed when she spoke of the child; the hard indifference was gone, pain flared, love flashed, and tears followed. It was her weakness—2 Corinthians 12:9 'for my strength is made perfect in weakness.' "I do want her," he called out, following her outside. He stood in the middle of the walkway with his eyes closed, speaking loudly. "'Suffer the little children to come unto me, and forbid them not,' Mark 10:14."

Braley spun around. People stopped to stare. "Stop it! Stop twisting the gospel to suit your purpose, that is not what that means, and you know it!"

He lowered his voice, "I do want her, and I'm coming for her." Jacob stopped where he was. The look in her eyes had changed again, and it was like nothing he had seen before.

"Then you're a dead man."

She walked away. Desperate to find Laith, but aware Jacob was watching, she entered a nearby shop and peered out the window until he went back inside. Then she went straight to the bank to find Laith.

He took one look at the set of her mouth and her pale face. "What's wrong?"

"Take me home. Now. Take me to Eliza."

He put his arm around her. "It's him, isn't it? Is he here?"

She nodded, and he led her to the sleigh.

"What did she say?" Leland asked.

Jacob Turner leaned back in his chair in the hotel dining room, where they had agreed to meet. "She said she is married," he answered with a scowl.

"I've never believed it. It's a trick. I don't think they got married, and if she is married to you, they can't be."

Jacob did not look up. His gaze was dark and distant. "She is my wife."

Leland's eyes glittered with anticipation. He had wracked his brain for weeks wondering how he could find this *Jacob,* who had earned a warning, in the letters he had intercepted. Then, at the dance on Christmas Eve, like a gift, Turner had come to him. The tall stranger had kept to the shadows but stood out like a sore thumb in his long coat. Leland, not distracted by the dancing, had noticed and watched the man who had eyes only for Braley. "You know her," he stated, taking a place in the darkness beside him, his heart beating faster.

The stranger shot him a sideways glare and continued to watch as the blond man twirled the object of his interest around the floor. "Do you?"

"She is *supposedly* my sister-in-law. That's my brother. Are you Jacob?"

The man stiffened and shot another glare in his direction. "How do you know?"

"Come on." Leland glanced around and grabbed his arm to usher him outside, but released him at the look he gave. "We'll talk outside. It will be better if no one knows you're here."

He pulled his thoughts from his past good fortune to focus on the present. He had a way to go before realizing his goal. "What about the kid?"

"The child is her weakness. She will be useful."

"But you want her back? You'll take them both?"

"I will." Jacob Turner nodded.

Leland's pulse quickened. The cold stare from this strange man brought a chill to his spine and a smile to his lips. He was getting closer to what he wanted. They both were.

Chapter 25

Despite Braley's fears, Eliza was fine. She kissed her cheek uncountable times while she held her and explained the circumstances to Ella, and Laith ordered extra guards around the house. They had left town right away, and Laith assured her if they hurried, he had time to travel up to the cabin and get out before Leland returned.

"I'll be fine. I'll be back before you know it."

She studied the confident stance, could feel the urgency that radiated from him, and saw the encouraging light in his eyes as he waited for her response.

Everything in her being told her something menacing waited there. *Could it be a trap? Was Laith in danger? Eliza was well guarded now.* She closed her eyes, treasuring the feel of the silken curls with a brush of her lips. "I'm going with you." She would go, praying all the while she was doing the right thing, and knowing she would never forgive herself if she had made the wrong choice.

They rode in silence. The cabin was not as far as she remembered from the day they had gone to repair the fences, although the more direct route had been slowed in places where they detoured around fallen branches. Luckily, the path was well-traveled by the ranch hands, and the hoofprints were likely to go unnoticed.

They waited and watched a few minutes to see if anyone else was around. "There's no smoke," Laith whispered, squinting at the chimney before urging his horse forward and waving for Braley to follow.

She held her breath as they entered the side door, feeling very much the thief, and then reminded herself she was there to claim her own possessions. It was obvious now that no one was there, but still her breath did not come easily as they made their way through the house speaking in whispers. The living room and the kitchen clearly showed signs of habitation, but the spare bedroom seemed to be as they had left it, right down to the partially opened drawers of the desk and the dirty coffee cup, which had now grown a fine, fuzzy mold. Braley wrinkled her nose, but claimed the letters and the telegram as old friends and held them to her heart. They were hers, a connection to Constance, and she hadn't wanted to leave them in the first place.

Laith stuffed his leather pouch into his pocket without a word, and with a last glance around, they went on their way.

Home before nightfall, Laith took care of the horses, while Braley, her heart in her throat, ran straight to Eliza and saw no reason to leave her ever again. Nothing had happened, but the ominous feel of the cabin had not lessened. Perhaps the aura of hate Leland left behind had permeated its very walls.

The weeks passed, every hour longer than the one before. The snow never seemed to stop, and the cold was brutal. Dog, much improved, was acting like his old self. The only place Braley ventured was out to care for and exercise the horses, and even then, only in the paddock. Always, she rushed back to be with Eliza, Dog at her side. The longer it snowed, the safer she felt, as travel was almost impossible. But the time would come. Jacob would come. And Leland would discover what they had done. Tired of living on the edge of her nerves, she found herself almost, but not quite, wishing for spring. That in itself held added consternation.

Laith stayed close and paced more, restless from inactivity. He spent time in the evenings playing chess with Monty, wondering how best to break the news of what Leland had done.

They retired earlier with the cold, so that the nights, too, were longer, deeper, and darker, and when they made love, it was with a hint of desperation. They were all too aware of the tension and the danger that hung in the air around them, and the passing of each precious day.

This night, as he held her, warmed by the embers of their loving, he thought to tell her how he didn't care. He didn't care about Leland or Turner or the ranch or anything else. If she were to leave him, nothing would matter, but she was sleepy and content lying against him; there was the damn promise, and the words didn't seem to come. Even if they had, he was not sure he could have gotten them past the lump in his throat.

Finally, there came a break from the endless snow, with a week of sunny days, and it was at breakfast one morning when Leland entered, blustering like the wind that accompanied him through the door. "You broke into my house!" He went straight for Laith, who jumped from his seat, his hands balled into fists.

"Lee!" His father yelled, getting to his feet.

The big man halted out of habit. "He stole my things!"

"I did no such thing," Laith replied, wearing a grin of disbelief at the audacity of the claim.

"Did too!"

"Laithram, did you break into the cabin?"

"I did not." Laith insisted without guilt, as the door had been unlocked.

Braley watched, her heart pounding, and tried to quiet Eliza, who had begun to cry at the unusual upset.

Ella looked from one to the other of the brothers and back again. "You boys, quiet down! And Monty, you've got to take it easy."

"Yes, sit down and let's talk this over," Monty ordered, taking his seat, but neither of the other men sat. "When did this happen?"

"I'm not sure," Leland mumbled.

"Well, what's missing, and what makes you think your brother took it? He hasn't left here for weeks in this cold, and you shouldn't be out in it either."

"Yes, why don't you tell us what's missing?" Laith challenged.

Leland, already red-faced from the stinging winds, flushed purple. "This isn't over!"

"You've got that right at least," Laith called before the door slammed.

Ella was the first to break the awkward silence, "My goodness, what do you suppose brought that on?"

Braley felt herself flush and hid her face behind her daughter.

Laith shrugged and took his seat. "I'm sure the truth will out eventually."

The weather had only teased at warming, and the snow returned with a vengeance. Cocooned in the fortress of white, they could only wait for the true thaw. Braley seemed to exist in a fog until the trickle of the streams running from the hills and the first touch of green in the meadows brought hope to the land and fear to her heart. She stood by the front window staring out at the snow that disappeared a little each day, the last of the barrier that separated them from the rest of the world. She jumped when Laith appeared behind her and wrapped his arms around her.

"I know what you're thinking. We'll be all right. You're safe here."

She nodded and rested her head back on his shoulder. She wanted so much to believe him, but found little comfort in his words. *Was she? Was he?*

Visits from Leland did not help the feeling of living on the edge of her nerves, especially when they became more frequent. Yes, these visits were on the pretext of concern for his father, but she had grown to know him well enough and could not shake the feeling that he was up to something. As Laith had said, *the truth would out,* and it was not long before he showed his hand, or so she thought.

"I need to talk to you, Pa." Again, he caught them at the table, but they had finished supper and sat over coffee.

"Well, sit down and help yourself," Monty answered, looking him up and down. "And you might try a proper greeting, for a change."

The chair scraped across the floor, and he dropped himself into the seat. "I've decided to get married."

Laith shot a glance at Braley.

Monty placed his napkin on the table. "Is that so? Well, who's the lucky woman?"

"Niki Paterakis."

Laith scoffed, "Does she know?"

Leland glared in his direction.

"You don't say." Monty looked from one son to the other. "I always thought it was Laith she fancied."

"Well, it's me now, and I'd like you to reconsider the future ownership of Riverdale. It's perfect. Their land is next to ours, and we'll have the biggest ranch in the country."

"But I've already promised this house to Laith. If you have the cabin section and if you truly marry her, that will work well, because your share of the land will border theirs."

"But Laith isn't really married and…"

"We've been over this before!" Laith threw his napkin down and got to his feet.

Monty's voice rose above them both, "Stop!" Eliza began to cry, and he spared an apologetic glance for Braley and a nod to Ella, "We'll move this discussion to the study."

"Now then, Leland, you can't keep spouting this nonsense about your brother's marriage. We've been over it numerous times, and it's getting downright ugly. You knew the agreement, and you had the same amount of time to act. It's too late now. The deal is done, you…"

"She's married."

Monty frowned, "Yes…"

"She has a husband! She was married before, and she still is. I met her husband in town."

Laith took his brother down in one leap. "That's not true!"

Monty struggled to pull them apart. "Stop! Stop!"

Laith gave one good punch and pulled Leland up by the shirtfront.

"You sit there, and you sit there!" Their father directed, stepping between them.

"It's not true!" Laith pushed the hair out of his eyes and sat out of respect for his father. "She was never married, it wasn't legal, and she was free to leave. She is my wife!"

"But for how long? I know it's some kind of arrangement. I know she's leaving!"

"And I know you tried to kill me, and you took my money!" Laith said, his heart twisting at the look on Monty's face. "It's true. My money bag was in the cabin, hidden in the desk. That's what he complained that I stole. He was so afraid I'd beat him out of the ranch that he tried to kill me before I even left."

Monty blindly felt his way behind his desk and sank into the chair, staring at Leland. "Is it true?"

"It wasn't me! It was Trotter!"

"Same," Laith said in disgust. "Trotter never does anything unless you tell him to. I guess that explains the bad shot." He looked to Monty for direction.

His face was flushed; his eyes on his elder son. "Is it true?" You tried to have your brother killed?"

Leland took out his bandana and wiped his brow. "It was Trotter, I tell ya. It wasn't me."

Monty looked at Laith. "Send for him."

Laith paced in the back of the study, and the other men sat in silence until the foreman arrived. "Hey, Boss, what…" He paused at the look on their faces as Laithram closed the door behind him. "What's up?"

"They know what you did," Leland warned.

"What?"

"Did you?" Monty stood on shaking knees. "Did you shoot my son and leave him to die?"

"Now wait a minute. It was Lee. He made me do it. He told me he would fire me. I… I couldn't do it. I followed him, and I was going to, but I pulled up and I missed. I went down in the gully and tried to finish it, but I couldn't. That's why I tied him up. I figured the wolves would take care of the rest." He spun to face Laith behind him. "I'm sorry. I'm sorry! It was never my idea. I had nothing against you. I was glad when you showed up. It was Leland; he promised me a share, and he kept all the money. *Please…*"

From where the women sat, they had heard the muffled arguing and the fighting, and after a long silence, the voices raised in anger again. Then it changed. It was louder now and more desperate.

"Help! Help!" Braley's eyes met Ella's in alarm, and they ran for the study, skirts flying. Laith crossed their path on his way to the front door, calling for the guards and all available men to start clearing the road to town.

It was Monty. He sat slouched in his chair with a hand on his chest, breathing rapidly.

"Have him lie down." Ella got his medicine while the two men helped him to the sofa. "Monty, can you hear me?" She administered the elixir and brushed the hair back from his forehead.

At his slight nod, she breathed a sigh of relief.

Braley hovered over them both, covering Monty with a blanket, when Laith returned, shooting his brother a glare. "We need the doctor. The snow is too deep for the sleigh. We've got to clear the road. I want everyone out there."

Leland nodded, his usually ruddy complexion turned ashen. "I'm on it. Come on," he said to Trotter, who avoided looking at Laith.

"Wait!" Ella spoke up, "I think we should move him to the downstairs guest room so he'll be more comfortable."

They worked together in silence, a truce born of the unspoken thoughts and the desperate hope held by all, until the men left to help clear the road. Laith kissed Braley goodbye, and she showed her bravest face. It was all about Monty now. It had to be. Whatever consequences might come from opening their haven to the rest of the world would be dealt with in their own time.

Chapter 26

The men worked through the night. Braley, dressed in her warmest clothes, drove a wagon back and forth with sandwiches and pots and pans of coffee to keep them going. By dawn they had covered a fraction of the distance.

"It's not enough," she said to Ella on a return trip. By the time I get there, the coffee is cold and half the pans have spilled, and there is not enough to go around. I think I should set up a camp nearer to where they are working."

"If you think that would be best." Ella joined her in the kitchen after checking on Monty.

"But that leaves you with your hands full with Monty and Eliza, and cooking too. I was thinking if we set everything up, they could take turns making the coffee on their breaks, and I could be here to help you with everything and go out once in the morning and once in the evening. I remember seeing another large coffee pot at the cabin. I could ride up and get it. Leland's not there, and he can't hate me any more than he already does."

"I don't know," Ella said. Do you think it's safe? What if you get lost? And if they can't get through…"

"I've been there with Laith. It's shorter through the woods, and that trail has been cleared by the men traveling back and forth. If I leave now, I'll be back in time for the next round. Don't worry." She kissed Eliza and ran out to saddle her horse.

It was eerily quiet as she wound her way through the woods, but the snow was less deep here on the well-traveled path under the heavy canopy of the pines, and she made good time. The cabin, too, was quiet and empty, as it had been before, and the premonition of dread returned in persistent warning. She had forgotten, but when she had come with Laith, everything had been fine. Again, she walked with caution and held her breath as she retrieved the coffee pot from the kitchen and retraced her steps.

It wasn't until she went to leave that her blood ran cold and she stopped and stared. On one of the pegs beside the door was a long black coat. *No, it couldn't be. Had it been there before?* She couldn't recall. With a trembling hand, she reached out and lifted the hem to see it more clearly. *Yes, a black frock coat, exactly like Jacob…* She spun to face the living room, her hand moving involuntarily to the gun on her hip.

There was no one there. Nearly paralyzed with fright, she forced herself down the hall to the first bedroom where she had found the letters. Straining to hear any sound above the pounding of her own heart in the gray void that had become her world, she peeked inside. The moldy coffee cup was gone, the bed was made up, and there were two white collars on the bureau.

Braley had dropped the coffee pot and now drove her mount recklessly through the woods, slipping and sliding on the downhill trail. *He was here. He was here the whole time. Holed up with Leland. The closed roads had not been protecting her. The consequences would not be from the open*

passage, and they were not to be dealt with later. They were here and now. She bent low in the saddle as she hit a level stretch and pushed the horse as fast as she could across the treacherous ground, skidding as she pulled up at the front of the house. She was out of the saddle before the horse had come to a full stop and running up the steps, praying as she went, her stomach dropping at the sight of the open door.

"Ella! Ella!"

Ella sat on the floor in the hallway, a gash on her temple. She cradled Monty, his head on her lap, his face an alarming shade of blue.

"He tried to help." She looked down, stroking her cousin's forehead. "There was a man…"

Braley's heart thudded as she scanned the room, already in denial, even as she braced herself for what she knew would come next.

"He took the baby."

Her jaw clenched, holding in the primal cry of terror that sounded only in her mind. She searched the next room, and the next, and checked the kitchen. There was no sign of her, and she sprinted for the stairs. Doors slammed back on their hinges, each louder than the last, as she checked each room, knowing her search was in vain, and her anger grew. Anger at Jacob. Anger at Leland. But most of all, anger at herself. She had let her guard down. The one thing she promised herself she would never do, and she left her. She had tried not to be too possessive, not to live in fear. She had learned to trust again. She had grown comfortable, and she had left her. *She had left her. So many times. Too many times. And Eliza was gone.*

Braley sank to her knees but pulled herself up. She couldn't feel her legs, but made her way down the stairs. *There was no time for self-pity. She didn't deserve it. She didn't deserve anything. Stupid! Stupid! How could she have been so stupid?*

She would not remember getting a cloth for Ella's wound and moving them both into the living room, dragging Monty on a blanket, and building up the fire before she rushed out to find Laith. Laith had been her first thought, her only thought, in her desperate need for help. *Help. What help was there for this? Where could she even begin? Laith. Laith would know.* With shaking hands, she gathered the reins and leapt into the saddle to ride into the gloaming, her heart as dark as the night.

"Hey, I was getting worried," Laith said when she rode up, but there was no wagon, and the expression on her face… His heart began to pound when she tumbled into his arms and then fell to her knees. He went down with her, holding her by the arms and fearing the worst. *"What is it? My father? Is he…"*

"Jacob. Eliza! Eliza is gone! He took her. And your father is worse, and Ella is hurt. You've got to send someone. They tried to stop him, and Eliza is gone. She's gone! I left her! I left her!" She dissolved into tears, and he held her, unable to understand the rest of her words.

"You're sure it was him?"

She nodded, wondering at the high keening sound that she didn't realize was coming from her own throat.

He held her tighter, and she clung to him.

Braley drew a deep breath and a wave of strength from his embrace. She straightened and tried to think clearly. "It was him. I know it. I went to the cabin for the coffee pot and I… I saw his coat." She closed her eyes in agony, trying to remember through the terror of that moment. "I saw… in the bedroom… I saw his collars and his coat. He's been there. All this time. He was there… He was there!"

Some of the men had gathered around to see what the commotion was, and Laith got to his feet pulling Braley up with him. He walked over to Leland, who stood hiding in the shadows, and punched him in the jaw, sending him to land on his back in the snow. In one move, he landed on top of his brother. "You knew he was here? You knew it the whole time? You sheltered that bastard?" He shook him by the collar of his coat, screaming into his face, his own tears streaming now, "Where is he?"

"I don't know!" Leland yelled back. "I don't know! He was supposed to wait until the road was open. He wasn't supposed to hurt Pa or Ella, just take the kid and go. She ain't yours anyway. She's his."

Laith hit him again. "You have no idea what you've done. And if anything happens to Pa or Ella, you're done. We're done now. You are no brother of mine. I don't even know you, and if we don't get that baby back…" He put his head back, emitting a cry of anguish, and delivered the surge of rage through another fist to the face, leaving his brother where he lay.

Some of the hands rode with Laith and Braley back to the house, leaving the others to work double time to clear the pass. Laith was sickened at the sight of his father's coloring, but there was little to be done until the doctor was summoned, except to make him more comfortable. Together they moved him to the sofa. He gave Ella a hug, sharing a reassurance he did not own, and turned his attention to the best course of action.

Braley, desperate to get moving, was busy back and forth from the kitchen, making coffee and packing food, and dissuading Ella, who kept insisting she was well enough to help, even though she never moved from her seat by the fire.

"You three, take the wagon back with the food and help with the clearing. You two stay and guard the house," Laith instructed the men, as he checked his handgun and loaded his rifle.

Braley came to join him at the gun rack and proceeded to load her own guns.

"What are you doing?" He asked.

"I'm going to look for her."

Laith frowned. "I was really hoping you would stay here where it's safe."

She spared him a glance, her lips pressed together, methodically loading her revolver, tamping each chamber with added purpose and a fierce determination. "I don't need to be safe. I need my daughter back. Besides, what makes you think it's safe here?"

Laith drew a long breath, the bitterness in her voice burning his soul. "Please stay."

"I can't."

"Hear me out. Please. It's dark now. It'll be hard tracking, and I'm afraid he'll be waiting for us. He could be anywhere, waiting to take a shot at us."

"My baby is out there in the cold." Her voice caught on a sob, "With a monster."

Her next words came so softly he barely heard them.

"And it's my fault. *I left her*. I promised her it would never happen again. I failed her."

"What if he gets us both?"

"What?" Braley stopped gathering her things to glance at him, afraid he was about to make a point she could not argue away.

He placed his hands on her shoulders, "He's probably expecting us. He had to be watching the house. He knew no one was here." He looked away. "I should have left some guards behind. I was so worried about my father. I wanted all the help we had, and I thought with the road blocked…"

"Don't," she said. "Don't blame yourself. You thought the same thing I did. That we were safe until the thaw." She placed her hand along his jaw to guide him to look at her. "Don't."

He looked into eyes brimming with unshed tears and nodded. "He knows we'll go after him, and he's probably waiting. I don't want to leave you, but we can't leave her out there." He raised a palm to still her protest. "Hear me out. I don't think he's stupid enough to go back to the cabin, and he can't get to town. There's only one other place he can go."

She blinked and wiped at the tears that spilled over and made their way down her cheeks. "Lime Rock." *He had followed them there that day with Constance.*

"I think so. It's a start at least. There's shelter, and he would be closer to town, and once the road is cleared, he could leave that much faster."

"Don't think for a minute he hasn't figured that out and knows that you will too. I want to go. I need to."

He shook his head, "I think we should split up. It doubles her chances. I'll go first. I know the way. I can find it in the dark. He could be waiting, or it could be a trap. If I don't come back by morning, you can come after me. It will be easier for you to follow the tracks in the daylight. Bring some of the men."

If he didn't come back. Her lips trembled as the horror of what he was saying hit home. "But you're not taking anyone."

"I'll be all right. I'd rather they keep working. By morning we'll see how close they are, or…" He pulled her into his arms and buried his face in her hair. "Watch over them for me," he pleaded. "Don't let my father die alone." He kissed her goodbye, tasting the salt of her tears mingled with his own.

Chapter 27

Ella dozed fitfully in the chair, refusing to go to bed, and Braley paced the floor, checking on Monty every few minutes. She had regretted her decision to stay as soon as Laith had left. She had considered going after him, but it was true she would probably end up lost in the dark and adding to the problems. She would wait for daybreak, and it would be one of the hardest things she had ever done.

Wes took up a post in the front hall, and Cody had gone down to the barn to take care of the horses. Braley walked again to the window and stared out, her heart racing, listening as she had when Laith left. *What had she been listening for? The cry of her child? No, that was what she longed for, but…* Her stomach lurched with the realization. *Gunshot. She had feared a gunshot that would have told her Laith had been right and Jacob had waited in ambush. A gunshot that would have shattered the frozen silence of the night and ended the world as she knew it.* Her eyes scanned the expanse of white ground in the selfish moonlight that revealed little between the rolling clouds. Now she listened for something more normal. The closing of a door, the clang of a metal bucket, the whinny of a horse, some small treasure of ordinary sound that would tell her Cody was going about his task unhindered. *Was Jacob out there? A glance at Dog lying peacefully by the fire helped to calm her fears. But what if he had not gone to the abandoned town? It was a logical choice. Too logical? What if he waited in the bunkhouse, knowing no one was there? Knowing Laith would leave, lured by that logical choice. There was food out there, it wasn't far away, and—no one was there.* Her heart raced again, and she struggled to draw another deep breath before returning to check on Monty.

Laith pulled up his collar and squinted into the darkness, waiting for the moon to show itself again, in its game of hide and seek. He had been right in thinking Jacob would head for the bluff, and the tracks were not hard to follow in the snow. He only hoped Eliza was warm enough and Braley had stayed put.

The snow was less deep as he entered the woods, but the same branches that sheltered the trail now blocked what little light there had been, and their shadows hid the tracks from his view. It did not matter. He knew where they were going.

His heart broke for Braley. The path wound up and down, the landscape so different than that warm autumn day he had traveled here with her and Constance. He considered their friendship and wished the woman were here now as a comfort to Braley. She was almost as feisty as his wife, and he admired their loyalty to one another… *Unlike his brother. Perhaps if either woman had been at the house, this would not have happened.*

He had not had time to give much thought to Leland and how he fared after their fight. He didn't care. The void of feeling gave him pause. The thought presented itself without the slightest trace of guilt. He had always fought with Leland, always felt the struggle of *one-upmanship* fostered by his half-brother, and maybe, if he were honest, fueled by his father. As the younger child, he had loved and looked up to them both without question, until he had grown, and it had become more and more difficult to pretend that his feelings were returned by his sibling. But still, the guilt of disloyalty had always been a heavy weight to bear whenever he questioned his brother's love. He did not understand the need for superiority and ego, and combating it had always felt like swimming upstream. He had tried to deny it, always thinking they could work out their differences, ignoring the greed and the slights, the jealousy and the comments, believing that the love was still there beneath the surface. Then he met Braley and learned what love was. She may or may not stay, but she had shown him what it was like to have someone on your side, and to be completely and utterly on theirs. He would have never dreamed Leland would go that far, or that the whole mess would lead them here. His thoughts turned to his father, and he closed his eyes as the horse plodded slowly but steadily onward.

Braley fed the fire and checked on Monty yet again. He seemed to rest peacefully, and his color had improved, but he had not regained consciousness. She did not know whether that was for the best or cause for greater concern. The less he had need of his medicine for his chest pain, the better. The bottle was almost empty, and she had no idea how close the men were to bringing the doctor. There were still hours to go before daylight. Cody had returned without incident, except for a slip on the ice, and he and Wes were taking turns sleeping. It was quiet, as it had been for the past hours, with nothing to distract her from her torturous thoughts of Eliza and Laith. She sank down by the sofa, placing her fingers on Monty's wrist. His pulse was weak and unsteady, and she held his hand, resting her cheek on the edge of the cushion. Dog moved reluctantly from his spot by the fire to curl up beside her, his head in her lap, and she closed her swollen eyes in prayer.

It was not quite light. Laith sat in the trees along the ridge overlooking the deserted town. The tracks he followed led boldly down the main street and disappeared around the corner with no effort made to hide or deceive. *But why? It was most certainly a challenge or a trap, but what? What did he want? Merely to be rid of him? Was it because he had married her? Did he think it would leave Braley vulnerable?* His stomach churned at the thought.

Yes, it was most likely an ambush, and he would be in the open. There were plenty of places for Jacob to hide, unless, of course, the baby gave him away. He cut off the thought that Eliza had come to harm, swallowing the bile that rose in his throat. *Jacob needed her. She was his best bargaining chip. Besides, she was his daughter, and Braley had been his wife. Maybe that alone was enough to drive him to this. It was why he, himself, was here. He loved them both. Oh, God, how he loved them, and he would make his move in the hopes that they would all be reunited.* He swallowed hard and nudged his horse forward down the hill, feeling very much a pawn in the game.

Braley opened her eyes. *It was almost daylight. Laith had not returned.* Monty's breathing was slow but steady. The hand she held was cold to the touch. She tucked it under the blanket, brushing aside thoughts of Papa Joe in his last hours, and rose, rubbing her neck.

"How is he?" Ella had started awake at her movement.

"A little better, I think. How are you doing?" She checked the cut under the bandage and kissed the woman's forehead.

"Just a bit of a headache, I'll be fine." She gazed at her cousin and shook her head, a single tear in her eye. "It doesn't look good, does it?"

"I don't know. I do think it would help if he could have some water and something to eat. The men are working hard. They should be through soon." She patted the woman's shoulder. "I'll make breakfast. You should eat too."

"I have to go out."

"I'll go with you."

Braley let Dog out the back door, hoping he would stay close, and he did. She helped Ella with her coat and armed herself, and they walked the path to the privy without incident. She handed the older woman the rifle while she took her turn, and Wes stood guard on the back porch.

Laith had not returned. She held the thought at bay while she made the coffee and hurried breakfast, making sure everyone was fed. *Laith had not returned.* She didn't eat. The few sips of coffee she downed seemed to burn in the pit of her stomach. *He didn't have any coffee, and her baby most likely had not eaten anything since yesterday. He had not made it back.* She wrestled with the full weight of the thought as she finished up. *Was he hurt? Or worse? And what of Eliza? Were they lying out in the cold? Were they...* She slammed the door on the dark corridor of her thoughts as Wes entered the kitchen with Cody hobbling behind.

"You sure that's what you should do, missus?" Wes asked, referring to her plan to ride out after the man he considered his boss. I could go, and you could stay, or I could at least go with you. That might be for the best." Laith had given strict orders that his wife was not to go after him if he did not return. *Apparently, he had not told her that.*

"I have to. I'll be careful. This house is too big to be guarded by only one, and Cody's hurt as it is. How is your ankle this morning?" She placed two plates on the table.

"Aw, it ain't so bad, Ma'am. A little swollen is all."

"Well, you could hardly run for cover," she said. "You would be better off to stay posted in the front hall."

Wes was not sure how much he should argue with the boss's wife. Especially this one, who was currently strapping on a holster and making her plans.

"I'd feel better if the two of you stayed with Ella and Monty. I'll ride toward town first and see how far they have gotten, and get a few men to come with me. Don't worry."

Cody shook his head and shot Wes an encouraging look.

"Please, Ma'am. Let me go." Wes tried again. "It don't seem right, you going out by yourself, and," he lowered his voice, "not knowing what you might find and all. And what if something happens here? I mean, Mr. Monty don't look too good, and Miss Ella don't seem herself. What if he should die with none of the family here?"

Braley paused and glanced at Monty, and then at Ella sleeping again in the chair, and recalled Laith's words—*Don't let my father die alone.* Her shoulders slumped. She wanted to be there. She wanted her child back in her arms as soon as possible. *They may be on their way back even now. What if she were to meet him halfway and they came back to find Monty had died in her absence, alone? And if he wasn't on his way back. If it had gone badly, did she really want to be the one to find them? What would she do?* She could not stop the tears that came, or the memories… *the couple she had buried on the side of the trail, the weight of the shovel in her hands…* She looked at Cody, who lowered his chin and gave her a sympathetic look. She then locked eyes with Wes and read the message he could not hide. *He should have been back by now. He would have been back by now.* "You would do that, then?"

He nodded.

"You would check on the road first and get some help? And then go to Lime Rock? There should be tracks. It might be a trap."

"I know, I know. I'll do my best. I promise."

She gave him a quick hug, handing him the bundle of food she had packed, and watched him head for the door, dying to follow. She gripped the back of the chair. "Wesley," she called after him.

Wes turned to see the fear in her eyes.

"Don't underestimate him."

Laith rode in the shadows as dawn peeked over the horizon, staying to the side of what had been the main street. The ice on a distant pond moaned in eerie warning, followed by the screaming cries of a small child. He pulled his horse to a stop and dismounted, walking close to the buildings to peer around the corner.

She was there. Sitting in the middle of the street, wrapped in a blanket. *Surely, she hadn't been there long?* In spite of the cold, he felt a trickle of sweat run down the middle of his back, wetting his shirt beneath the heavy wool of his coat. *This is it, Laithram, you're about to die.*

Trying to ignore the voice in his head, he looked up and down the row of buildings. *Where would it come from, the shot that would end his life? But there was no light, no shadow, no hint of his adversary, and he couldn't leave her in the snow. In the cold.*

He ran and dove for her, skidded on the icy crust, rolled to his feet, and kept running into a building on the other side. The shot came too late. *What the hell just happened? How did you get away with that? You're fast, Laith, but you're not faster than a bullet.* "I was pretty quick, though, wasn't I, sweetheart?" He kissed her cheek. She began to cry harder, and he tried to comfort her. *Poor thing was probably starving, and she was soaking wet.* Whether from the snow or a wet diaper, he could not tell, and held her up in the air for closer inspection. *Both. It was both.* He turned his face away. "It's all right, little girl, it's all right. You're not half as surprised as I am."

"Who's there?!" A voice demanded from somewhere down the street. "That you, Demoranville?"

"Yep!"

There was a long silence. "Where's my wife?"

"She's *my* wife, and she's not coming!"

"That's a lie! That's two lies." The sound echoed down the empty street. "She'll come for the girl. I know she will!"

"Not this time! She has me to help her!"

Another silence followed. "Come out!"

"So you can shoot me? I don't think so."

"I won't!"

He had moved closer. "Why don't you fight me fair and square? Man to man, winner takes all?" Laith challenged.

"Because I don't have to. You have no food, no water, and no heat. Think of the... *child!*"

Laith was busy searching his surroundings. There was a back door, but the drifts were deeper in the open space behind the buildings, and his horse was out front. "I'll never give her up to you!" He was not prepared for the laugh that followed.

"I don't want *her.* I never wanted her."

What the hell? "What?"

Turner's voice came flat and cold. "You'll not push her back on me. She is the spawn of the devil. I'll have naught to do with her!"

Laith swore under his breath. *It wasn't about Eliza. He wanted Braley. Only Braley. He would have separated them again, and what would have become of the baby?*

"Surrender and I'll leave you alone. You'll have a fair chance. I don't care what you do with that abomination."

Think, think! Laith was slow to answer until he saw the glowing light and smelled the kerosene. "No."

"I was going to wait you out, but I don't have time. If you don't come out now, I'll burn you out so I can be on my way. It's up to you."

"No! Wait!" Laith could see the torch to his left if he pressed his face against the window. *Save Eliza. He must save Eliza at all costs. Worry about Eliza now, and then Braley. Because he could never face her again if he failed. She was smart. He could trust her to look out for herself, and the sooner Turner went on his way, the sooner he could follow. It wasn't much of a plan, but the flame was moving closer.* "Okay! I'm coming out, but I want your word to God, you won't harm her."

"I swear it to God Almighty, beloved Jehovah, Author and Perfector of my faith. He laughed again. A haunting sound that sent a chill down Laith's spine before it dissolved into the cold dawn, only to echo back at them from the canyon walls. "I wouldn't dirty my hands with her. I only pray she has not defiled my soul."

Too late for that. God help me. Laith whispered his own prayer and stepped out onto the covered boardwalk to face him.

Jacob held a rifle at the ready and tossed the burning torch into the snow, where it guttered and smoked as it burned out. "Give me your gun."

Laith did, carefully, with one hand, steadying Eliza against his shoulder with the other. She had stopped screaming, but he wasn't sure if that was good or bad. The man said nothing about the knife in his belt, so neither did he.

"Walk. Down there to the left. The sheriff's office."

They crossed the street, Laith sheltering Eliza inside his coat.

"There," Jacob managed to lock the old cell door with one hand while holding his rifle with the other.

His prisoner, still not trusting him to keep his word, kept a close eye on his every move until he stepped toward the door. He saw now that he walked with a stiff limp. "Hey! You just going to leave us here to die?"

"I said I'd leave you alone." To Laith's disgust, he smiled at his own joke. There's some food, and enough water for a day or two." He nodded toward the corner of the cell. "When I'm finished with my errand, I'll send someone. In fact, I'd be shocked if someone wasn't already on their way. I am not a murderer." His eyes burned a hole through Laith. "*I am not!* He hit me first! He did! It wasn't my fault!" He looked around the room. "Now, if you'll excuse me."

Errand. Laith knew exactly what that errand was. He gritted his teeth as his eyes scanned the room, searching for a way out. It was obvious Turner, or someone, had spent some time here. The room had been cleaned and straightened, and judging by the supplies on the nearby desk, the lock on the cell had been repaired and freshly oiled. *Supplies likely stolen from his own ranch. Damn Leland!*

Eliza squirmed in his arms, and he sat her on the bare bunk to change her, cutting up her blanket for new diapers, and wrapping her in his coat before opening the bag of food, and finding her something to eat. He sniffed and then tasted the bread and water and looked over the other contents before feeding her small bites, all the while trying to think of a way out. The bars had rusted, but seemed to be sturdy enough. The keys were on the desk. Even his gun was on the desk. *But how to reach them?*

Wes had ridden toward the road in hopes of gathering reinforcements, but there was no sign of them. The crew must have made more progress than he thought. The road was cleared ahead as far as he could see. *But how far? It would take too much time.* He would go alone. He traveled back toward the ranch and joined the trail to Lime Rock on the next path through the woods, intersecting the trail at the halfway point. *Damn.* He pulled up, studying the ground and stared back toward the ranch, frozen in indecision. There were two sets of tracks heading to the town and one heading back in the other direction. *Was it Laith? Had he been successful, and was he heading back to Braley? Or was he still out there? That would leave the Missus to fend for herself, with only an injured Cody to help her. But the baby... What if they were out there waiting for help, and he left them too long in the cold? There was no question what Braley would want.* His heart slamming against his ribs, he wheeled the horse around and continued on his way to Lime Rock.

$$Chapter\ 28$$

The sun had risen, but her hopes had not. Braley wished she had gone herself. Anything would be better than this endless waiting. She checked on Ella, who had been dozing in her chair since breakfast, and on Monty yet again. There was little change, except that Monty had begun mumbling in his sleep, and she was becoming more and more worried about Ella.

"Where you going?" Cody dropped his chair from where it was tilted back against the wall, eyes wide in alarm.

Braley finished buckling her holster and pulled on her coat. "To feed the horses, of course."

"I can do it." He struggled to stand, gaining only doubt from a raised brow.

"I'll go. But maybe you could be a bit more vigilant while I'm out there. She moved his chair to the front window beside the door and helped him to sit.

"What?"

"*Vigilant. On guard, alert.* Just in case… And lock the door."

Dog carried out his usual morning inspections, stopping to christen a few select spots along the way, and greeted each of his friends in the barn. Braley glanced around the dim interior and went about her chores, feeding and watering the horses, her anger growing when she found herself trying to be extra quiet and straining to hear at every little sound. Her heart pounded and her hands shook.

Ella came awake and looked around the room. She was feeling better, after her nap, but she had to visit the necessary again. There didn't seem to be anyone around, but that was alright. She could certainly go by herself. She sighed and pushed herself up from the chair, heading to the back door.

Braley stopped mucking the stall and leaned on the rake, closing her eyes. *Eliza. How had this happened, and where were they?* Her sudden sob startled Pappy, and he stepped away from her, tossing his head. I'm sorry, boy. I'm sorry. She was stroking the horse, crying into his neck, when she heard a sound, and Dog whined and ran out of the barn.

Was it a shot? Braley stared up at the house, hesitant to cross the open area of the yard. The dog was nowhere in sight. *The sound was muffled. Inside? Cody?* She scanned the yard as she traveled along the edge of the clearing, keeping to the trees until she reached the front door. Silently, she turned the knob, holding her breath. It was still locked, and not daring to call out, she made her way to the back and tried the handle.

The latch lifted. *Unlocked.* Her heart pounded and she spun around at the noise behind her, reaching for her gun.

Ella stepped from the privy, closing the door.

Braley had no time to breathe a sigh of relief when Dog bounded up beside her, and they went together to get Ella and usher her into the house, locking the door behind them. "I need you to wait here, Ella. Do you understand?" She whispered, seating her in the kitchen.

"Of course I do." The woman whispered back, wondering what was wrong with Braley. "Don't worry about me, but shouldn't we check on Monty? I heard something."

"I will," Braley said. She, too, had heard the painful moan and peered cautiously into the living room. *Odd, the fire was still burning brightly, but it was cold.* It wasn't Monty. He lay much as she had left him, and the sound came again. *Cody?* "Cody?" She said aloud, her hand resting on her gun as her eyes darted around the room. The cold air drew her to the hall. Cody lay bleeding, the front door was wide open, and Dog bounded through it, heading back to the barn.

"He came in the back," Cody said. "A tall man in a black suit. *A preacher!* He's looking for you. I'm sorry, I wasn't ready for that. He thinks you're in the barn. I told him. I'm sorry. He's gone down there."

"Shh. You're hurt.".

"It's my leg. Same leg, damn it. Because I wouldn't tell him… He just shot me. A preacher!" He gritted his teeth against the pain.

She checked the wound and went to the kitchen to get towels and a pan of water. "Cody has been shot."

Ella got to her feet, "I'll take care of it."

Together they made him more comfortable so Ella could tend to the wound. "Hopefully the doctor will be here soon," Braley said, as a shot shattered the living room window, causing them to huddle together on the floor. "Stay down. I'm going out there. Ella, I want you to lock the door, and don't open it for anyone unless you are sure who it is."

Ella nodded.

"I think you should wait, ma'am, if you don't mind my sayin' so," Cody dared.

She glanced toward Monty and placed a hand on Ella's shoulder as they knelt in the hallway.

"We could probably hold him off." Cody offered.

Braley smiled sadly at the young cowboy lying flat on his back in agony. "He wants me, not them."

Three heads turned as another shot was heard, and Braley scrambled to her feet. *Dog!* "Ella, the door."

"Got it!"

Laith sat on the floor, cuddling Eliza in his coat. It was freezing. She seemed warm enough, but he was worried. The night would be colder, and there wasn't that much food. He had tried everything he could think of, chiseling at the stone around the bars with his knife until it broke, playing with the lock, testing the hinges. He had stopped to feed and change the baby. He had thought it would be easy, that he would be on his way by now. *On his way to help Braley. Or that they would have come for him. Unless something had gone terribly wrong. He couldn't just wait.*

He was no different than an animal in a cage. Yes, it was a jail. It was made to keep people in, but with years of neglect, it should be falling apart. He rested his head back on the bunk behind him. It was like the other buildings, most of them were in good shape except for the roofs… He got to his feet. *There were a few bad spots, but could he reach them?*

Jacob lowered the rifle. He had missed. *Damn dog! He would give himself away. Where the hell was that woman? He had planned so well. Making his move when all the men were out shoveling, so there were no guards. Getting rid of that heathen who had tried to steal his wife. Of course he would not send someone to find him. No one would find him, and he had not condemned himself by killing. He had left that to God. He would have broken in the back door, but then the old woman came out and made it so easy to surprise her. It was divine intervention; he was sure of it. It would have been perfect. But she wasn't there. The young buck in the hallway*

talked easily enough when he shot him in the leg and threatened worse, but he lied... or did he? The cursed dog was sniffing around, running in and out, growling and threatening. It was obvious someone had stopped in the middle of cleaning the stalls. Was she hiding? He stood listening, his eyes searching the dark shadows. *The dog was always with her. All the days he had watched and waited the dog had followed her in her routine. She must be here somewhere. He was running out of time. The men would surely have reached town by now and would be returning with the doctor. He had to capture her and be back in hiding so he could ride out as soon as they rode in.*

Wes looked down on the small deserted town and a sight that nearly made him sick. Laith's horse wandered alone, foraging for what bit of grass might be had along the edge of the boardwalk. That answered one question, he thought, and raised another. *No, it had not been Laith's tracks leading back toward the ranch... And where was he?* There was no movement, no signs of life, except for the horse with an empty saddle. A loud bang echoed in the stillness, and his eyes darted across the rooftops. One of them was moving. There was a splintering sound as some of the wooden shingles by a hole in the roof broke away. The noise came again, and he guided his horse down the hill as fast as possible.

Laith stood on the cross bars of the cell, jamming a piece of the broken bunk into the rotted shingles above him. He had managed a small opening. He could barely reach it with the length of wood and didn't know how he would get out, even if he were to succeed in making the hole large enough. The door opened, and he looked down in alarm before his shoulders fell in relief. "Thank God."

Wes took in the scene with a glance. "That's what I like about you,

Boss. You never give up."

"Yeah? Well, I was about to. What took you so long?" He jumped down and gathered Eliza in her makeshift covers.

"Doubt it." Wes was already unlocking the door, the look on Laith's face all the thanks he needed. "He's headed for the ranch. I'll explain on the way." He glanced back over his shoulder at the attempted escape route as Laith holstered his gun and they went out the door, "It might'a worked."

Braley stood on the porch and listened to the lock turn behind her. She had to keep him away from them, she thought. It was her he wanted, and it was clear he would not hesitate to shoot anyone who stood in his way. But he would not shoot her. That would defeat his purpose. She would do whatever she had to, but *God help her*, she would not go with him. She walked toward the barn, gathering her courage and her faith. *A shield of faith. There was a verse. How did it go? 'Take unto you the whole armor of God that ye may be able to withstand in the evil day'—Ephesians? No. Yes, Ephesians six… something. Thirteen? God forgive me. Sixteen? 'Above all, taking the shield of faith.' That was it, Ephesians 6:16.*

Jacob still searched for her in the barn, convinced that she was there somewhere. Every move or whinny from a horse, or scamper of a mouse, drew his attention. Every shift, every creak of the aged beams in the cold air. A drifting straw from the loft above almost drew fire. He closed his eyes. He had no need to fear. *'Put on the whole armor of God that ye may be able to stand against the wiles of the devil'*—Ephesians, 6:11. *'Stand therefore, having your loins girt about with truth, and having on the breastplate of righteousness'*—Ephesians, 6:14. He had no need to fear because he was doing the right thing. *Yes, He was righteous in his mission, and no man would think differently.*

There was no point in hiding, but she would not go into the barn. Into the darkness. He would have to face her in the light. She did not see Dog anywhere, and fearing the worst, she stopped in the middle of the yard, looking around. *Surely, he would have run to her by now, unless… Unless he was off chasing rabbits.* She finished the thought with pure determination and called him, but he did not come.

An answer to a prayer. Jacob wheeled around, his heart soaring, and went to find her.

Braley eyed him as he appeared from the depths of the barn and walked toward her, her stomach turning at the sight of him. *How she hated him. God help her, she hated him with every fiber of her being.* "Where's my daughter? Why would you take her if you don't want her?"

"Because you do. Common sense, woman. You cannot be angry with me for using common sense. I thought you would come for her, but I guess you didn't care enough."

She would not be baited. He did not have common sense or any other kind; he wasn't even human. "Where is she?"

"She should be fine."

It was her first glimmer of hope that Eliza was alive. *"Should be?"*

"They are in a safe place. If we leave soon enough, I will let you send someone to rescue them."

They. That was good. They. But rescue? They needed rescuing. And he must not know about Wes. If they were there, he would find them. "Did you shoot my dog?"

"Not yet, but I will if he interferes with our leaving."

"I'm not leaving."

"Of course you are." He began to walk away from the barn, as though he would circle her, causing her to turn with him, so she no longer stood between him and the house. "You must. Otherwise, I will go back and take care of things."

"You misunderstand," she said, keeping her face to him. "You're not leaving either."

A chill ran down his spine, and for the first time in months of planning, he was uncertain. "You would kill me, then, and live out your life the sinner that God knows you are? A fornicator and a murderess? I'm offering you a chance at redemption."

She gave a wry smile and shook her head at his insults. He would never change. It was in God's hands. *God and the law.* "No. You have shot a man and kidnapped a child that is no longer yours, and God knows what else. The sheriff will deal with you, and the Good Lord later."

He was not hearing her. His face was red, and sweat beaded his brow in the cold air. "Go ahead then. End this misery, because if you refuse to marry me and right our trespasses, my life is worthless. I have sinned, and will burn for it."

His eyes lit with a strange intensity even as she watched.

"Revelations, 21:8." He closed his eyes. "'Murderers and whoremongers…shall have their part in the lake which burneth with fire and brimstone.'" But it is your fault! I was a good man. A faithful servant! You have ruined me. Yes, I see now that I must die, but you must come with me! This is how it can be made right. I see it now. We shall go together and stand before our loving God and together ask his forgiveness. He will forgive me. You will tell him it was your fault, and he will forgive me. *He will!* But you… Are you not afraid? Are you not afraid to go to Hell?"

"No. I have already been there."

He scowled at her words, and fear gripped her by the throat when he raised his rifle. She struggled to speak and keep her voice steady. "He will forgive you now, Jacob. There is no need for this. Do you not believe he is a good and understanding God? What happened with Eliza wasn't a fault. It was in good faith. She is not a sin. She is a miracle. God loves her, and you are not her judge." *Was he listening? Would he consider her words?* "Go home. Go home and build your church. It's not too late. But if you kill me now, it will be. I will only be freed from this torment, but you will not. You will be condemned to the hell that you fear. It would be a far greater sin than giving life to an innocent child."

"My church? My church is gone." His mouth twisted in disgust, and fury lit his eyes. "You did that! It's too late for that. It's too late to start again."

"It's not. You could do it." *It was a mistake to mention the church. Had he heard anything else?*

"No! This is the best way. The only way." His grip tightened as he settled the rifle into his shoulder, and his head tilted as he sighted down the barrel.

Dear God. It would end for one of them here. She took her stance and a deep breath. She heard the hammer click and lock into place. A low growl sounded from the right, and there was a blur of gold.

All Jacob saw was teeth as Dog charged from the brush.

Braley yelled, but it was too late to deter her defender.

The rifle swung away.

"Don't!" She screamed.

The ivory grip was smooth in her hand. There was the familiar pull of the barrel as it slid sideways, and the release as it cleared the well-oiled leather, the ice-like metal of the hammer beneath her thumb… From somewhere far away, she heard three shots and watched Jacob fall.

The face of Herkules rose in memory. *Three shots. One for the Father, one for the Son, and one for the Holy Ghost. A prayer for them if you don't miss, and a prayer for yourself if you do.* She had not prayed for Jacob, but she had not missed.

Dog, deprived of his full-on attack, skidded to a halt and inspected the body before trotting to Braley, who dropped to her knees to hold him with shaking hands.

Chapter 29

They traveled in the biting cold. Laith had taken off his coat and buttoned it around Eliza. He rode as fast as he could, fearing he was too late. At the halfway point, he sent Wes to check on the work crew, hoping against hope they would not have additional need for the doctor, or worse. He reached the yard to spot Braley sitting on the ground down by the barn, Dog standing beside her. *Was she hurt?* He spurred his horse on, closing the distance, and it was then he spotted Jacob. He swung down beside her. *"Braley?"*

Braley, stunned almost beyond comprehension, saw only that the small bundle he carried was covered over. She clenched her jaw and held her breath, her asking eyes holding his until he realized his mistake.

"No, no! Oh, Jeez. Here. She's here. I was keeping her warm." He knelt and placed the child on her lap, undoing the buttons of his coat until a wide-eyed Eliza peered up at her mother.

"Oh," she cried, hugging her with her whole heart. "You did it! Is she all right? And you? You're not hurt?" She touched his cheek, and he took her hand, kissing her fingers. "You saved her, and…" *Was it all too good to be true?* She looked behind him. "Wes?"

"We're fine. He's gone to help the crew. Let's get her in the house. I'm sure she needs to eat." Laith helped her to her feet.

"Yes, Cody's been wounded, and Ella's taking care of him."

She did not discuss Jacob, so neither did he. *That would come in time.*

"The doctor should be coming soon, don't you think? I'd like him to look at Eliza too…" No sooner had she said it than the jingle of harness and hooves was heard in the distance, and a group of riders accompanying the doctor's buggy turned into the drive. Wes was leading the way.

The doctor had his hands full. Cody was rebandaged and carried off to bed. Eliza had a full checkup and would be fine with food and warmth, and Ella, who, in spite of the hit to her head, was declared to be doing well.

Monty was not. There had been little change, and according to the doctor, there was little to be done. "We'll have to wait and see. I'm sorry," he told Laith in a quiet corner. "He may regain consciousness or he may not, and there is no way of telling whether he will be his former self if he does. You know, sometimes, men as big and strong as your father, who have been active all their lives… I mean men who have lived big and strong, taken life by the horns, taken chances, and built things, accomplished things. They can't handle being laid up. They don't do well."

"What are you saying?"

The doctor put his hand on Laith's shoulder. "I'm saying it takes the will to live. That type of man doesn't want to live confined to a chair or a bed. They can't *be* weak; they don't know how. If they can no longer do what they want, for them, life is already over. Do you understand?"

Laith nodded and went to sit with Ella, who filled him in on some of the story while he waited for Braley.

Braley, after a warm bath for herself and Eliza, was prescribed a shot of whiskey that she did not want.

"It's good for the nerves," the doctor said, "and it will warm you."

She took the drink and went to sit beside Laith, Eliza on her lap. "What I really need is the sheriff. I won't sleep until I know what kind of trouble I might be in. I think you need to send someone for him."

"But clearly it was self-defense." Laith offered. He broke into our house, he shot Cody. He stole our daughter and locked us in the stone-cold jail. We could have died there."

"*What?*"

He had clearly stepped on the wrong path. "I'll tell you later. I'll send for the sheriff, and you can clear your mind."

"I'll go," Wes looked up from cooing over Eliza.

"But you've done so much already." Braley protested. "And you just got back. That's crazy."

Laith smiled. "Not so crazy. The rest of the men are still celebrating in town. Wes met the good doctor halfway here. He didn't get to go." He went to the desk in the study and handed Wes some bills. This will cover you and anybody else who's still there. Drink your fill, and then get them back here."

Wes grinned. "I'll be back before nightfall."

Laith walked him to the door and kept his voice low, "No need to hurry back, but I'd like you to take the buckboard and bring the body to the sheriff. I don't even want him buried here."

Braley hardly took her eyes off of Eliza, while she shooed Ella from the kitchen, coaxing the woman to rest before supper.

Laith filled the wood boxes and fed the fires, keeping an eye on Braley. She hadn't talked much about what had happened, except to say that she thought she might be in trouble. He hauled in more wood for the upstairs and went to talk to Cody.

"He came in through the back." Cody hung his head. "I was

watching the front. I was sitting because I had hurt my ankle. I looked up and he was there. He was looking for her, the Missus, and I said she wasn't here, and he shot me. Just like that. He said, *Tell me the truth,* aiming at my face." He lowered his voice and looked away. "So, I told him she had gone to the barn. I'm not sure what happened after that, but then she and Miss Ella came through the back… Maybe she heard the shot. I don't know. After that, she went out again. I tried to get her to stay. She wanted to keep us safe. She went out there. Told Miss Ella to lock the door." This time, his eyes met Laith's, "It was about the bravest thing I've ever seen."

Laith nodded, wondering what she was thinking as she went out the door, *how she felt.*

"I didn't see any of what happened after that. I only know what Miss Ella told me from looking out the window, that he was aiming at her when the dog ran out. He was going to kill the dog, and that's when she shot him."

"So, he did threaten to kill her?"

"Yes, sir, as far as I know. After that, she just sat there. Miss Ella wanted to go out to get her, but I thought maybe she needed a little time. She didn't seem to be hurt. It wasn't long after that you came. I'm sorry I wasn't much help."

Laith paused before leaving, "You did fine, Cody. I'm sorry you got shot."

Braley sat with her dog resting beside her chair. She cradled Eliza in her arms, watching her sleep, listening to each sweet breath. *How long?* Now that she was free of Jacob, how long could she hold her? Was it truly self-defense? She had been defending Dog at the time, but if he hadn't run out when he did, it might have been her. Would the other things Jacob had done count in her favor? Not the beatings, of course, although she carried the evidence with her every day. She was considered his wife at the time. The courts didn't care about that. Those were *private family concerns.* After all, a husband had to keep his wife in line, *didn't he?* It was his job, and if the poor man was forced to beat his wife, surely the wife had done *something…* The kidnapping, too, was most likely not a major concern. Like it or not, Eliza was his daughter, and he probably had the right to do that, too. True, he had shot poor Cody, and broken into the house, and Laith had said something about being locked up… but she had *killed* him. She drew a quick breath, causing Eliza to start in her sleep before the rhythmic sounds of her repose continued. *She had killed someone. God forgive her.* What would Papa Joe have thought?

She had known for a long time that it would end badly between them. The knowledge was embedded in her soul and festered like a splinter over the years. A nagging intuition by day, and a harbinger of terrors in the night. One of them would come to harm. *She had always thought it would be her.* But she was still here, and he was not. *Because she had killed him. Would she ever get used to it? Would she be different? Different from what she would have been?* She rather thought she would. *Could she learn to live with it? If only he had stayed away. What would other people think? What would Eliza think when she was old enough to understand? Would she tell her?*

She lifted the child to her shoulder because she needed her closer. Dog rose, circling several times before he settled again, and she absently ran her fingers through the fur at his neck. *How long?* Would the sheriff take her away, now that Eliza was home? *Perhaps it was their destiny to be separated.* She looked up as the answer to her questions came through the door.

True to his word, Wes brought the sheriff. Unfortunately, he was followed by a drunken and blubbering Leland who went straight to his father's side.

Laith colored a deep shade of rage and looked to Wes, who could only shrug.

"I'm sorry, boss," I didn't think it was my place to tell him he couldn't come in, it bein' his father an' all."

Laith nodded, trying to stay calm, a task that became more difficult when Trotter quietly entered and went to stand beside Leland. He turned his attention to the other matters at hand.

"Sheriff. Thank you for coming out. You remember Braley…"

In the privacy of the study, she told her story from the very beginning. Laith told his, until it ended here, wondering at the consequences. The sheriff consulted with Cody and Ella. And that was all. Braley couldn't believe it. She was free to stay with Eliza, for which she would be forever grateful, but no one mentioned self-defense. She was not allowed that small bit of redemption. It was not because she had been beaten, or burned, or scarred. Not because she had once been abducted herself, or deprived of her child, or tracked like an animal, or threatened with a gun—*It was because she belonged to Laith*—And because he had assaulted *Monty*, and locked *Laith* in an abandoned jail where he might have perished. It had nothing to do with Eliza. Children mattered even less than women. It seemed the main concern was that Jacob Turner had dared to darken the halls of Riverdale and threatened the men who lived there. They were untouchable. Because they had gotten here first and claimed the biggest piece of land. Out here, land was everything. Land was survival, and money. Land was power. This wasn't justice. It was worship. She wanted to scream at them. All of them. She swallowed her disgust and rocked Eliza, holding her tight. She understood now why the house was so important to them. It was the symbol of triumph. It was the flag raised on the hill to lay the claim. The claim to the land. The land that hadn't really been theirs to begin with.

Laith shook hands with the sheriff and walked him to the door of the study, not daring to breathe a sigh of relief. Braley was free. It was over, and spring was almost here. *She could go home now.* With great effort, he summoned a smile and went to put his arms around woman and child. "Thank God that's over."

She nodded, but he sensed a reluctance. She did not lean into him as she usually did, nor did she return his smile. That was understandable, after what she had been through. He only hoped that was the reason.

"That's it!?" Leland's voice rang loudly from the front room, and Laith rushed out of the study to see what was wrong.

His brother had tailed the sheriff to the front door and stood calling after him. "That's it? Aren't you going to arrest her? Why aren't you going to arrest her?! She killed a man!"

"Leland! Shut your mouth or go! This is your fault!" Laith had not decided what to do about Leland, who had stayed by his father's side, whining and making apologies until now.

"It wasn't my fault! I didn't want this to happen. This wasn't supposed to happen. I didn't know… I didn't know. He was supposed to just…"

"Kill Braley? It's not the first time you tried to get rid of her, don't think I don't remember!" Laith found no sympathy for his half-brother. They were not alike. They had never been alike, as much as he had tried to think so.

"No, he was only going to take the kid so she would follow. It was supposed to be her who went, not you! It should have been fine, but he came too soon, and Pa wasn't well. He would have been in his study or out working… I told him to wait."

Laith grabbed him by his shirt. *"Do you hear what you're saying?* You were part of it! You planned it! You invited that bastard in! You housed him. *You almost got my wife killed!* I should have sent *you* with the sheriff. *This is all your fault!* You don't deserve to be here." He turned to Trotter, who stood silently in the corner. "And you! You must have known. How dare you come back here? You shot me in the back. Get the hell out of my house! Get out of my sight!"

Trotter scurried out, Laith slammed the door, and Monty opened his eyes.

"I don't know," the doctor told Laith. "I've seen it before, but it may not mean what you think it means."

Monty had been given a sponge bath and a change of clothes. Ella was constantly at his side, feeding him broth, seeing to his needs, and holding his hand as he sat up in the bed.

Leland took full advantage of his father's attention to talk about Niki and the plans he was making to get married. "I could do it, Pa. I could be like you. I could run this ranch and make it even bigger and better. Don't let Laith turn it into some sad corn farm. There's no glory in that. That's not what you worked for all these years. Someday I'll inherit the Paterakis place too, and rename it. Riverdale will be the biggest spread in the country. It will be your legacy. Leave it to me. Leave it to me and you won't be sorry."

Laith listened to Leland badger their father from outside the bedroom door. *'Leave it to me.' Did he mean the ranch or the monumental task of besting Paterakis?*

"Seems awful sudden." He heard his father say, his voice just above a whisper. "Do you love the girl, and does she have feelings for you?"

Was the old man actually interested in the idea? Would he change his mind about the ranch?

"Of course, Pa, we've been sweet on each other for years."

It was Leland again, lying through his teeth.

"Well, if you're going to marry the girl, I would like to see it."

Laith listened to the doctor above the loud thudding of his heart,

"I think that's enough for now. He's very weak," he backed the larger man from the room, while Ella followed them out.

"I'll go get her!" Leland spoke over the doctor's shoulder. "I'll bring her and her Pa, and I'll get the preacher too! We already got a license. You think about what I said! I'll be back!"

The doctor spoke aside to Laith as Leland rushed out of the house. "He does need his rest, but if you need to ask him anything important, you should do it now. Just do it quietly. You must keep him calm."

Chapter 30

The hour grew late and the house grew quiet. Braley had let Ella help a little with supper and the cleaning up, to appease her, and seen her off to bed. Now she was putting Eliza down for the night, still reluctant to let go of her. Leland was unlikely to return at this hour, and she was relieved, at least for the time being. It would be easier to deal with whatever disaster he wrought in the morning, she thought, as she climbed into bed.

Laith had spent time with his father, both before and after Monty napped. He returned to have supper with him. Afterward, Monty insisted on visiting his study, and with the doctor's permission, Laith helped him to his chair. They spoke of the future, but the older man was most content reminiscing about how he had started the ranch when he was young and telling his favorite tales. He stopped to smile. "Now listen, Laithram…"

Was this it? Laith wondered. *Had he changed his mind? Would he change the arrangement? Would he leave the ranch to Leland?*

Motioning Laith closer, he placed something in his hand, covering it with his own.

The burn of unshed tears stung as he faced the truth he had tried so hard to deny. Laith struggled to keep his voice steady. "Oh, but I can't…" He felt the small chain trickle into his palm and the coolness of the metal case, worn smooth through the years, polished with the very essence of his father's everyday life.

Monty looked into his eyes and smiled, "You can. I want you to have it. It was a gift from your mother, but I would have given it to you anyway. You've always been the best of us. That was her doing. I'm sorry that I didn't take a stronger stand against Lee. I found it hard to believe. Deep down, I've known for years he wasn't what he should be. I guess I hoped he'd turn around." He shrugged. "The things he did to you and to Braley were inexcusable, and that was before this last…" He shook his head. "I can only say, I'm sorry."

Laith nodded and swallowed with difficulty when his father placed the watch in his hand.

"Doc?" Monty called, and the doctor appeared in the doorway, "I want you to see this. I'm giving Laith my watch, and I'm signing these papers. Call Ella, would you please?"

Laith helped him back to bed, and they talked until the wee hours. When the old man dozed off, his son pulled the blanket up to his bewhiskered chin, hesitated a moment, and bent to kiss his forehead.

"How is he?" Braley asked when he let himself into the room. She was not reading, but she had not been sleeping.

"He was in good spirits. He's resting now," he said, going first to check on Eliza.

Braley found great comfort in the familiar gesture and the thumping of Dog's tail from the corner.

"He had a lot to say. I'm sorry I'm so late." He put his arm out and she moved closer, but he felt the same distance he had earlier. "Is everything all right?"

"I don't know."

"You don't know?"

"No."

"Do you… What do you mean?"

"I don't know."

"Are you unwell? Do you have a headache?"

"No. I don't know how I feel. I feel… empty."

Of course, he thought, less than twenty-four hours ago, she had faced death. She had found his father and Ella on the floor and seen Cody wounded, and then she had… done what she had to do. *And what had he done for her?* They had barely spoken or spent much time together. "Do you want to talk about it?"

"I don't know."

Laith thought for a moment. "Can I talk about it?"

"If you want to."

"First of all, I want to apologize for not telling you this earlier. Thank you for taking care of my father and Ella, and you probably saved Cody's life by stopping the bleeding. You probably saved everyone's life, and I'm very grateful."

"Do you think I'm different?"

"No. Why?"

"Different than the person you thought I was?"

His arm tightened around her. "Of course not. Do you *feel* different?"

"I'm not sure. Did you know… Did you ever think I was the type of person who could kill someone?"

He was quiet for a moment. "Well, yeah."

"You did?!"

"Sure. When I first met you, I thought you were going to kill me. And the way you looked at that old biddy that tried to keep you from Eliza at the children's home… Mrs. Clark, wasn't it?"

She nodded.

"Thought she was a gonner for sure."

Braley smiled, and tears sprang to her eyes. The first for his kindness, the latter for the memory, or vice versa. She wasn't sure. "I was upset by the sheriff."

"That couldn't have been easy. Especially the waiting. I'm sorry I wasn't there for you before he came."

"No, not that. Well, yes, but that's not it. It's that my story didn't seem to matter. What happened was barely a consideration… *I* didn't matter."

"Why would you think that?" He brushed her hair back from her face and tilted his head to read her expression in the shadows.

"He didn't seem to care what I had done, or why."

Oh, God. No one had told her. He, of all people, hadn't told her… "Braley Stuart, you had every right to do what you did. If you hadn't… I can't even begin to think what might have happened. I do know one way or the other, he would have taken you away, and you wouldn't be here now. Dog would be…" Dog thumped his tail at the mention of his name, and Laith smiled down at her. "The sheriff knew that too."

"But he wasn't aiming at me when I shot him. I think if I had been anyone else, anyone but your wife…" She did her best to explain how she felt about the law and the land and the privilege it gave.

"You may be right, and I'm sorry. I'm sorry for this whole mess and the unfairness of it all. But I cannot be sorry that if it's true, you're free because of it. I don't think that's it though.

She studied him, hopeful for something to hold onto.

"You can't think because you're my wife, you would be allowed to go around killing people and getting away with it. That part, at least, is not true. It's not some backhanded justice. It's only right. All of those things mattered. You matter more than anything. No one should have the right to do the things he did. He targeted you for years and wounded you unmercifully. It makes my skin crawl that he could get away with that. What were you supposed to do, wait until he shot you? He certainly would have." He sat up and held her by the shoulders.

"Don't you remember what you told me? Have you forgotten the beatings? How it felt to be locked in that room with your child ripped from your life? The miles and the months you went without her, not knowing if you would ever see her again?"

Her heart broke when he began to cry, *really cry*, in spite of his clenched jaw and his determination.

"He locked us in a stone cell and walked away. Me with Eliza. A child. *A baby!* With no heat and damn little food, knowing very well we would die there without help. I knew you might come, but after he left, I also knew you might not. I knew he was going for you. I was never more scared in my life… *And he laughed.* Laith looked up at the ceiling, trying in vain to stem the flow of his tears. *He laughed and said he didn't want her. He never wanted her.*" He dropped his hands to stare at his palms. "What kind of man could do that? He got better than he deserved." His eyes shifted to hers, "I only wish it had been me. I wish I had done it, because I wouldn't feel bad. *Not one bit.* I would have done it gladly. Do you think less of me now?"

"Of course not."

"I'll tell you something else." His gaze seemed to challenge her, "I hate that he was her father. I hate it."

Her lip trembled and her eyes filled with tears even as he watched, and he shook his head, placing his hands on her arms again.

"But I don't hate *her*. I love her more. Because she deserves it. She needs me, and I will always love her." His voice broke, and he went into her welcoming arms.

She held him until their tears had long subsided.

"There," his voice was muffled against her, "I hope you feel better now."

She gave a small laugh as he had hoped.

"I do, actually."

"I'm sorry that you don't have good memories. Especially here. I brought you here to keep you safe."

"I have some." She offered after a moment.

"We will make better ones."

"We could."

"Yes," he said, trying to think of something.

"Would you?"

"Would I wha… Oh," he said, when she kissed him.

"Show me. Show me that I am no different in your eyes. That's the only thing that matters."

He did. Braley's breath caught as she melted into his kiss. A kiss that she would always remember as never-ending. Not for its length, but for its depth, plunging the dark abyss of her doubts and her fears to bring her back with him into the light they shared when they were together. He made love to the old Braley, paying tribute to her past and her pain and all the things that made her who she was. He worshipped this new Braley, a knight coming to the rescue, to save her from her demons of despair, covering her with kisses that said all that his words could not, tempering her strength with the flames he created.

Braley writhed beneath him as he kissed her in places she never thought possible, caught in the inferno he created, too weak to return his favors… and then he stopped, rolling onto his back, leaving her to wonder, her eyes seeking his, her heart pounding.

Laith held out his arms, and she followed his lead as his strong hands lifted her above him. *Above him, where she belonged,* he thought.

He lowered her to enclose him, piercing her layers of self-doubt and misgivings and unleashing her reserve.

This was different. Being in the open, uncovered and on display. She might have been shy, except that she could see the pleasure and admiration in his eyes. It was a feeling she could not name, and she rather liked it.

Laith clasped her hands and arched his body, lifting her high, and smiling up at her before bringing her back to earth.

She moved, adjusting her seat, and he moaned, giving her a new sensation and a name for her feelings. *Power. The power to love him and pleasure him as he had her.* His love renewed her, as always, making her a queen. She leaned low to capture his mouth and, with a trust that was new, brought his hands to her breasts, offering them up for his kisses.

Laith was wild with wanting but waited on her, empowering her to the end.

She began to move, slowly at first, and then with more purpose as the fires she had been caught in earlier leapt back to life, leaving her little choice. She felt his urgency, which fueled her own, and matched him stroke for stroke, gladly sharing her power and surrendering all at the end.

Chapter 31

Monty did not die alone. His youngest son was at his side, and his cousin held his hand. He had declined breakfast earlier, and at nine o'clock in the morning, he closed his eyes and went to his final rest.

Niki entered with a handsome gentleman, *who could only be her father,* Braley thought. The pastor from their church followed them in, and the three stood chatting and wiping the mud from their feet. It was well after noon, and Leland had just arrived with the small party, his expression bright with expectation until his gaze fell on Ella.

She sat on the sofa crying into her handkerchief, comforted by the doctor who spoke in soft tones. Leland's eyes swung to Braley, who spoke to Laith in much the same manner, and his stomach dropped. *No! He couldn't be too late. He couldn't.* But the eyes of his brother told him differently. *He was. He was too late to see his plan come to fruition.* He looked to the doctor, who nodded, the sympathy in his face an unwelcome assurance of his defeat. "But he was fine! *He was better.*" Leland went to the bedroom to see for himself. "Pa? Pa…" He fell to his knees beside the bed, the sheet covering his father's face cementing the undeniable truth. *He was too late.*

He wouldn't get the main house, but maybe he could still merge the cabin and its added acreage with the neighbors.

Laith entered the room with the doctor, and Leland looked up, his face red with distress. "I told him I'd be back. I told him to wait. Why? Why didn't he wait?"

"We can't control these things," the doctor said. "Sometimes there's just no telling."

Laith looked on with disgust and quit the room.

Braley had been left to deal with Niki and the imposing man in an elegant gray suit, whose hair was as dark as his daughter's, but graying at the temples. She was more comfortable with the reverend with the thick white hair. A kind man, he was their regular pastor and had come several times to visit Monty. Something about his soft-spoken manner had always reminded her of home. "Please come and sit down," she invited, in the awkward moments before Laith returned to take over.

"Niki, may I take your coat? Reverend Pittsley, come in. Mr. Paterakis, I'd like to speak with you later if you don't mind." He helped the young woman with her coat and shook hands with the gentlemen as they offered their condolences. "Braley, I don't think you've met Niki's father. Mr. Aristidis Paterakis, or *Mr. P,* to a lot of people."

"Ari, is fine." The striking gentleman bowed his head, hiding the broad planes of his face and his pleasant smile.

Braley nodded her greeting and sat, not really following the conversation. She eyed Niki in her beautiful silk gown. *The woman was exquisite, with every hair in place, but she looked extremely unhappy. Was she sad about Monty? Did she know him that well? Then of course, it would stand to reason… but she had looked that way when she came in.*

Laith rose from his seat. "If you'll excuse us, I would like to speak with Ari in the study."

Braley rose too, shifting Eliza to her shoulder. "I'll make coffee." Would you like to come with me, Niki?" She offered, leaving Ella to be comforted by the reverend while the other two men retired to the study.

Niki followed Braley, who had said nothing else. "Thank you," she broke the awkward silence. "I never know what to do in these situations. I *am* sorry about Mr. Demoranville."

Braley had only been waiting until they reached the privacy of the kitchen, where she offered her a seat at the table. "Are you all right?" She placed Eliza in her playpen and turned to study the other woman.

"Yes, I'm fine," she said, but glanced away.

"You're lying," Braley said.

The woman's mouth opened at the unexpected assault, "How rude! Why would you…"

"Don't bother to deny it." Braley glanced toward the living room as she measured out the coffee. "We may not have much time."

"But, what…"

"Look, we may have gotten off on the wrong foot, but I'm trying to help you. You looked pretty unhappy for a woman who was about to marry a man she cared for."

Niki brightened at her words. "What do you mean *was*? *Do you know something?*"

"I might. Do you want to marry Leland?"

Niki studied her hands.

"Well, do you?" She set the pot on the stove.

The pretty girl wrinkled her nose. "Of course not," she whispered. "Would you?"

Braley made a face of her own and drew a breath. *"Is it Laith?"* She asked, watching for the other's reaction.

Her shoulders slumped. "No. I like Laith, but he was always more of a friend, and I don't think he likes me very much. I'm afraid I didn't always make the best impression."

Braley failed to see what love had to do with impressions, but held her tongue.

Niki traced the pattern on the tablecloth with a slender forefinger. "When I saw him with you at the dance, I guess I was jealous."

Braley almost laughed aloud. "*You were jealous of me?*"

Niki nodded, looking sad again.

"Is there someone else?"

"Why are you asking me all these questions? What business…"

"Is there?"

The young woman scowled. "Yes. If you must know, I met someone while I was away."

"Then why would you marry Leland?"

"For the land."

Braley stopped what she was doing, the heat rising in her chest. *"How could you…?"*

"No, my father wanted the land. Just like Monty did. They were great rivals in their younger days, and now Leland wants it."

"Do you mean your father is trading you for the land? You're a bribe?"

Niki shook her head, her tears spilling over. "It's not like that. It's not his fault. I mean, he does want the land… Years ago, when he staked out his original acres, the parcel included part of what is now Riverdale, but Monty beat him to the claim office. My father always said he moved the markers. They became somewhat friendly, out of necessity, I think, being out here alone, but it has remained a sore spot over the years. With Leland as his son-in-law, Riverdale is as good as his…

"But?" Braley prompted.

"But he thinks I am in love with Leland."

Braley looked at her sideways. "Why?"

"Because that's what I told him. Leland said my father would say yes to the marriage either way, whether I wanted it or not. And if I didn't pretend that I did, he would… *do things.*"

"What things?"

The young woman looked down at her hands again. "He said he

would beat me after we were married and never allow me to leave the house, and that he would have the right to do that, and… I think that might be true." She wiped at a tear. "You see, Leland thinks he will inherit our land when my father dies, that's why he wants to marry me."

"And you couldn't talk to your father?"

"I was afraid. And after I told him I loved Leland the first time, I was afraid to tell him I had lied.

Braley could barely breathe. "So, you were just going to go ahead with it?"

"I didn't know what else to do."

"Wait here."

There was a quick knock and the door to the study flew open.

"Braley?" Laith looked up from shaking hands with his guest as she rushed into the room.

"Stop! Whatever you're doing, stop," she said, going back to close the door.

"What's wrong?"

"Niki does not want to marry Leland." She answered Laith and faced Aristidis, "You can't make her. Please. Please don't do this, Mr. Paterakis. You can't."

"Of course I will not, my dear," he looked at her with warmth in his dark eyes. "My daughter means the world to me."

"Well, you should tell her that."

"Braley!" Laith came around the desk to put his arm around her.

"I'm sorry, but she should know. It is a beautiful thing to say, but what good is it if she doesn't know?"

"Of course she must know. She is the light of my life."

"Then why is she afraid of you? Afraid to come to you with the truth?"

"This cannot be. Surely, she is not. She is free to tell me anything."

"She doesn't want to marry Leland."

"I knew that," Laith said.

"How did you know?" She asked.

"Well… because he's Leland, for one, and she never liked him."

"But do you know about the blackmail? And the threats?" Braley fought through tears to tell them what she knew.

"If you will excuse me?" Ari bowed and went to find his daughter.

Braley turned to plead with Laith, clutching his arm with both hands, "Sell him the land. Give him what he wants, but she can't marry Leland. Don't let that happen."

Laith held her. "Don't worry, I won't."

Ella insisted on preparing a late lunch. The group sat drinking coffee or whiskey, each according to their preference, discussing arrangements for Monty, and listening to Mr. P share stories of the early days, when he and Monty started out. Rivals, whose squabbles made them stronger, as each strove to best the other. "But no matter our differences, in the hardest times and the coldest of winters, we always helped each other when it was needed." He stood and raised his glass in a touching tribute, and the others followed suit.

"Let's get on with it." Leland stood in the doorway expectantly. In the answering silence, everyone but Reverend Pittsley turned to glare at him.

"Get on with what?" Laith asked.

"The wedding, *sheep dip*, just because Pa died, doesn't mean we shouldn't go ahead. It's what he would have wanted."

"Out of respect, there will be no wedding." Ari put down his glass and exchanged a look with his daughter.

Leland's concern showed in his face. "But the preacher's here and Niki's all fancied up. I see no need to wait."

Ari raised his voice, his words clear and precise. "You misunderstand me. Not only out of respect for your father, which you should show, but out of respect for my daughter. There will be no wedding. Not today. Not ever. The wedding is off. And if you ever dare to threaten my daughter again, you will answer to me. Do you understand?"

Niki, nearly faint with relief, shot a look of gratitude to Braley, who was just as relieved at the woman's narrow escape.

Leland, seeing another part of his scheme slipping away, came forward. "But you promised!"

"I did no such thing. I merely gave permission for what I thought was my daughter's wish. I am simply withdrawing that permission, because I now find that it was not."

Leland charged the older man. Laith couldn't reach them in time, but Ari stepped aside and dropped him with one swing.

"Get up, Leland. And get out," Laith shouted. "You've embarrassed our father and this house. You've embarrassed us all."

"I have a right to be here!" Leland picked himself up off the floor, rubbing his jaw.

Laith stepped closer. "No, you don't."

"For the wake, I do." He backed toward the door, "And we have things to talk about. It doesn't end here."

Three days. The body was lovingly cared for, washed and dressed by the family, and laid out in the side parlor. People came from miles around, and for three days and nights they took turns to guard against demons, to watch for signs of life, and to do their best to comfort the family. They brought food, and advice, and good intentions. Laith ordered a coffin in town, built from lumber Monty himself had cut from Riverdale land. It took three days, which was just as well, because it took the men almost as long to dig through the frozen earth in the little family cemetery on the hill.

Braley closed her eyes, swaying on her feet. She had stayed up the first night, making over a long-sleeved black muslin Ella had given her, so she would have something proper to wear. It was a good thing she had finished, because the first mourners arrived with the dawn, and she had been busy playing hostess ever since. There were plenty of hands to help with Eliza, and she was never far away, but she had barely seen Laith outside of the parlor. He spent the days meeting and greeting, except for the times she stole him away to the kitchen to make sure he had something to eat, and the few hours they had tried to sleep.

Leland had been there too, on and off, but she did not see him now, on this, the third evening. She frowned, searching the crowd for a glimpse of her husband. *There.* She wove her way through the throng until she reached his side, taking hold of his arm. "You need to rest a minute. Come, you haven't eaten all day."

"I don't want to leave Ella alone." He glanced around on either side of them.

"I have already stolen her. She's in the front room sitting down. It's allowed, you know. Everyone is here to help. They won't mind."

"Thanks," he said, as they passed the study on their way to the kitchen. "I'm afraid if I sit down, I will never get up."

She smiled in understanding and squeezed his arm. "What's the matter?"

He had stopped, scowling. "There's a light."

She followed his line of sight to the study where a light shone beneath the door. *He would not have left a lamp burning unattended, and he had not been in there all day.* "You have guests!" She reminded, as he threw open the door, leaving her behind.

"You won't find it, Lee."

Leland looked up from the papers he had strewn across the desk. "Find what?"

"The paperwork that was left to my care. You'll have to wait until after the burial for the lawyers and the witnesses, like everyone else. Get out there and show some respect. Try to pretend you care."

"I do care. You have no idea how bad I feel. He was my father. I was here first! *You don't know! You don't know!*" He pushed past Braley in the doorway, giving her a shove.

Laith started after him, but she grabbed his arm. "Not now," she whispered.

He nodded, but seeing the look on his face, she did not dare to let go.

Chapter 32

The silence at the table was louder than the conversation had ever been, the empty chair marking a passing of something greater than its occupant. The house itself was not the same, nor would it ever be again. Its founder was gone. The blood, sweat, and tears remained in the walls, but the spirit of the home had departed, much like the soul leaves its host behind. There was an echo within that would never find rest.

Laith shifted in his chair, considering all that was ahead. It was spring. A busy time, with floating the logs they had cut all winter down the river to the sawmill, calving, castrating and branding, repairing winter's damage to fields and fences, driving herds to the summer pastures and to market. He hated spring on the ranch. At least with the railroads coming in, the drives would get shorter and easier… *It was time for planting. Acres of corn. A new crop that would rise up and shine golden in the summer sun, waiting for harvest. A harvest that could better the stock and feed the world. But not this year. It was already too late.*

"Laith?"

He jumped, his heart pounding. It was Braley. Braley, looking lovely, sitting across the table, requesting his attention. *Would she still be there tomorrow? That was the part he had been avoiding. Every time.* Every time the thought crept in, he turned his mind to the massive number of tasks at hand. Spring had come, and every time she spoke, he was afraid. Afraid she would remind him of his promise. Afraid it was time for her to go. As a result, he had been short with her. *Hell, he had even avoided her at times, defeating the very purpose of wanting her to stay.* "Hmm?"

"I am planning on going…"

No, no, no.

"…for a buggy ride with Ella today. It's warm enough for her, and I think the outing would do her good. She won't socialize yet, of course, and we won't shop. I want to check the mail and send my letter to Constance. I thought the main road would be all right. Do you think it is good enough for the buggy?"

"Should be."

Braley knew her pleasant chatter was forced and she hated that she sounded nervous. She wasn't afraid of him, but he had been so short with her lately. He hardly bothered to converse and limited his answers to one or two words, as he did now. She glanced away, battling unpleasant memories.

Laith left the table before she could read the fear in his eyes, and before he saw the tears in hers.

Perhaps she had overstayed her welcome. Was he angry because she was still here? He had what he wanted. The house was his. Was it that he no longer needed her? She picked up Eliza and went upstairs to finish her letter. The letters from Constance had been less frequent of late. Braley understood she was busy with her family, but desperately hoped there would be one today. She needed the comforting voice of her friend, even if it were only on paper.

The ride had been good for both women, who had set out bravely, still in their mourning dresses. Ella found solace in the warmth of the sun and the new spring buds attesting life's return to the valley, and

Braley got her coveted letter. She had had time to think as Ella dozed on the way home. *She would confront Laith.* She would not live with this distance between them. It was not as bad as it was with Jacob, of course, but it could not go on.

Laith waited for Leland. The snow had returned and the dark clouds suited his mood. His problem with Braley was one thing, he thought, as he sat at his father's desk in the study; the settlement with Leland was another. He had managed to dodge a confrontation with her so far, hoping the answers would come. *Only the nights were the same… The nights of passion beyond his wildest dreams. Nights filled with all the loving they seemed to be unable to share in the daytime. She came to him without resentment, and he worshipped her still. Every touch, every movement, more meaningful, enhanced perhaps, because of the words they could not speak.*

"What do you want?"

Laith looked up as *the other problem* showed his face. "Took you long enough."

Leland dropped his frame into a chair. "Just because you got the house doesn't make you the boss. I have things to do."

"You're right, I'm not your boss, but you should know, as it stands, I am in charge of the estate. As soon as the lawyer can draw up the papers, I'll be dividing up the properties." He watched as his brother broke out in a sweat.

"Everything? I mean, I thought it was all done."

"You should have stayed. He changed it. Your recent behavior and your last-ditch lies did not go over well."

"But I'm the oldest. And how do I know you're telling the truth?"

"Because there were witnesses."

He scoffed. "Who? *Ella?*"

"Yes. And the doctor and the reverend."

"He never knew I lied about Niki."

"No. But I do."

"But I was only doing it because I loved him! I loved him."

"And yet, in the last moments of his life, you were still plotting and scheming instead of staying by his side. You could have spent time with him. He was awake. He was himself. You could have apologized for the things you did—the problems you caused all of us.

"But I…"

"And when you came back… You didn't cry because he was gone. You cried for yourself. You grieved because your plan didn't work. A plan that you hoped would challenge an agreement already made. And I'll say it—*He was wrong*. He was wrong to pit us against each other. To make marriage a contest, and love a game."

Leland stared, unable to deny the truth. *He had so desperately wanted the house, and had lost it anyway, and at what cost?* "So, what happens now? As if I didn't know. You get the house, I get the cabin, and we split the herd in half? What about the lumber?"

"I don't know. It would seem to me, with the cabin being smaller, three-quarters of the herd and the land would be more fair, don't you think?"

"Yes! Yes, it would. That's only fair."

"That's what I was thinking." He stared across the room at nothing, "It all depends on Braley."

Leland threw himself out of the chair, his voice strangled, his face a brilliant crimson, "She gets to choose? After all this, it's up to *her* how things are divided? That's not right!"

That was not what he meant, but Laith did not bother to correct him as he stormed out.

Spring flirted and retreated like a shy lover, uncertain whether to surrender her charms to the fullest. As a result, a light snow blanketed the ground under a starlit sky, but the breeze was warm. Braley needed only a shawl over her black dress as she stepped out onto the back porch where Laith had taken refuge after supper.

He stood with his back to her, but still took a few steps away, needing the distance. *This was it.* He knew what was coming, and the worst part was, it had been his idea. *'I need to talk to you,'* she had said, and he had run away. Run from the tension that had been building between them. He was a coward. Why wait? It was inevitable. He could not avoid it forever. She was not entirely happy here, and he had no right to ask her to stay. With one sentence, he gave her the opening she needed, handing her the knife that would cut out his heart. "I expect you'll be leaving."

There it was. He hadn't even waited to see what she wanted. He must have known, and left no opening for her carefully rehearsed speech about why they belonged together. The time was up, and he still expected her to leave. *"Yes,"* she whispered, sorrow squeezing her throat.

The pain struck his heart as a solid thing, taking his breath. His hands tightened on the railing.

He didn't speak again, and she reached for the handle on the screen door.

He stood looking into the night, at the pasture, the meadow, and the moon. Its silvered light did not show him her tears, flowing freely now, nor the last pleading look she gave, as her heart cried out, *Look at me! I thought you loved me!*

Moments passed, his mind and heart screaming in protest.

When he could stand it no longer, he spun around, his hand raised beseechingly as the door closed softly behind her. His shoulders bowed under the unbearable burden, and for one brief moment, stubbornness crowed its victory. *No!* A voice cried within, promise or not, he'd be damned if he would let her go without even asking her to change her mind. The door flew back, straining its spring as he rushed into the house, intending to race up the stairs and have the matter out.

She had barely moved.

Laith stumbled to a stop.

She stood at the stairway, staring straight ahead, her hand on the railing, one foot resting on the bottom step. When the door slammed of its own accord, her spine stiffened and her chin raised.

He knew that look, could almost feel the strength of her resolve, and his own determination wavered. *Was he wrong to do it? Was it unfair of him to ask? To beg if he had to?* Time stood still until she spoke.

"Laith," she began in a whisper, stopping to take a deep breath. "I don't want to leave you." She swallowed her anguish and closed her eyes, her chin raising another notch before she continued, "Because, you see, I love you. I love you so much, I'm not sure I can." There, she had said it. She had broken the bargain, but he hadn't kept his part either. An eternity passed while she waited for his reaction.

She turned to him and he read the mixture of fear and hope in her eyes. She needn't have worried. His heart lifted, relieved of the weight he had carried, and the answer was in his smile as he lifted her in his arms. "Oh, Braley, I couldn't let you go, but I was so afraid you'd be angry. I know I promised, but I can't do it. I love you too much to ever let you go. He kissed her over and over, and then withdrew to kiss her eyes, her forehead and her cheeks in rapid succession, until she laughed with joy.

"So, it's true," Leland spoke from the shadows. "I was right. All this time. You lied to Pa!"

"What are you doing here?" Laith wheeled around, shielding

Braley from his brother's wrath.

"I came back to ask what happened to Pa's watch."

"The watch is mine. He gave it to me."

"How did you get him to do that, another lie?"

"The watch was a gift from my mother, and I never lied. I loved Braley before I married her and I always will."

Braley's heart soared.

"Of course, she is free to go if she is unhappy here, but either way, it is no business of yours."

Leland seethed, feeling he was somehow being made the fool. There had been plenty of reasons for her to be unhappy here, yet she chose not to leave. *What more would it take?*

Chapter 33

Braley had written to Constance to let her know she would be staying, for now. She still hoped to visit. An extended visit with Laith, but she did not see how that would be possible with the amount of work to be done. Perhaps in the middle of winter, but then there was the lumber camp to run, and travel would be dangerous at best.

At least travel was easier here, now that the weather had improved. She tooled the buggy around the largest ruts, trying not to jar Ella overmuch on their trip to town. The vehicle pitched and tilted. "Whoa!" Fortunately, they had barely been moving when the wheel came loose and leaned outward, leaving them sitting at an odd angle. "Are you all right?"

"Sure I am. Takes more than a little jolt to damage this old bag of bones. It's not my first broken wheel, dear." She shifted Eliza on her lap. "Question is, as always, what do we do now? It'll be a while before they come lookin' for us."

It was true. They were closer to the ranch than to town, but it was still a good distance, and it would be hours before they were considered late. "I could take the horse and ride back for help, but I don't want to leave you alone." She searched the surrounding hills, her heart racing at the thought of Ella and Eliza sitting alone in the wilderness. *She hadn't even brought the rifle. What was she thinking?*

"We could walk," Ella offered.

"I think it's too far." She gave her a hug. "Can you shoot? I could leave my gun with you."

"I can, but what if you need it?"

Braley thought for a moment, looking over the damage. "The wheel isn't broken at all." She turned a frown to the older woman. "It's only come loose. And look…" She began to walk back the way they had come, searching the ground, until she stooped to pick up the square axle nut and waved it in the air toward Ella. "It's full of sand, that can't be good." She searched the buggy and, for lack of a better alternative, began wiping the sand from the greasy mess with her shirttail.

How to get the wheel repositioned on the axle was the problem. The buggy was fairly light, but to try to lift it and adjust the wheel at the same time proved too difficult, until Ella took the horse by the bridle and began to walk him forward while Braley watched. The crooked wheel wabbled but stayed in place until she steered the opposite side of the carriage into a deep rut, tipping it enough to lift the problem wheel off the ground.

"How clever!" Braley complimented.

"I saw my daddy do that once." Ella smiled, happy to be of help and pleased with the memory.

It was then a small matter to work the wheel into place and replace the nut. Without a wrench, Braley could only hand-tighten it and give an extra tap with a rock for good measure. They headed back, checking every so often to see that the nut stayed tight enough to get them home.

Laith was crossing the yard when he spotted the buggy coming up the drive. *It was too soon. Way too soon. They couldn't have made it to town in that time, never mind returned, and Braley was walking, leading*

the horse, her shirt covered in… blood? Was that blood? He ran down the drive toward them. *Grease?* "Is that grease?" He called, by way of greeting, catching his breath.

She nodded.

Thank God! "What happened?"

"We almost lost a wheel. It came loose, but we managed to get it back on."

"Everybody all right?" Laith frowned, pushing back his hat. Braley pointed out the offending wheel and told the story as he took over leading the horse up to the house. He frowned harder.

"What's the matter?" She asked, walking beside him.

He took Eliza and handed her to her mother, and helped Ella down from the buggy. He shrugged. "It's odd, is all. I just greased those wheels, and they were tight. Besides that, the hubs are threaded to tighten as they turn…"

"About that," Braley interrupted, holding out the tails of her shirt, "It fell in the sand. I tried to wipe it off. You probably want to check and make sure it's not ruined."

The frown was still there.

"I'm sorry. We did the best we could."

"No, no. You did fine. You did the right thing." He put an arm around each of them.

There were more odd things after that. Little things at first. So much so that Braley questioned whether she was imagining them or if they really meant anything. Her saddle had fallen into the muck of the stall. *Had she left it on the partition? Could Pappy have knocked it off its perch?* Her jacket went missing from the front hall and was found hanging in the outhouse, *or had she left it there?* And on several mornings, there were no eggs. *No eggs from dozens of laying hens.* Another time, the cow was let loose, and she had to chase her down.

When the garden she had started was trampled by cattle who happened to find themselves inside the latched gate, she drew the line. It had to be Leland, and if he thought he could make her feel like she was losing her mind, he'd better think again. She had played this game before. She had yet to involve Laith, but she kept an even closer eye on Eliza and made sure Dog was always nearby. She also made sure to keep the doors locked.

It wasn't long, of course, before she found herself explaining to Ella about the missing eggs. And soon after, Laith, returning to the house in the middle of the afternoon and finding himself locked out, demanded to know why.

"Why wouldn't you tell me?"

"I wasn't sure myself at first. I'm still not entirely certain, but I can't think who else it could be, or… if you'd even believe me."

"Of course, I believe you. Why would you say that?"

She looked at him, her eyes filled with doubt.

"Tell me."

"Well, the things he's done in the past don't even seem to matter." She threw her hands in the air and turned away. "I mean, why would you even speak to him, much less allow him back in your house?"

Laith came up behind her and she turned into his arms. "I'm sorry, she said, I didn't realize I was that angry."

"Do you think for one moment I've forgotten? The things he did to my father and Ella, and Eliza, and especially to you? Anything that Turner did was his fault, too, because he made it possible. He is responsible for all of that. As far as I am concerned, he caused my father's death, and the sight of him makes my skin crawl. I have not forgotten. Trust me."

She buried her face in his shoulder.

"I'll order the guards back, but there aren't too many available. Most are out on the drive. I trust Wes and Cody, but I'm not sure about the rest. I think some are hedging their bets, waiting to see who they will be working for."

The summer flew by, the days indiscernible. She supposed living each day on the edge of one's nerves had that effect. Braley resented living with guards, and yet she wished there were more. She had finished in the outhouse and turned the latch to step out when the door was ripped open, startling her and revealing a grinning Leland.

"Sorry," he said, the smirk never leaving his face. "I didn't know anyone was in there."

"Clearly, you did. Clearly, you have been watching and waiting. To what end, I cannot possibly guess. Go home, Leland. This isn't it. You don't belong here." Braley made sure to walk as slowly and steadily as she could back to the house. This time she did tell Laith, not because she wanted him to do anything, but because she had promised that she would keep him informed. It was not to be the worst of it.

It was a Saturday, and Laith was yet to come home. Ella and Braley had built the outside fire for heating the bath water, its warmth welcome in the crisp autumn air. She dressed in her trail clothes to work around the fire and wore her gun, even though Wes and Cody were nearby. Eliza had had her bath and was tucked in for the night. Ella had gone next, and Braley finished refilling the tub while Ella emptied the last few buckets of dirty water outside.

Braley stepped into the tub but could not relax, in spite of the steaming warmth. *Something was off.* "Ella?" She heard the door open,

"Ella?" She called again, making sure the older woman was all right, when there came a low whistle, followed by a chuckle.

He was behind her. She glanced at the nearby stool, her gun hidden beneath the pile of discarded clothing, and reached for a towel, hunching forward to cover herself. She looked over her shoulder. "Get out! Get out, Leland, or I swear I will track you down and shoot you myself."

"Yeah, you're good at that." The whistle came again, louder this time, as he stared at her back, at her shoulder, and the lash marks that appeared to wrap around her side. "Well, look at that. Fire, I'm guessin'. That had to be fire. That must have been scary. *Poor Miss High and Mighty, not scared of anything.* I bet you were scared then. *Does fire scare you?* I bet it does. I had no idea what my little brother's been sleeping with. Does he know, or do you keep the lights out? *You really should, you know, it's not pretty.*" He laughed. "Then again, you're all marked up like one of those road maps that help you find the important places. I might like to visit some of those myself." He stepped further into the long, narrow room, unfastening his belt.

It had been a hard day searching for strays, and Laith looked forward to his supper and a nice hot bath, and, of course, spending time with Braley. He thought about her as he rode. How she would greet him with a kiss. The way her eyes spoke to him when no one was looking. It was time to head for home. He yawned. He would have missed Eliza's bedtime. She always had the first bath on Saturdays. He'd have to stop at the barn first and take care of his horse. That was all right. Braley would be waiting. She made everything worth it.

Dog rounded the corner in full charge, the door rebounding against the wall. Alerted by Leland's whistle, and spurred by a rising sense of danger as he raced closer, he was more than ready to defend his mistress. For once, undeterred, he took full advantage of his good fortune. In a heartbeat, the predator became the prey; the focus changing from pleasure to pain in one clamp of the strong jaws.

Leland screamed, turning in circles, finding no escape. Dog growled, shaking his head and adjusting his hold somewhere near the left buttock and upper thigh. Braley took the opportunity to jump from the tub, wrapping herself in the towel and grabbing her gun, but she remained silent, fascinated by the power of the animal. She had last seen him settled by Eliza in her room.

"Get out!" Ella appeared in the hall, holding a rifle, blood dripping from her hand.

"Sit!" Braley shouted, startled to awareness. Dog sat.

To Braley's amazement, Ella cocked the gun and kept a steady aim on Leland, looking like the mistress of death in her black mourning dress.

He glanced at the older woman and back at Braley, as a second hammer clicked in the stillness. He backed from the room, keeping an eye on Dog, fumbled for the lock on the back door, and limped from the house.

"I'm so sorry." Ella kept her eyes on the door. That was my fault. I didn't see him. I was coming in, and he pushed me down and locked me out. I went around to the front, but it's locked, of course, so I had to break the window."

Braley put away her gun and picked up a small towel, but didn't move from her spot. "You did fine. That was good thinking. We're all right, thanks to you… You can put the gun down now."

Ella gave a short laugh and released the hammer, lowering the rifle she was still aiming at the back door. "I'm sorry, did I scare you?" She turned the lock. "I was thinking of all the times I wish I had done that before."

Braley came forward to examine her wound and dab it with the towel.

"It's just a scratch from the window." Ella took the cloth from Braley's hands. "You check on the baby and get dressed before you catch cold. I'll clean up the blood."

Braley looked at the splotches of blood Leland had left across the floor. "I'll do it. Just let me see to Eliza."

"I insist." Ella gave her a pointed look. "Maybe you should lie down." A tear formed and rolled down her cheek.

"Oh, I'm fine, Ella," Braley embraced her with sudden understanding. "You were there in plenty of time. He didn't get anywhere near me, and he wouldn't have. Neither of us was going to let that happen."

The woman nodded, another tear falling. "But he's so awful. I'm ashamed. I'm ashamed to call him family. She paused and then looked at Braley. "I don't think I want to stay here much longer."

Shocked to hear the words that had echoed through her mind for months, Braley fell silent again. She didn't want to leave Laith, but how could she stay here? Ella's next words pulled her from her thoughts.

"I never liked Leland." It seemed to Braley as though the woman had surprised herself, but having spoken the thoughts out loud, she continued. "He was a horrible child, and he's a horrible person. He is always mean to me when no one is around, because he knows that I know. That I am not fooled by the show he puts on. I kept my mouth shut around Monty, of course. When you're the poor relative… When you have no place to go, sometimes you have no choice."

Braley nodded and touched her hand.

"Monty kept him in check somewhat, but he was always one of those kids, picking and prodding, especially at poor Laith, and whining when he got as good in return. It wasn't often, though. Laith couldn't seem to see it when he was younger. He worshipped his big brother. I think solely because he *was* his big brother. I can see no other reason for it. He has this sense of family and loyalty, and Leland does not. It's so heartbreaking to watch. I stuck it out when Monty was here, but it's not the same without him, and to be honest, I'm getting too old for all this work. This is a big house to take care of, and I'm just plain tired, and now all this commotion…"

Laith finished up in the barn, even more exhausted than before. He was not so tired, however, that he didn't notice the somber attitude of the two women and that Braley's greeting was not the same as usual. "What's wrong?"

'*Nothing,*' they assured him, too much in unison, turning the conversation to small talk.

"Anything unusual happen today?" He asked, finishing up his supper.

Braley shook her head and hid behind a sip of her coffee, still undecided on how much she should say. *It wouldn't do any of them any good to have him jailed for murder, but she had promised to keep him informed.*

"Funny thing," Laith began, looking from one to the other. "I got back to the barn late and found Wes and Cody locked in the tack room. They'd been in there quite a while. Pretty odd, I thought, but as long as nothing happened, I guess it must have been some kind of weird accident, or a practical joke." He looked at each again and shrugged, draining the last of his coffee. "Guess I'll take my bath."

"You have to tell him," Ella whispered as soon as he had stepped outside to lug the buckets of hot water from the fire pit.

"I'm afraid he'll go after him," Braley whispered back.

"But he's your husband. He has a right to know. *You know what Leland intended.*"

"One of them could very well end up dead, and either way, I would lose Laith. *It's not worth it.*"

Laith poured the last bucket of water, filling the tub, and removed his boots and socks. He stopped and lifted his foot, and set it down again on the stone floor, testing. *Was there something sticky?* He tried another spot, and another. *Yes, definitely something…* He scowled, holding the lantern closer, but saw nothing. On his hands and knees now, with the lantern on the floor, he ran his hand over the stone and sniffed. *Soap?* Yes, but at this angle, he could barely make out a faint pattern of splotches and stains leading across the room and out to the back door. It was difficult to see in the limited light, but here and there the stains were darker, and there, in the corner, tiny red droplets. *Was that…* **"Braley!"**

The women exchanged glances, and Braley winced, but neither moved before Laith entered the room barefoot, his shirt hanging open, and fire in his eyes. He gritted his teeth, "Who's going to tell me what happened?"

"Why don't you take your bath first?" Braley suggested.

He crossed his arms and lowered his chin.

"Well, at least sit down." She waited, as stubborn as he, until he sat. She shot Ella a warning look, "Leland came into the house, and Dog attacked him."

"In the bathing room."

"Yes."

"Why in the bathing room?"

Braley developed a sudden fascination with the handle of her coffee cup.

Laith felt his blood turn cold. "Was someone in there?"

She nodded, still not looking at him.

"Oh my God. Were you in there?"

"Now calm down." She bit her lip.

"Were you in the tub?!" He gripped the edge of the table. *"Did he…?"*

She shook her head, and this time was quick to answer, "No. Dog came, and Ella, with a rifle, and I had my gun."

"Ella with…" He turned his gaze on his cousin.

"He tried to." What Braley couldn't bring herself to tell him, Ella did. All of it, including the crude comments about the *road map* and prospects of visitation, Dog's attack, and the gun she had gotten from the front hallway.

Braley blushed scarlet, her eyes lowered. "I didn't know you heard that," she whispered.

Laith felt her pain. Her scars were such a private thing to her. He knew she regarded them as a mark of shame, somehow representative of blame she took upon herself. She never spoke of them. *Another reason to go after Leland.*

"I did." Ella, caught in a righteous anger, stared straight ahead. "Every bit of it. And I saw him unbuckle his belt. I was behind him, but I could tell. If it hadn't been for the dog…"

Chairs scraped across the floor. Laith and Braley leapt from their seats at the same time, he, barely able to think straight, she, pushing him back toward the bathroom, before he realized her intent. "Let me go," he warned.

"No, please. Please. You're not even dressed. Calm down first. Take your bath and we'll talk about it. I'll tell you everything. We can make a plan. Please!"

Laith pushed back, blinded by rage and deafened by determination, wanting to get by, but careful not to hurt her. "Let me go! You can't expect me to let this pass."

She tried everything, and still he moved her backwards, to the point where she could barely hold on and thought she was going to lose him. The thought scared her and the cry came from her heart, *"I need you! Please don't leave me!"*

She slid to her knees in tears, her arms wrapped around his legs, begging him to stay, and his heart melted. He went to the floor and held her, rocking her back and forth, fighting tears of sympathy and frustration. *He had said he would never hurt her.* "Don't cry. Don't cry, Braley Stuart. I'm here. We'll figure it out."

Dog had taken refuge under the table, confused by the exchange. *His mistress was distressed but did not seem to need his help this time. Besides, he knew this one. They both liked this one.*

Ella gave the dog a pat and took herself off to bed, doubting she would sleep with all the thoughts spinning in her head. *She hadn't cleaned the floor as well as she thought. Her eyesight wasn't what it used to be. And if it hadn't been for the dog, she most likely would have shot Leland dead and would be in jail now. It was definitely time to leave.*

Chapter 34

Laith kissed her until she stopped crying, his love for her the only thing stronger than his anger and his lust for vengeance. He helped her to her feet and kissed her again, long and lovingly, desperate to tell her how much she meant to him.

Braley twined her arms around his neck, backing into the bathing room, still afraid to let him go. She pressed herself against him, holding him against the wall and pushing his shirt back off his shoulders and down to his elbows so he couldn't move. "Now I've got you," she teased, looking up at him through the tears that still filled her eyes. The corner of his mouth lifted, and she kissed his chest, his shoulders, and his neck, running her hands over him and resting her cheek against the beat of his heart, closing her eyes. "Thank you. Thank you for staying with me."

He nodded, calmed from his rage and aroused by her caresses, and awaited her pleasure, still not sure he knew everything that had happened in this room, or how she would feel about it. *Damn Leland.*

She unfastened his trousers and slid her hands inside to slip them down, knowingly or not, teasing along the way. She helped him step out of them, running her hands back up his thighs as she stood, welcoming his interest with both hands.

He moved to embrace her, meeting the gentle restraint of his sleeves, and she smiled, pulling his shirt off, freeing him to caress her back and pull her closer. He kissed her gently at first, until the flame she started inside him burned free and engulfed her with its heat.

She coaxed him to the still hot tub and he stepped in, welcoming its warmth, but reluctant to leave her.

She washed and rinsed his hair and began to soap his back. "Why do you call me that?"

"Hmm?"

"*Braley Stuart*. Why do you still call me that?"

His brow rose, his eyes a deep gold in the firelight as he searched for the answer, "Because it's who you are, and I like who you are. I don't know, maybe because it was plain as day when we met, you did not want to let anyone in. But you did. It was a gift you gave me, I thought, when you told me your name. It was my privilege to know and to use, and so I do. Turns out, it was the best gift of my whole life. I'm as blessed and proud as I can be that you're Braley Demoranville, don't get me wrong, but you will always be the tough and determined Braley Stuart that I met on the trail. The Braley Stuart that... I like to think needed me, if only a little bit... Does that make sense?" He turned his head to look at her.

She nodded, unable to speak for the moment, shifting her eyes to the rough stubble on his cheek.

"What are you thinking now?" She asked, easing him back, and soaping his chest, conscious that his gaze had never left her.

"That you should be in here with me."

Her brow rose. "I don't think there's room."

"You'll have to get close," he whispered. "You're already wet."

True, the edges of her sleeves were damp, though she had rolled them back. She glanced at the front of her blouse, which showed several spots that were now wet through. "A little," she said, and caught her breath when he splashed her, wetting the front of her blouse.

"You should probably take that off."

She grinned, "It's not that wet."

He put one arm around her and placed the other at the back of her neck, drawing her in for a kiss, teasing with his tongue, and pulling back so that she followed him across the rim of the tub to come to rest against him. His hand slid up to capture her breast, now submerged in the warm soapy water.

Braley felt the warmth of the water seeping through her blouse and the heat of his kiss sinking into her soul.

"How about now?" He murmured against her mouth.

She drew back and nodded, reaching for the buttons of her blouse.

"You wouldn't want to catch cold."

"I don't think there's much chance of that," she whispered, standing to step out of her skirts and into the tub.

She was right, there was not much room, and they laughed as they twisted and turned trying to get settled, and water spilled over the edge. He traded places with her, flipping her onto her back and bathing her chest and arms, as she had done for him. "But I've already had my bath," she reminded, putting her head back, and leaning into his touch while he played and teased, leaning over her.

"Not like this," he rasped.

"No, not like this," she agreed, her voice no more than a breath of a whisper in the lamplight.

He watched as she shared the abundance of lather he had created, taking it from her own body, unknowingly teasing him with each swipe of her hand, each glimpse of her beauty unveiled anew. She continued his bath where she had left off, reaching as far as she could, in the close quarters of the tub.

Laith, his muscular arms on the sides of the tub supporting his weight, did his best to make sure she had no trouble reaching wherever she wanted. He held his breath as she passed the soap over him again and again, reveling in the way her hands slid across his skin and the pleasure she gave.

He drew a sharp breath, bringing her play to a stop. Lifting her hips caused a wave to wash over her, revealing the whole of her from her soapy covering, as he sank beneath the water and into her welcoming warmth.

He bathed her again, this time with his mouth, his tongue teasing until she begged him with her body to move with her in a rhythm as old as the sea and as endless. He matched her move for move, letting the waves swell and crash around them, carrying them to the far ends of the earth, where he followed her over the edge.

The fire on the hearth burned to embers, and what little was left of the water grew cool. The rest had surged over the sides of the tub, cleansing the floor, washing away the horrid encounter of the early evening, and leaving a cherished memory in its wake.

"Where are you going?" Braley sat up in bed to see Laith already dressed and about to leave the room.

"Did you think I forgot?"

"No. I hoped… Oh…." She put a hand to her neck, capturing his attention.

"Are you all right?" He came to sit beside her and massage her shoulders, his strong hands easing the muscles that pained her.

They had fallen asleep in the bath, he resting on top of her and she spending most of the night in a sitting position. Then they had gathered their clothes and run through the house wrapped in towels, racing like children. Now he had grown serious again, and she was worried.

"Where are you going? It's still early."

"I have some things to take care of."

"I'll come down with you," she said, putting on her robe. "Please tell me you are not going to confront Leland. I'm afraid of what will happen."

"You shouldn't be. *He should be,* but you shouldn't. But don't worry, I'm going to see the lawyer. I have an idea. Something I've been working on. I'll tell you about it later."

"Promise me you'll be extra careful," he said as they sat over coffee.

"We will. But Dog did quite a bit of damage. I don't think he'll be up and around anytime soon."

Braley was right. For the next months, there was no sign of Leland. The pranks stopped, there were eggs and milk every morning, and nothing seemed amiss in the stables. Still, she could not shake the feeling that he might be watching and could jump out at her at any time. She wore her holster, stayed close to the house, and kept Dog inside as much as possible. She wrote to Constance and continued her occasional letters to Astrid and Herkules, but she sent them with Laith when he went to town. The time for the fair came and went, but with all of their problems and Monty's passing, they did not attend. Laith was still dealing with the lawyers, planning for the day when all would be settled, and they waited. *To what end?* She wondered. *Would there ever come a day when they were free of Leland? Was it even possible? In the meantime, must they put up with this? The very air they breathed was heavy, a suffocating blanket of dread that smothered the joy from their days. How long must they wait?"*

It didn't take as long as she thought, but neither was it the plan they had hoped for.

It was an ordinary Sunday. They hadn't gone to church, choosing not to make the trek into town in the light rain. Ella prepared a delicious dinner, and they had spent a quiet day at home playing with Eliza, watching her practice her steps, and trying to teach her new words. She and Laith even spent some time on the back porch, bundled against the cold, gazing at the stars before they went to bed. Everything was fine. An ordinary Sunday.

Braley woke. It was pitch black. *The middle of the night.* Laith was there, warm by her side, and she waited for her eyes to adjust to the darkness, listening.

Dog whined and paced, his nails clicking on the wooden floor. *But why? That smell…* She sat up and lit the lamp, the jolt of fear that shot through her like nothing she had known before. "Laith!"

They jumped from the bed. Tendrils of smoke curled upward from beneath the door, floating through the room like a specter. Braley broke from the chill that paralyzed her and went immediately to Eliza, wrapping her in her blankets and covering her little face. Her eyes darted around the room looking for answers. She had faced fire before, but not like this. The other time, she had seen a way out. There had been a way out. *What to do? Where to run? The windows? How far from the ground? She looked out, but could not see the porch roof below. Too far for Eliza? A last resort. The smell was stronger now…*

Laith went to the door, feeling the heat before he reached it. *How bad was it? He would have to open it to find out, and then it might be too late. Should he? Would it fan the flames?* He eyed the single pitcher of water on the bureau and glanced at Braley, holding her child, her eyes feral and wide with fear. *It was up to him. Dear God, it was up to him!*

He grabbed a shirt to turn the knob and open the door a crack. Flames devoured the frame and covered the floor in front of their room, but he could see across the hall, an island, a refuge, a spot of rug, untouched. He closed the door and grabbed the quilts from the bed, locking eyes with Braley, his holding a message for all eternity. "Close the door behind me," he said, slipping into his boots, and then, when she did not respond, "Do you hear me?!"

She nodded.

He opened the door and dove through the flames, tumbling to the other side of the hallway, using the quilts to smother the flames in front of the door, beating and stomping through the blankets. The walls proved more difficult; the fire was up above his head, and he had to reach up to fight it.

He had to get them to the stairway. He turned his head, searching through the smoke and saw… *Nothing?* Thick smoke billowed and burned his eyes, but on either side of him in the hall, he saw no flames. The only damage was outside of their room. He could smell kerosene. *Damn you to hell, Leland!*

Braley's fear had only multiplied when Laith yelled at her and then disappeared. She used her shoulder to push the door shut, sheltering Eliza. *What could she do? The way he had looked at her… so brave. She could help. She could at least try. She wasn't giving in without a fight.* She placed Eliza on the bed and used the shirt to open the door as Laith had.

His first swings overhead had only fanned the flames, causing them to burn brighter. Now, he patted and blotted with what was left of the smoldering quilts, when a bite—*the sting of a thousand bees*—attacked his forearm and crawled upward…

She opened the door and saw him, covered with soot and drenched with sweat—*and his arm—his arm on fire!* Her thoughts froze for what seemed like forever, remembering the piercing agony.

"Good girl!" It was Laith, hugging her, holding her as though he would never let her go, the sleeve of his long johns dripping wet. *"Thank you."* He waved the smoke away from their faces, coughing and choking, the scent of kerosene heavy in the air. "Get Eliza downstairs, I'll make sure it's out for good."

Braley held the pitcher in her hand, empty now, but she did not recall grabbing it from the bureau after she had put Eliza down. *Eliza, she must get Eliza, and Ella!* Braley gathered the baby, called to Dog, and rushed down the hall, her face buried in the child's blankets, confused at first, to find when she passed from the main cloud of smoke, there was no more fire. Not in the rest of the upstairs, and nothing downstairs. She checked every room. *But how?* Her steps faltered and she came to a halt, remembering Leland's words as he taunted her, *'Does fire scare you? I bet it does.' Would he go that far? Of course he would. How on earth could she keep it from Laith? How could they stay here putting Eliza in danger, and how would she tell him?*

It was only three in the morning, but she had made coffee when Laith came downstairs.

"Is Ella okay?" He asked, as she prepared to bandage his arm, which wasn't as bad as she had feared.

"Yes, I looked in on her, but there is really no reason to wake her."

"The fire's out, and I opened all the windows, but the smell is terrible.

Braley stared into space and nodded. "Everything is ruined." Her words hung heavily in the air between them.

I have to talk to you, they said at the same time.

"Maybe we should go into the study," Laith suggested.

Braley followed, her heart racing.

"You know it was Leland." He wasted no time. As soon as Braley had settled Eliza on the sofa and surrounded her with pillows, Laith spoke his mind. "The buggy wheel, too. You knew that."

"I know." She sat with her hands folded in her lap; her nightgown spotted with soot. "I am not a coward, but I am afraid for Eliza. Tonight was too close. If it were just me, I wouldn't care what he did, but I have to put her first. "Tonight was about me." She closed her eyes, "That night in the bathing room, when he saw my scars, and said… *those things*. He asked me if I was afraid of fire. *Did you see? Did you notice it was only near our room? I think he wanted to scare me.*"

"I did, and I promise you he will pay for it." He took his seat and drew a deep breath. "In the meantime, I want you to leave."

Alone? She waited, her eyes wide.

He saw the pain fill her eyes and hurried with his explanation. "I don't want you in danger."

"We are all in danger." Without realizing it, she had moved to the edge of her seat, "Will you not come with me?"

Laith went to kneel in front of her and hold her hands while he spoke the words that would break her heart. "I have to stay. I need to take care of things here. I'm waiting for some paperwork, and there's the herd and the horses and men due back from the drive who will have to be paid. Please try to understand."

Of course he would not leave. He had the house now, and the enormous responsibility of filling his father's footsteps. She had known the answer before she asked, and could only nod. "It's the house, isn't it?" She dissolved into tears, and he could barely make out her next words, "It means more to you than I do."

Laith shook his head and held her by the shoulders, "Listen to me, Braley. Nothing means more to me than you do. I'm leaving. I need to do it my way. I've been working on something, and it's almost done, but I think it's too dangerous for you to wait here. I want you to go to Cheyenne and wait for me…"

She almost breathed a sigh of relief.

"Wait until Christmas. If I'm not there…"

"Why? Why would you not be there? What do you mean? Will

you call the sheriff? I don't want you to get in trouble."

"Don't worry."

"No. Promise me. Promise me you won't touch him. I couldn't stand it if you went to jail. He's not worth it!"

Laith took his time answering. "I promise I won't touch him."

"You can't shoot him either," she added, thinking he had agreed too easily.

He grinned and hugged her. "I won't shoot him if you'll trust me. This is something that I need to do."

"What you need to do is come with me. I'll never forgive myself for leaving if something happens to you."

"I will be fine. And I will find you, I promise."

He held her for a long time until she spoke again, "I hate that he will think he scared me off. That he will think he won."

"He won't."

"What does that mea…"

Laith talked over her question, "Could you face him? If he came here?"

"If I had to."

"I think he should see you leave. Or at least hear about it. We could stage a fight, that way it will look like you are leaving angry with me and not because of what he has done."

"Either way, he has won," she said, tears falling at last.

"It will be all right. If you stayed and something happened, I don't think you would forgive me, and what's worse, I don't think you could forgive yourself. You are doing the right thing putting her first. You are very brave." *And so am I*, he thought. Braver than he had ever been. Still, he could not keep his voice from breaking when he told her, "I once said I love you too much to ever let you go. I was wrong. I love you more than that."

She stared into his eyes, placing her palm against the side of his face and the lightest of kisses on his lips.

Chapter 35

The fewer the days, the more precious they became, but as always, much of the time was spent working. Braley and Ella had washed all of the clothes and hung them out to dry, and then washed most of them again. "I think this smell is impossible to get rid of completely," Ella complained. "We've about run out of soda."

Braley gave a half-smile and stirred the large wash pot that sat over the firepit. They had moved their belongings out of the room and cleaned and aired what they could. The books she had given Laith were laid out in the sun along with their other favorites, the pages sprinkled with more of the baking soda to try to salvage them. That was it, though. Braley frowned in thought. They had moved their things, but Laith hadn't made any repairs or had any work done. The ruined rugs and damaged walls, the smell and the mess, remained as they were. The only thing he had bothered with was the brass bed. It had been dismantled and now stood in the front hall minus its ruined ticking. Braley felt a stab to her heart each time she passed, a cutting reminder of the memories it held and their time together coming to an end.

She smiled her thanks to Wes as he added a few more logs to the fire. He and Cody were now her constant companions whenever Laith was absent from the house. She hadn't seen Leland for some time, and she was less nervous about him making an appearance. She had a feeling he was done. At least for now. *Maybe he had done his worst.*

After all, she was leaving. She closed her eyes, denying the tears that hovered always at the ready. She wondered if Laith had said anything to him, but she rather thought not. He hadn't come home bruised or bloodied, and she was almost certain he would have if there had been any contact. He had been livid after inspecting the outside of the house and the grounds the day after the fire. The porch and back of the house were charred where a fire had been started in several different places, but had not caught. Perhaps it was the dampness from the morning's rain, or, as Laith said, *Leland was too damn stupid to start a proper fire.* Braley preferred to think someone was watching over them and hoped they would continue to do so. In any case, the fire was not meant only to scare them.

The women said their goodbyes and did their crying in private, Ella holding Eliza on her lap as she had so many times. "I'm going to miss you," The older woman said.

Braley nodded sadly. "You could come with me."

"Oh, I couldn't leave Laith here alone. He might need me… Oh, I'm sorry!" She immediately apologized at the look on Braley's face. "I didn't mean that you shouldn't. I am certain you are making the right choice after what's happened. It is not safe as long as Leland is around. Besides, I'll keep an eye on things." She gave Braley a wink and kissed Eliza on the top of her head, hugging her again. "I'll never understand how Leland is allowed to rule the roost. He gets away with everything. Why hasn't Laith called the sheriff, especially after the other night?"

"I don't know. Not enough proof, I would guess. He said not to worry. We'll have to trust him."

She was right to trust him. The sheriff came that night to talk to all of them. He wrote down every word and had them all sign the paper. Braley didn't know how that would help, but hope rose in her heart. That was, until he said he was returning to town.

"*That was it? That was all?* Did he not come to arrest Leland?" She questioned Laith after the sheriff had left, her hopes taking a hard fall.

"Don't worry," he said again, and bid Ella good night before leading Braley off to bed.

They now slept in the bedroom at the other end of the hall, as far from their old room as they could get. Braley resented every minute spent in that room, another reminder of Leland's interference in their lives. Especially tonight. *Their last night. It was a terrible time to leave, with the holidays coming and the winter weather, but there would never be a right time. She had stalled as long as she dared. The weather was already turning bad.* All of these thoughts had her angry and upset until Laith took her in his arms and made her forget where she was, where she was going, and anything else but their love for one another.

She had not slept afterward. She had stayed awake until the dreaded morning light crept between the curtains. *She might have stayed. If only he had asked her. Against her better judgment, she still might have stayed by his side.* But he did not ask. He was letting her go at last.

She left in the morning, with more strength than she knew she possessed. The buckboard, hitched to the black team, was loaded with her things. Eliza snuggled beside her, and Dog rode in the bed, with Pappy and the mule tied to the back. Wes and Cody would escort her to town, and from there they would travel north to the newly established city of Cheyenne, where she planned to take the train back to the East. She took a breath and slapped down the reins, her silver bracelet glinting in the first rays of the sun.

Laith had decided not to have Leland present for her departure. He saw no need for that added insult to his wife, and would not give his brother that satisfaction. Braley was not pleased with his plan, but did as he asked. They *had words* down by the barn where he went with her to pick up her horse and mule, and tie them to the back of the wagon. Several of the men were there, so Leland would be sure to hear about everything.

"Go ahead then, if you want to go! See if I care!" He had said, the words tearing at his heart, because he did care. Almost more than he could stand.

Braley had pleaded one last time before they left the house. *"Please come with me. Whatever you're doing can't be more important than being together,"* she had said, but he had turned her down, and she had played her part well. "Stay on your precious ranch! I hope you're happy. You love it more than you love me anyway!" Although it hurt her to say them, the words came a little too easily for her comfort. The anger was for Leland. Her tears were real.

Laith glared at the men for good measure and walked back to the house. He had watched her go from the porch. She did not look back, and he died a little more inside. It wasn't until he went up to bed, not sure he could sleep in the room they had shared, that he saw she had left something behind. On the side of the bed sat a brown valise with a little stuffed rabbit strapped to the top.

It was two weeks later when a messenger brought a note from his lawyer, and Laith had rushed into town, and another week before everything was settled to his satisfaction. He now sat in the front room and read the message again while he waited for Leland—*Mr. Paterakis has returned from his trip. All is well. Everything is ready*— He was oddly calm. This was what he had waited for. What he had risked the best thing in his life for. Ella had chosen to stay in her room.

"Come on in."

Leland looked around warily.

"Don't worry, she's not here. Neither is her dog."

"I heard, but I didn't believe it."

"Yeah, she set the house on fire, so I threw her out."

Leland's face grew red, and his eyes grew round.

"She denied it, of course, but I know it was her. Who else could it have been? It was the middle of the night, and Ella was sleeping. She never liked this house. *Damn women.* More trouble than they're worth, wouldn't you say?"

"I sure would. I knew she was trouble from the beginning." He laughed uncomfortably, wiping his forehead.

"I think I knew right away."

Leland grinned and raised his eyebrows. "But I bet it was fun while it lasted, hey?

His younger brother did not smile.

"I say good riddance. Don't forget, she killed a man. And she had those ugly scars."

Laith closed his eyes and remembered his promise to stay out of jail. "Yeah, kind of like this one," he said, pulling back his sleeve.

Leland colored several shades deeper, and then he remembered his pretense, "What happened?"

"I guess she didn't like feeling alone in the world. Can you imagine what that would be like?"

Leland stared, not sure they were still talking about the same thing, and not wanting to make a wrong step.

"Anyway, that's not what I called you here for." Laith led the way into the study and stood behind the desk. "How did you know?" He asked, pretending ignorance.

"How did I know what?" Leland eagerly took a seat.

"How did you know about her scars?"

There was a lengthy silence. "She said so, one time. She told me about them. Complaining about it, I think."

Laith eyed him until he squirmed in his chair. "I see." He took a deep breath, "Well, here's the story, I've decided to let you have this house." He watched as his brother's face lit up and then dimmed. "You might want to do some repairs to the upstairs. I'm sure you know where."

"But you said three-quarters of the land and the herd go with the cabin."

"Yes, and you said that was fair."

"But now you're keeping it? That's not right! I changed my mind!"

"I'm not keeping it. I've sold it to Ari. The cabin, the land, and the better part of the herd. Most of the hands are going to work for him as well. And if you've got any more ideas about blackmailing a bride, Niki is happily married to the man she met on her trip. She will inherit everything. I was only waiting for Ari to return from the wedding. What I am keeping is the sawmill, and I have a deal with Ari for the timber rights. Wes and Cody are going to run it for me. I'm making them partners. I'll check in now and then, of course. It will be a lot easier to travel back and forth now that the railroad has reached us."

"*Check in?* You're leaving? But where are you going?" Leland leaned forward.

"Does it matter? The house is yours. This grand, glorious house, that you sold your soul for. Other than a few things I'm taking with me, it's all yours. Your very own albatross."

"What?"

Laith only shook his head, and when it was clear he wasn't going to explain, Leland put his head in his hands. His shoulders began to shake. "This isn't what I wanted. I wanted it the way it was, only bigger and better."

"You mean before you tried to have me killed? I should thank you for that; it was how I met Braley, if you recall." He stared across the room. "It was big enough. There was plenty for all of us."

Leland caught his breath on a sob and slid to his knees. "I want it the way it used to be. I want Pa in his chair." He looked up, his nose running, his cheeks wet with tears. "I want you here, and Ella making breakfast. We could run it together. It's no good now. I don't want it now. Please don't go. *You're my brother! You're all that's left.*" He tried to grab Laith's leg as he walked away.

"It's a little too late for that now." He stopped when he reached the door. "By the way, Ella is coming with me, and the sheriff is on his way. He has a warrant for your arrest. You and Trotter, wherever he's hiding."

"But what's going to happen? What will happen to me? Don't you care? Don't you care what will happen to the house?"

"Did you care, Lee? Did you care when I was shot and left to die? Did you care when you plotted to kill the woman I love? And when that didn't work, you attempted to… *to attack her? How far would you have gone?* How far? If the dog hadn't come? If Ella hadn't been there? You drove her away. She wasn't afraid of you. She feared for her child. *A baby!*" He turned to look at his brother with a look of disbelief, as the thought struck him anew, "*You almost burned us to death.* And what you caused to happen to Pa, and Ella… *All over this damned house.*" He looked around him at the walls that had once meant so much and felt the emptiness. "There's nothing here now. This was *his* dream, not mine, and I don't even know who you are anymore. No, I don't care. I'm done." He only hoped he would be in time.

Chapter 36

The train was leaving on time. Its steel bulk stood reassuringly solid, a stark contrast to the wisps of softly falling snow that had just begun, and the uncertainties that lay ahead. People loaded with bags and baggage bustled about, full of importance. The whistle blew a long cry of joy for those who were eager to be on their way, and of sorrow for those who were not.

Braley was one of the latter. Still undecided as to whether she would leave—*could leave*—she stood out of the way of the swarming crowd in a gray travel dress and cloak with a dark velvet collar. She had only moments to decide. Her baggage was onboard. Her animals were loaded, except for Dog, who waited at her feet. *What was she waiting for?*

She still believed he would come as he had promised, but the truth was, if he didn't, she would go back. *Was he all right? Had the pull of the house proved too much?* She shifted Eliza on her hip and nuzzled her face in the soft blankets to hide a wayward tear before taking one last glance down the busy street.

He worked his way through the throng, his eyes pinning her in place, and her heart lifted until she saw he had no luggage. *Would he not come with her? Had he only come to see her off?* He moved closer, and she could see Ella walking at his side.

Laith kept his eyes locked on hers as he approached. *How had he ever let her drive away? It was something he had had to do. To see it through until the end. Leland had to be made to pay for the things he had done, and he had to be certain he would never bother them again. But she was right, it had not been more important than being with her. He had known it as soon as she had left. Would she forgive him?* He searched her face before he spoke, his heart in his eyes. "You forgot your valise."

Ella held out her arms, and Eliza went to her willingly. Braley smiled, "I didn't forget it. It was my way of making sure you would come after me."

The corner of his mouth lifted. "But how do you know if I came after you because I need you, or because you left your valise?"

Warmth infused her heart at his choice of words. "You're right," she said, "I don't." She looked away across the crowd, unsure of what her next words should be.

"All aboard!" The conductor called out, as the bell rang and the engine began to hiss and spit, building up the power to tear them worlds apart.

"Well… where is it?" She glanced around expectantly.

He studied the toe of his boot. "I don't have it."

Her heart fell, and her gaze followed his to the ground.

"It's on the train. With my luggage."

Her eyes met his with a clash of understanding that filled her soul and set her heart to singing. She waited, their eyes locked, until he continued.

"I needed to know that you would sit with me and let me explain."

She smiled and tried to speak calmly despite the frantic pounding of her heart, "How will you know if I'm coming because I can't live without you, or because I need my valise?"

He grinned. "You're right, I don't."

"Don't you?" She whispered, moving into his arms and kissing him in front of everyone, laughing at the remarks and applause from the crowd. "Don't you?" She asked again, as they broke apart. She closed her eyes and rested her head against the soft wool of his coat, snowflakes kissing her cheek, her heart near to bursting.

Laith looked up through the dizzying snowfall and laughed, reveling in the promise found in her kiss.

"I do now, Braley Stuart. I do now."

"But you're certain this is what you want? You're sure?" Braley asked, after he had told her all that had happened, and how Leland would be arrested and the house would be left to sit empty. She glanced at Ella and found great comfort in her nod of reassurance, as the train chugged along.

"Yes. I'm not going back, unless there's a problem with the mill, and only if you'll go with me."

They stopped to change trains in Iowa before continuing east. "Where do you want to go? "Did you have someplace in mind?" She wanted very much to stop and see Constance. She had even thought she might settle there so they could be close again, but she knew she would follow him anywhere.

He grinned. The grin he grinned whenever he talked about his dreams. That grin, and the faraway look in his eyes… "Well, I know the best place in the world to grow corn."

Braley nodded, unwittingly holding her breath. "And where is that?"

"Wherever you are."

Her smile broke like the dawn. "Will Ohio do?" Her heart was in her eyes as she looked from one to the other.

"Fine with me," Ella said. "As long as I can spend the rest of my days watching this baby grow."

"I'll get the tickets," Laith offered, returning her smile. "But you should know, I promised Ella a trip to see your ocean after we're settled. And I think we should pay a visit to that neighbor lady of yours." He whispered in her ear, barely able to contain his laughter, "Maybe you could teach her a few things." Braley blushed and swatted his arm, even as she returned the smoldering look in his eyes.

They watched as the horses were transferred to a different car. Laith's golden, along with Pappy and the mule, the team of blacks, and, to her delight, the cow. There were their trunks, and several large crates she assumed might be his books, and one large, long box that caught her attention. Her hand flew to cover her mouth when Laith answered her questioning look.

"Oh, that's the bed."

"You brought the bed?"

He would explain to her later when they had more privacy. It was the one thing worth saving in the house. Not the bed itself, but what it represented. The place where she had learned to feel safe, and desired, and beautiful. She should always feel those things. She should always feel loved, and he would see to it, because no one could love her more. He pushed his hat back, "Jeez, Braley, of course I did."

Epilogue

August 1869
Ohio

The wind swirled across the surface, causing ripples and waves under a late summer sun. Braley paused in her sweeping of the porch and looked out across the sea of green and gold, so like the ocean they had visited two months past, long after the planting was done. Acres of corn stood tall and proud, fading into the horizon.

They had made a home here. A good home. A happy home, for which they would always be grateful. A home with a big brass bed where they found comfort at the end of the day, and a calendar stick that hung by the door to remind them of other days that did not end as well. No one could have known her road would end here in blissful contentment, a few miles from the town where her journey had begun in paralyzing terror, a few miles from the house where Constance once lived.

Constance no longer lived in that house. The Murphy family had grown, and Braley had enlisted Laith's help in convincing them to build a new home next door to them. Thanks to Rusty and the crew Laith hired, the large white house, so like their own, was up in no time at all. Twin houses, waiting to be filled with love, their window boxes overflowing with color. Warren was now the farm manager and a new partner, and with his bad knees, was able to spend more time at his desk than on his feet, and out of danger.

She looked across at the barns and spotted Dog running toward her, followed by Constance, Ella, and the children. They had met at the barn to visit the baby goats and the horses. Constance's older boys, although a great help, were too grown for such foolishness, of course. The little group was slowed by Eliza's small steps, but Curtis and Olivia were happy to hold her hands and help her along. Constance had her daughter and a new, adorable son, Curtis had his sister to watch over, and Braley couldn't be happier.

Constance had taken her letters about the brother and sister to heart, but hadn't told her how she planned to stop in Kansas to adopt them on the way home from her visit, in case it didn't work out. Olivia, being too small to be of much help to anyone, had still been in the children's home, and Curtis had been returned several times as a runaway. By the time Constance showed up, those in charge were more than willing to be rid of them both.

"You'll never guess!" Constance said as they joined her on the porch.

"You'd better tell me then," Braley laughed, greeting each child in turn, and exchanging a glance with Ella at their friend's enthusiasm.

"I got a note from Lucy, and the committee may have two more children who need our help. She is coming tomorrow with the reverend to celebrate with us. The whole town is coming!"

Braley put down the broom and hugged her friend. "I can't believe it's finally here."

"The more the merrier, I say. No sense letting all that room go to waste, honey." She looked out over the shifting crop, "And they for sure won't go hungry."

"That's true," Braley agreed, "Laith is going to plant winter wheat and beans, and add to the squash crop next year." She looked from Constance to Ella, returning their smiles, "This is better than I hoped. Can it really be happening?"

"Well, I think you're about to find out," Ella pointed out as Laith rode up.

He dismounted and grinned up at them. "We're all set. The wagons are ready. The first children will be here tomorrow."

Braley ran to greet him, and Laith, a captive of her smile, nearly bursting with happiness for her, twirled her in a circle before setting her back on her feet. "You're not going to turn into Mrs. Clark, now, are you?"

Her laugh floated across the yard on the summer breeze. "No. I promise never to be like Mrs. Clark, and this house will never be like hers or some of those others. It will be a house full of kindness and hope, where the children will know love and laughter. Where brothers and sisters will not have to be separated, ever, and…"

He kissed her, distracting her momentarily, while her arms went around his neck and he became her only thought. She leaned against him, resting her cheek on his chest. "Thank you for this. It is something I've dreamt of for a very long time."

"I would still like to have a few more of our own," he teased. "But this just feels right. They'll all be ours."

It warmed her soul, as it always did when he claimed Eliza, and now the others, too. "That is my dearest wish. But this is… this is…"

He tilted his head and looked into her eyes, his own full of understanding. "This is bigger than everything. I think this may be what you were meant for. What we were meant for."

"Do you?" Her heart swelled with love for this man, this gift she had found along the way.

He nodded. "Maybe I was meant to trade a house with a dark history for your house of hope. And your journey, the road you traveled, everything you suffered, everything you saw, and lost and gained, has led you here, to this. Don't you see? This is not the end of your road, Braley Stuart, this is the beginning."

Author's Note

This story is set in the years after the American Civil War, a pivotal period of growth and change in American history. One of the most important achievements in the history of the country, the completion of the Transcontinental Railroad, was accomplished around this time.

In 1863, the Union Pacific Railroad started from Nebraska heading west, and the Central Pacific Railroad began building from Sacramento, California, heading east. The two companies met in Utah in May of 1869, connecting the coasts and opening the country to endless possibilities.

It is not my intention to give an elementary history lesson. I would like, instead, to take a moment to call attention to this remarkable feat, and to acknowledge the men of many nationalities who made it possible. I would especially like to mention the twelve thousand Chinese immigrants who worked on the western section, many of whom did not survive the terrible winters and poor working conditions. Added to this were prejudice, unfair treatment, and low wages, and it's a wonder they stayed at all. But they did. They stayed and organized and fought for fair wages and better conditions for all in one of the earliest and largest strikes in our history, and the railroad was completed. For this, we owe a great deal of appreciation.

How sad then, that only thirteen years later, an influx of Chinese laborers was blamed for the scarcity of jobs and low wages, and President Chester A. Arthur signed the Chinese Exclusion Act. The act banned Chinese workers from entering the United States for ten years and blocked those already here from becoming American citizens.

The Chinese Exclusion Repeal Act was passed in 1943, allowing 105 Chinese immigrants per year. Further allowances were made in 1952 and 1965. * While history may be fascinating, it is often disheartening.

It was not my intent to condemn or insult the Children's Aid Society, the Orphan Train, or marriage by correspondence. I'm sure much good came of these, and many did find decent homes and loving spouses. I only imagine and acknowledge that, as in all things, there was likely good and bad.

I wish to make it clear that I have great respect for the Scriptures, many of which are beautiful and poetic. In this story, I am simply saying that they are sometimes used in the wrong ways and for the wrong reasons.

Domestic violence of any kind is only to be condemned, and I beg anyone in need to seek help.

~National Archives, archives.gov

In Acknowledgment

With heartfelt appreciation and love for my circle of
family and friends who have encouraged, assisted and
supported me on this crazy path.
You know who you are and I could not be more grateful.
My circle is a dream catcher.

Special thanks to Lisa Gentile Horsemanship and Chai.

Coming in 2026
Book two in the Keeper of the Light series
'STEP FROM THE SHADOWS'
Ilene's story

About the Author

Lesley M. Avery grew up in New England, where her appreciation of history began. She loves autumn, candles, Christmas, and of course, romance. When not reading, writing or gardening, she may be found spending time with the best of friends or letting the dog in or out… or out and in… or out.

If you enjoyed this book, kindly leave a review
or contact the author at:
Lesleymavery.author@gmail.com
Follow at
Faceboook.com/LMAveryauthor/
Or
Lesleymavery.com